THE
ADVENTURES
OF ISABEL

THE ADVENTURES OF ISABEL

A POSTMODERN MYSTERY, BY THE NUMBERS

An Epitome Apartments Mystery by

CANDAS JANE DORSEY

Published by ECW Press
665 Gerrard Street East
Toronto, Ontario, Canada M4M 1Y2
416-694-3348 / info@ecwpress.com

Cover artwork and design by Brienne Lim
Author photo: © P. J. Groeneveldt

Adventures of Isabel poem copyright © 1931 by Ogden Nash, renewed. Reprinted by permission of Curtis Brown, Ltd.

This is a work of fiction. Names, characters, places, and incidents either are the product of the author's imagination or are used fictitiously, and any resemblance to actual persons, living or dead, business establishments, events, or locales is entirely coincidental.

LIBRARY AND ARCHIVES CANADA CATALOGUING IN PUBLICATION

Title: The adventures of Isabel : a postmodern mystery, by the numbers / Candas Jane Dorsey.

Names: Dorsey, Candas Jane, author.

Description: Series statement: An Epitome Apartments mystery ; 1

Identifiers: Canadiana (print) 20200248480
Canadiana (ebook) 20200248499

ISBN 978-1-77041-555-3 (softcover)
ISBN 978-1-77305-601-2 (PDF)
ISBN 978-1-77305-600-5 (ePUB)

Classification: LCC PS8557.O78 A38 2020
DDC C813/.54—dc23

The publication of *The Adventures of Isabel* has been generously supported by the Canada Council for the Arts which last year invested $153 million to bring the arts to Canadians throughout the country and is funded in part by the Government of Canada. *Nous remercions le Conseil des arts du Canada de son soutien. L'an dernier, le Conseil a investi 153 millions de dollars pour mettre de l'art dans la vie des Canadiennes et des Canadiens de tout le pays. Ce livre est financé en partie par le gouvernement du Canada.* We acknowledge the support of the Ontario Arts Council (OAC), an agency of the Government of Ontario, which last year funded 1,737 individual artists and 1,095 organizations in 223 communities across Ontario for a total of $52.1 million. We also acknowledge the contribution of the Government of Ontario through the Ontario Book Publishing Tax Credit, and through Ontario Creates for the marketing of this book.

ONTARIO CREATES

ONTARIO ARTS COUNCIL
CONSEIL DES ARTS DE L'ONTARIO
an Ontario government agency
un organisme du gouvernement de l'Ontario

Canada Council
for the Arts

Conseil des Arts
du Canada

Canadä

PRINTED AND BOUND IN CANADA

PRINTING: MARQUIS 5 4 3 2 1

MIX
Paper from responsible sources
FSC® C103567
www.fsc.org

ISABEL MET AN ENORMOUS BEAR,

1. POSTMODERN DILEMMAS

I hate show tunes.

Las Vegas show tunes, that is, crooner stuff, the kind of thing one associates with Frank Sinatra and Carol Channing. The neighbour was playing them: one of those big-band-pop-singer recordings where the linguistic distinction between *po-tay-to* and *po-tah-to* is deconstructed in detail by a hard-voiced pop-mezzo with platinum-bleached Attitude. Sun and hot wind had us all with opened windows for a last-gasp September summer moment, and I couldn't avoid the experience of hearing paean after paean to the dysfunctional love affairs of stupid heterosexual people.

I live in a suite on the fourth floor of something called the Epitome Apartments. The landlord and locals call it "The EP-ee-tome", with a silent final *e* and no irony at all. My balcony, where I have a few straggly window boxes, my feeble tribute to the Earth Goddess, is a three-foot-square iron grillwork cage, the landing of the fire escape, really, floating above a grimy urban alley that leads to the best — in my opinion — Chinese restaurant in town. But for months the budget hadn't allowed eating out even at the rock-bottom prices to be had there, and depression and unemployment had me trapped in the epitome of epitombs, with someone canned asking me what you get when you fall in love.

If the cat and I could have borne the stifling air, I'd have closed the apartment against the racket. As it was, Bunnywit sat out on the fire escape, and I had Ian Tamblyn's *Antarctica* on, hoping if not to drown out the brassy voice, at least to turn it into some kind of postmodern sound collage. That was mostly working.

I wasn't.

Finances had gone beyond desperate and into hopeless, and even blue sky after weeks of rain and Bun purring like a motorised bread pudding couldn't cheer me up. What *I* needed was a dysfunctional love affair of my own, one that lasted for two nights of hilarity and imported beer and ended with drunken protestations of eternal love just before the other party passed out and I slunk away without leaving my telephone number — or even my real name. No, what I needed was a lottery win.

I realised as I sat there that I could do two things well and I couldn't get a job doing one of them: hadn't gotten a job after the government "downsized" grants to social agencies and I was "transitioned" from six years perfectly happy as a helping professional onto unemployment insurance, which had run out nine weeks earlier. Job search being what it is in a land of twelve percent unemployment, I hadn't found anything but frustration yet.

I was seriously considering making a business of the other thing I do well — not that I've done any of *that* for a while either. Tomorrow, when the classified ads office opened at the local tabloid rag, I'd be there. *Aaaandrea. Hot bisexual. In and out calls. No Greek. Party girl. Says* to-may-to.

I was revising the ad — *AAAAbelard. Post-surgery, loves teddy*

2

bears, silk, and fur, threesomes. Will Come to you — when the phone rang.

"Yeah, what?"

"Munchkin, what *are* you doing home on a day like this?"

"Transitioning my career into the private sector. What are *you* doing phoning me on a day like this?"

"You now accept that *transitioning*'s a verb?"

"Don't change the subject."

Since the bright Titian cellophane job last week, my friend Denis was the guy the term *flaming faggot* was invented to describe. Why he wasn't out cruising the park on possibly the last day of summer sunbathing I didn't know, but it had to be important.

It was.

"Honey, you busy?"

"That's a loaded question."

"Sorry. It's Hep." That's what we called his next-door neighbour out in the suburban crescent where he'd inherited his parents' house and turned it into a monument to gay kitsch. Her real name was Maddy Pritchard, and she was a woman in her sixties who looked like a five-foot-tall duplicate of Katharine Hepburn and had been an activist for everything long before either of us was born.

"What's the matter?"

"You know the body on the riverbank?"

"What body? What?"

"I thought you watched the news every night?"

"Cat broke the TV. Can't afford to get it fixed."

"A body was found on the riverbank yesterday. When they started sorting out all the stuff in the pockets, they called Hep. They think it's her granddaughter, Maddy. I'm stuck at work, and —"

"Wait, wait." Denis was the best crisis worker I'd ever met, and at work he was solid and serious, but he was used to the lightning reporting style of emotional triage, and after a year away from it, I wasn't. The most exciting thing in my month had been Bun throwing up into a stone age TV, and the subsequent tiny implosions. Perhaps he wanted me to buy a twenty-first-century one, but tough luck on that.

"For Judy's sake, what's wrong with you, girlfriend? Concentrate! I can't go, so can you meet Hep and keep her company?"

"Where?"

"At the morgue."

2. CHANGES IN ATTITUDES, CHANGES IN LATITUDES

That changed the tenor of the day.

I was wearing a silk camisole and tap shorts. I swiped a Thai stone across my underpits, put on some overwear undemanding, neutral, and appropriate for hot weather, put the last of yesterday's fish sticks in the cat's bowl, and left for the suburbs.

3. UNDERWEAR MY BABY IS TONIGHT?

This is something my granny used to say. I remembered it as I stood on the subway platform, hoping it wasn't the day for Canada's second-worst subway disaster, and trying surreptitiously to tug down my underwear, which had climbed the crack in my butt on the short, sweaty walk to the subway. What can I say: they were *cheap*, and there was a reason I only wore them when I needed to do laundry. I was to meet Hep (we always called her that: she herself had a thing for her doppelganger) and drive her in her own car to identify her granddaughter.

There was a homeless Asian woman (hey, not racializing — her accent when she asked for a quarter was Hong Kong, if I had to guess) rummaging through the garbage. We talked a little about what food was safe to eat out of the garbage. I gave her all that was left in my pocket: a bus ticket, a dime, and a penny. She gave me a piece of paper with the sign language alphabet on it, which she had rescued from the street — muddy Gucci-loafer prints all over it, and one corner was torn off so *A* wasn't very clear — so we were both satisfied that we had shared commerce, not charity.

The train pulled in just in time. The salvaged fries she was eating were starting to look good.

4. WITH THE BENTFIN BOOMER BOYS . . .

I stopped being hungry, possibly for the rest of my life, at the morgue.

I also decided that I want to die before everybody I know, so I will never ever have to do that again.

I had picked up Hep and her car at her house. She was doing a pretty good Hepburn that day, hat and all, but her hands were shaking. The photos of her granddaughter that were usually propped up on the fireplace were lying on the kitchen table, and beside them a couple of crushed, wet handkerchiefs (Hep used the linen kind) added to the evidence of her reddened eyes. I took a closer look at the pictures than I ever had, and was disturbed to feel, from the image of the waif who stared defiantly out at me, strong echoes of my teen years. The kid even looked a little like I had.

Hep looked over my shoulder. "I just saw her last week. I gave her some money for her birthday. Here are the car keys . . ."

Hep's granddaughter looked even worse on the slab than in her photos. This is not a corpse joke. You could kind of get past the post-mortem lividity and the blotches of settled blood showing that the body had lain on its side, to see that the kid had had horrible skin, makeup up the kazoo, broken fingernails, tracks, bruises, and bad hair.

She was not mutilated around the face, upper chest, or arms, which was all they showed us. They also showed Hep the cheque with her signature on it that she'd given the kid, which had been tucked in the inside secret pocket of her leather jacket.

"Yes, that's my granddaughter. Madeline Pritchard. Yes, Madeline Pritchard. Yes, she was named after me."

5. GETTING TIGHT WITH KATHARINE HEPBURN

I let Hep off at the front, then parked the car. When I came around the house, she had already shed her hat and scarf, kicked off her shoes, and was coming out the back door with two tall glasses of iced tea gathering condensation and tinking with ice cubes.

"Madeline Pritchard," she said thoughtfully. "Same as mine. Maddy's mother never bothered to get married. Just as well. The guy was a bum. We found out after he took off that even his name was fake, and certainly the story of his life was made of whole cloth. Why they say that, I don't know. Whole cloth is solid. You could spit through that guy's reputation. We never found out who he was."

"But she was named after you?"

"Her mother loved me. After she died, the kid lived with me for a while. We had to figure out what to call each other to avoid confusion. We used to invent new ones. Names . . ."

"Artemisia Gentileschi is mine," I said, taking a glass and then shaking her outstretched hand. She laughed.

"That's a new one."

"I'm practising for the paid personals. Artemisia sounds like a wellspring of delights, don't you think?"

You can talk that way with Hep, and she talks this way: "Too erudite. They want Angela, all tits, French and Greek, available for parties."

"So I guess you were pretty hip to what your granddaughter was doing."

"'Hip'? Yes, she and I were . . . tight."

I looked at this woman in her sixties, slim, trim, and self-disciplined, and I looked around the suburban, well-mowed lawn on which we stood. "Tight?"

"As in, we were fond of each other. As in, we could talk, though Lord knows I wasn't always pleased with what I heard —" She turned abruptly and led the way into the shade. "You know, I don't think I was ready for the change in the personals. 'Likes dogs, hiking, and romantic dinners' was about my speed. Now 'likes dogs' means something else."

She set her glass carefully on a white-painted wrought-iron table and sat down in one of the matching chairs.

"Stir it — I didn't."

As I sat, she suddenly leaned forward, snapped up her glass of tea, drained it in several gulps, then very precisely threw it against the glass-embedded stucco on the side of the house. The pieces fell into the perfect English garden beside the walk.

I had just started to take a sip myself. I almost dropped my own glass when I tasted it. If there was any actual tea in it, I was a suburban housewife. Hep had just chugalugged a Long Island iced tea, four ounces of dynamite in a glass. Instant indeed.

It didn't take me long to follow suit. When Denis came by after work, he found us still there, and Hep still had enough presence of foot to mix him one of the dogs which by then had bitten us several times.

6. DELIRIUM TREMENDOUS

Denis and I slipped into our triage mode and did vaudeville all afternoon to try to distract Hep. "Hey, Denis, you think I'd make a good call girl?"

"You're too old. Phone sex your only option, girlfriend." And so on. It was hard work.

Finally Hep stopped us. "Enough of that bullshit. Pay attention. Somebody killed Maddy, and I want to know who. And I want you to find out." And she pointed at me.

"Me?"

"Don't squeak like that, you hurt my ears," said Denis.

"I love Madeline very much," Hep said precisely, "and I speak in the present tense on purpose. She is dead. I am not. I have spent the day in a melancholic state of self-pity, grief, and fury. With the onset of drunkenness, fury has won. I am determined that Maddy's killer be found."

Hep always talked like my high school English teacher. He had been a little, elegant guy with the same great green eyes and white hair. Come to think of it, I'd had a crush on him too.

"The police . . ." I said, knowing I was being the perfect Canadian, and knowing too from my days working with difficult people that the police have certain, shall we say, limitations.

"I believe in the police. I believe in law and order, all that shit. But the police see a dead *hooker*, probably killed by a *trick*." Coming from her classy lips, the words sounded properly epithetic. "I am not content to leave a busy policeman with too many similar cases, and too many preconceptions, to solve this. And I am not capable of doing it myself."

She was, as she often joked, a hale old bird. She saw my sceptical look and correctly read it. "Not because I am infirm," she said tartly. "Because I am too angry. I would bully and badger witnesses. I would try to kill whomever I found guilty. I would not be successful in either endeavour. And besides, look at me. You must know something about what Maddy's world was like. Do you think they would pay attention to me?"

"And you think they would to me?"

She laughed. "The ring in your nose, and the one in your nipple, should convince them."

"I don't have one in my nipple," I said involuntarily.

"You're blushing," she said. I looked away. The liquour loosened the self-discipline which so far had prevented me from vamping her, and even drunk I could not tell whether she in her dignified way — though how she stayed dignified after matching me drink for drink my fuddled brain could not imagine — was vamping me or not. Besides, these days, I was so deprived that I didn't trust my impulses. Anyone warmblooded, intelligent, and healthy interested me. Even some people who weren't. So I acted on nothing, which made the situation worse. Is life sensible? Mine certainly doesn't prove such a premise.

"This is silly," I said. "I am an involuntarily retired social worker. To be blunt, a downsized social worker. A *transitioned* social worker who hasn't said an empathic thing for over a year, except to my cat. Not even to my cat, the little creep. So what qualifies me to be Sam Spade or whoever?"

"Your sexism is showing. What happened to Miss Marple —"

"*You're* Miss Marple . . ."

"— or Kate Henry, or Victoria Warshawski, or Kinsey Millhone, or Joanne Kilbourn, or Aud Torvingen, or —?"

"Oh, put a sock in it," I said, forgetting I was talking to The Madwoman of Chaillot.

"Now we're getting somewhere," she said.

7. PROZAC TOMORROW?

"No we're not," I said. "You may as well hear the truth. I spend my days staring at the wall and fantasising about disembowelling my cat as an offering to whatever bitch goddess has been organising my life lately. I am so depressed that if I could motivate myself to

9

it I'd commit suicide, but it's too proactive for me. Furthermore, I know nothing about the real world of crime. I read Dick Francis mysteries, which are too damned nice, and for that matter, they are set in another country."

"And besides, the wench is dead," Hep said, quietly.

We all fell silent.

8. LOVE OF MONEY IS THE ROOT OF ALL EVIL

"Look, kiddo," said Denis finally, "you need a job. Hep needs someone who can ask hard questions to people without offending them. Nothing like a registered social worker to do that on an hourly basis. Hep has the money for the hourly basis."

"When did you two talk this over and decide I was the next Nancy Drew?"

"Before I called you," Denis said, enough less drunk than we were to still be shamefaced. (We, more simply, were just shitfaced.)

"Why the fuck didn't you tell me this then? I'd have stayed home with Bunnywit and eaten flies. Forget it. I've got my new career all mapped out. 'AAAAAlthea. Poetic but lusty. By the minute, hour, or week. Anything you want.' How's that sound?"

"It sounds stupid. These days you gotta have a dungeon and six thousand dollars' worth of video equipment just to turn a trick. And besides, Althea? Really? Why don't you just use your own . . . shit, no way you're distracting me. You need a source of income, if only to pay me back the big bucks you owe me. Not that I'd be crass enough to mention that as a way of trying to influence you."

Hep then named an hourly rate which made even my over-inflatedly self-indulgent subconscious blink, and between the emotional blackmail of being reminded how much I owed Denis, the memory of my empty cupboard, evocations of the pitiful dead kid, and greed, I was persuaded — provisionally, with confirmation to be given once I sobered up — to give up my career as a call girl and become a detective.

9. FISH STICKS

I stopped on the way home and spent some of my advance on food. Lots of my advance, actually. Which pretty much put paid to backing out.

When I got back the cat had disembowelled the leftover fish stick in the centre of the braided rug in the living room. Apparently he had found nothing edible there. I couldn't blame him. I had had the same experience myself the night before, but the half-empty pack of frozen fish wafers had been the last thing in the freezer, so I'd been forced to try them. Nevertheless, I gave him thirty seconds of scolding as I picked up the larger bits, threw them out, and opened the tin I'd brought home. He fell upon it as if he were starving. He probably was. I know it smelled pretty good to me, which showed the state I was in.

The other thing I'd brought home was steak. Later, Bun and I lay on the couch, replete and somnolent. If it hadn't been for the pictures of Maddy that her grandmother had shown me, I would have been able to sleep.

10. HAD A CAT ONCE — TASTED LIKE CHICKEN

My cat is called Bunnywit. Actually, he's called Fuckwit, but I realised after I'd had him for a while that whenever what passes for my family these days came over to visit, I had to stifle my yelling at him, and he got away with a lot of crap during those visits, so I Bowdlerised him to Bunnywit. In true cat fashion, he mostly only answers to Fuckwit. It's been a couple of months now, and we're still working on it.

Fuckwi—er, Bunnywit is the perfect sounding board. Stupid, feline, Rorschach, he moves in another world. I can pretend to be talking with him and, like the tarot or the I Ching, arrive at truth by impressionism. So when I say I consulted Bunnywit, I don't want you to think I actually asked him anything. The process was more like divination with entrails. Except, because I can't afford a new cat every time I have a life crisis, I leave the entrails in situ. It did have something to do with entrails though. After I'd been staring silently at him for about twenty minutes, Bunnywit, obliviously unflappable, walked over to his empty food bowl and miaowed. It wasn't exactly a sign from heaven, but it got me out of my chair, and there was a certain symbolic weight to it.

ISABEL, ISABEL DIDN'T CARE.

11. THE SOUND OF MONEY AND CIRCUMSTANCE

I decided the next morning when I woke up that counting every dangerous situation I had ever been in at work or play, this was one of the stupidest things I had ever agreed to do. Well, it was the next noon, actually, but that was because I had been up most of the night thinking about how to approach the task of solving a murder. I had reviewed every cheap thriller memory, trying to learn something from them, and it all seemed outrageous. Why had I allowed all that money to get to me?

All that money, Bun's entrails reminded me, *and* the sound of Hep's — Maddy Senior's — voice as she talked about her dead granddaughter.

The photos of Maddy lay on my table now.

"She had no originality," Hep had said, "but she had irony. It was going to be her saving grace. She was talking about kicking her habit. She was talking about getting out of the life. She was talking about settling down with Vicki, her roommate — her girlfriend — and living happily ever after."

In the first photo, Maddy looked awful. She'd tried to spruce herself up for dinner at her grandmother's, but it hadn't worked. Not much could change the condition of her overdyed hair, her bad skin, or the rings under her eyes. Her friend Vicki looked as bad. They leaned on each other, a couple of very thin flying buttresses holding up nothing. They wore hackneyed hooker clothes and grinned like high school kids. Hell, they *were* high-school kids — or Maddy could have been.

Not that I knew much about high-school kids any more, except from a long, long distance, watching them, bristling with earrings, clumsily capering in their black armed-forces surplus boots down inner city streets and calling pomo chatback to each other under my apartment's front windows.

When she gave the photos to me, Hep had put another photo down on top of the first. This was printout of a snapshot which she said Vicki had taken. In it Maddy wore thigh-high fuck-me boots, a microskirt, and a cropped T-shirt. She had too much make-up on and looked like a drag queen.

Hep had regarded it sadly. "She was so definite," she said, "that I decided to treat her as another adult. Was I wrong, I wonder? I have wondered. Should I have abducted her home, deprogrammed her like those idiots who try to convert their gay sons? Should I have abandoned some exaggerated idea of respect? She really wasn't much, just a scrap of life lying on the street, but I loved her. I love her still. That's all it adds up to, really."

"That may be all there is," I said, and Hep looked at me, hearing, I think, the compromise I'd drawn between "that's all that matters", which is what the social worker would have said last year, and "that may count for something . . . or not", which is what I was afraid to think now.

In the cold light of morning — which was actually the warm light of noon on another hot day — I shook crunchies into Fuc—er, Bunnywit's bowl. I was so tired I could hardly move. It wasn't physical. I was climbing a mountain of despair and lack of self-esteem. It doesn't matter how well I know it from the counsellor's side, it's still the same black cloud. Bunnywit was in an unusually kind mood: he rubbed against my hand as I filled his water dish, then licked my fingers. I imagined that I was a cat. A big hand was rubbing me behind the ears. It was offering me crunchies if I would do tricks. I wanted to bite it.

I shook myself. Bun's jaws split the hard cat food with a sound like the foundations of my self-image crumbling between the jaws of an army of rats. I had to laugh at that one. I was getting maudlin, and the sun was barely over the yardarm.

Wednesday afternoons I volunteered in the abortion clinic, but not today. I called in sick-and-tired, and picked up my wallet. To the bank first, to get rid of some of these fifties, and then to the police station.

12. I'LL HAVE IT IN FIFTIES AND THREES

The bank was glad to see me — my line of credit had topped out the day before, and they had called me at five yesterday to say I had to be in with a deposit before two today or I'd have my rent cheque bounced back. Since the slumlord was the leader of a vocal anti-gay-rights lobby and I was an equally vocal out bisexual,[1] it was better not to come to her notice. When I left the bank, my account was in the black for the first time in months, and I still had two hundred bucks in my wallet after buying a transit pass.

---

1. The correct word, of course, is *ambi*sexual, as in *ambidextrous*, but I'm reconsidering both words in light of my complete lack of interest in the gender binary. I've decided I should start saying *pansexual*, which is more accurate, but given the luck I've had changing Fuck—er, Bunnywit's name, I will warn you to allow for a bit of backsliding ongoing.

13. ROGER

The detective handling Maddy's case was in, typing a report into a computer terminal and chewing on a doughnut. Not only that, it was someone I knew. He used to be in Vice, when I worked with teenaged girls, lo these many years ago. When that institution was shut down due to budget cuts and I moved on, I lost touch with all the people uptown. But here he was.

"Is Homicide a lateral transfer?" I asked from the doorway. "Or did you get demoted for eating doughnuts?"

He didn't recognise me for sure at first. Then he jumped up to his full 6'6" (what the hell is that in metric?) "Is . . ."

"Is it really me? Yeah, it is, Rog. Strange as it seems."

He hugged me. "Didn't recognise you looking so femme." When Roger knew me, I'd had a brush cut and more Attitude. Ironically, it was before I started sleeping with women as well as men, and yet it had taken some time to convince him that I wasn't a dyke — maybe all of half an hour, as I recall, before he unbuttoned. But that had been a long time ago.

"Madeline Pritchard."

"What about her? You had something to do with her? What agency are you with now?"

"Well, none, any more. I've been re-efficiencied. I'm a friend of her grandmother. She wants some help figuring out what happened."

"She got killed. What, you doing grief counselling now?"

"Nah. Asking questions."

"What, some kinda private detective schtick? You need a licence for that, don't you?"

"Roger, I have no idea. I've been unemployed for aeons, and Hep — Maddy Senior to you — offers me a job asking questions about her grandkid. I admit, my head was turned. My rent cheque was bouncing sky high and I really needed the universe to cut me some slack. Since it's you and not some TV cop with testosterone overdose, can you maybe give me some idea of what happens next?"

"Well, we'll put it in the media . . ."

"What, you're that hard up?"

"Yeah. It's the usual bullshit. Dumped hooker. But there's something wrong."

"What?"

He was staring out the window.

"What, Roger?"

"No semen. No semen, no lube, no rubber glove dust, no professional-activity traces at all. And the level of dope in her tissues is too low."

"Too *low*?"

"The tracks are fresh, not post-mortem or anything, but fresh. We're supposed to think OD, maybe? But the girlfriend said the kid was quitting. And according to the pathologist, she really was. So what was that? Window dressing? What could I see if I found that window? And . . ."

"And?"

"And she hadn't cashed the cheque."

14. SHE SHOULD HAVE DIED HEREAFTER

I was haunted by the image of the dead girl. When I was in child care, at the beginning of my career, I had taken a lot of kids to hospital to treat a lot of self-mutilations and overdoses, but I hadn't been on duty for any of the three suicides. I had never regretted missing that experience. I'd seen two other dead people before Maddy, and found the difference between dead and alive spooky, mysterious, thought-provoking, and shivery. But this feeling wasn't me confronting mortality and the cold clay: the fury that Hep felt had its echo in my anger, reawakened from my caregiver days, at the brutal way the kid had been used, while alive and in death.

Just as Big Rog had done, I kept calling her "kid" and "girl". She'd been twenty, it turned out, though her thinness and vulnerability and bad hair had made her look like a teenager. I'd been twenty when I started working with "delinquent" kids, and (especially given what I'd gone through myself before that) I'd felt old. Now I was almost twice that age, and Maddy, who must have felt like she'd lived a millennium in her short life, had seemed like just a child, lying there in the mortuary.

Bad skin, she'd had, but young skin: not much in the way of wrinkles, laugh lines — she'd been real short on laugh lines — or weathering. The unhealthy life she'd led had given her skin a texture like mid-leavening dough, puffy and pasty, rather than charring her into smoked leather or shrinking her into an apple doll as it would have with a woman my age.

I looked closely at my own face in the mirror. Laugh lines, sure, but I still looked younger than I am, enough that in my work it had occasionally been a disadvantage. A moment ago I'd felt old, thinking about her. Now I felt young — young and fortunate to be alive. I was swinging on the emotional yo-yo, spinning on the string of the human condition.

15. A WHITE SPORTS COAT AND A PINK CARNATION

Vicki was a bleached blonde with such an amazing silicone job that she looked like a tiny version of one of the "gorgeous she-males" who advertise in the business personals, but the tatty pink nylon teddy she was wearing, combined with the recent wax job, left no doubt as to her genital configuration. She'd been crying, and along with her hooker-red rayon housecoat and hot pink undies, she was wearing big stuffed slippers shaped like chickens. I deduced that Maddy had given them to her, but it was an easy one: there was another snapshot, printed out on flimsy 20lb. typing paper and tacked roughly above the mantel, a selfie of sorts that showed the two of them, blurry and laughing, with wrapping paper around them and matching slippers kicking in the air.

She poured a Coke™ for herself, and one for me. "We don't have any booze in the house," she said. "We were the two stupidest drug-usin' sluts you ever saw: no booze, and no Twinkies. Can you imagine? We were thinkin' we were healthy, eatin' two squares a day and keepin' fresh lettuce in the house." She snorted. "When we went to the clinic, woman there told us to put a hunnerd'n'fifty-watt bulb in the bathroom light. Man, any time it was hard to keep our promise, we usta go in there and look at each other in the mirror. It was easier to see in the mirror. If I looked her in the eyes, man, I still drowned in them. I s'pose you think that's sick."

"Why sick?"

"Coupla lez hookers, dopers, pitiful."

"I don't usually do this on the first date," I said, and pulled up my skirt. Up high on my thighs, where hardly anybody ever looks in sunlight, the old tracks still show. Not many of them, I was lucky, but I have enough to have broken the ice in a number of situations, therapeutic and otherwise. "I may be twice your age, cupcake, but you didn't invent fucking up. People have been fucking up like you and Maddy since the dawn of time — or at least since the invention of the hypodermic."

"You got clean."

"I got locked up in a secure ward when I was fifteen. Why I became a social worker — I thought they saved my life."

"Yeah," she said. "With me it was the teachers in the home for unwed mothers. Can you believe it? I made one semester of college. I kept sayin' I'd go back."

"How old are you?"

"Twenty-three."

"You look thirteen. Except for the tits."

"Yeah, well, it's my schtick. School uniforms. The tits are for later in the scene."

"Do you do dungeon stuff?" I said, diverted. "Do you advertise? 'Bouncing Betty, 44-24-34' and all that?"

"You thinkin' of gettin' into the trade?"

"Well, until yesterday I wasn't making any headway anywhere else. Now I seem to be working for Maddy's grandmother, trying to gather data."

"Like a detective?"

"Well, I'd need a licence for that. I think. Besides, I'm not an idiot. Find out anything, it's to the police in a New York minute. Let them break the doors down and make the big arrests."

She laughed. Her face split down the lines of the mask, she was herself for a moment, and I could see what Maddy had seen. What had she seen in Maddy?

I asked her.

16. VICKI'S STORY

I dunno. She was cool. She was just always cool in every situation. She gave me the idea to stay alive. Before then I didn't much care. I was like, movie-of-the-week profile, I got fucked by my stepfather and pregnant, and gave up the kid, and tried to make college, and just fell apart. And by the time I met her, it was almost gamers. Listen to those bitches down in detention talk about self-respect, what do they know? They wear silk shirts and gold chains in the hot tub, man. They never have a hangnail even.

She was getting it together. She was. She never OD'd, that Roger Rabbit cop told me. Don't know if we were gonna quit the life, but we were independents: no pimp to chain us to a bed. We prob'ly woulda advertised, like you said, come to think of it. But maybe in Vancouver. Or Victoria, I heard it was pretty there.

17. LONG DISTANCE TRUCK DRIVER SEEKS COMPANION ON LONG TRIPS; WILL TEACH TO DRIVE

We kicked around a lot of useless ideas. Finally we decided we would fit me with some high heels and on Sunday night, a week from when Maddy had died, I'd go out trolling with Vicki. See what turned up.

"Sundays are pretty dead," she said, then flushed with despair, and her eyes filled with tears. She got up, rushed into the bedroom, but clearly only to find a distracting topic: in a moment she was back with the fuck-me boots Maddy had been wearing in the photo Hep had.

"One good thing, she had big feet," she said. "Try 'em."

Thanks, kid, I thought, but she went on obliviously, "Five inch spikes like this, you gotta have big feet. Man, we used to envy the trannies. When you got size eleven feet, five inches is nothing. When you got size five like me, you gotta stuff the toes, and they still hurt like hell. Probably why I do the Suzy Creamcheese act. You only gotta wear Mary Janes."

"*That's* why drag queens never complain about the shoes!" I said. "Hey, they fit."

At the odd mix of slightly-stricken and proud on Vicki's face, I leaned over to touch her shoulder. "We'll find out something," I said. "Maddy would want to be in on it, even if it's only by the spirit sticking to her boots."

"That's *so* tacky," she said.

We laughed, but we sounded like the teenaged boys who can't help, to their mortification, laughing at the rape scene in a movie.

18. LITTLE SHIP OF DREAMS

I dreamed about Maddy Junior that night. I woke up because F— . . . Bunnywit was sitting on my head, purring. Purring for him just means "here I am, serve me", it isn't a sign of anything special. At least, that's what I'd always thought, but his dishes had food and water, the litter box was clean, and he wasn't in the mood to play. When I sat down in the big rocker, he climbed up and sat on my head again, his heavy hips anchored on the back of the chair, his paws embracing my temples, licking the part in my hair.

I dozed off there, in the chair. Woke with the air cooling my saliva-soaked head to hear Bun scratching in his box in the bathroom, and stumbled back to bed. He returned to my head for most of the night, and I figure the only reason I didn't dream again was that it was too damned uncomfortable.

Only benefit to Bun being a Manx is that at least his tail wasn't up my nose. Morning, for a change, was welcome. I had to thank him, though. He'd done his best. I hoped I wasn't as competent as a detective as Bun was as a therapist.

I had to wash my hair before I went out, which must have been why it rained.

THE BEAR WAS HUNGRY, THE BEAR WAS RAVENOUS,

19. THE STORIES OF THE STREET ARE MINE

The inner city is a hungry beast feasting on the lives of children: jailbait pickups sucked into silver Lincoln Continentals so that sexually-incontinent old tourists from the 'burbs can spill their worthless lust into people they consider as disposable as the condoms they use to protect themselves from infection.

They drive home sated and smug, believing they've outwitted the street once again, not knowing that the street has their number, the kids have learned much more from them than they have learned in the transaction, and unable to imagine that the human beings they leave behind as trash have more to say to the universe than their rich, white, and much more trashy clientele.

I stood in a doorway in Maddy's boots, my feet and my spirit hurting. I was wondering already if this caper would cause permanent damage to both.

Denis and Vicki had had a ball tarting me up. Denis had pulled out his drag gear and outfitted me with an astonishingly brief hipster microskirt and a gigantic set of eyelashes (all evening

I'd felt like tent caterpillars were invading my eye sockets, but I'd managed not to counterattack — yet). They'd laughed uproariously while backcombing my hair into a frightening anti-halo, and Denis convinced me that the archival stretch marks on my belly added piquancy to the view exposed by the halter top. More like poignancy, I thought, but had to admit that until someone looked closely at my heavily made-up face, they would probably take me for a well-used twenty-eight instead of my real age.

What the devil I would do if anyone got that close, I didn't know.

When they were done, even I was scared by how much I looked like the Maddy in the photograph. If the right — the wrong — people saw me, I was going to press some heavy-duty buttons, all right.

20. ENTER, A MURDERER?

Hep had come over for supper on the weekend, Hepburn hat and draperies, high collar, and booze — a malt whiskey called Laphroaig, don't ask me to pronounce it, that went down like silk — and I made seafood vol-au-vent, and only social work ethics prevented me from suggesting an appropriate after-dinner activity.

Clearly she had the same set of ethics, or else was oblivious to the vibe, because after dinner it was all business. She went through her last visit with Maddy for me, minute by minute. She'd gone down to see Maddy, given her a cheque for her birthday, a week before the murder took place.

"She told me she didn't want it. 'I'm scared what I'd use it for,' she said. But I told her I trusted her, and put it into her pocket. She'd been arguing with two men there, and she told me to go home. She said she had to be in 'Attitude' mode for them, and she couldn't switch back and forth like ping-pong. I understood that, so I went."

"These guys, what did they look like?"

"Seedy."

I laughed immoderately. "Come on, Hep, *I* look seedy. Denis looks seedy. Seedy is fashionable! I need something a little less generic."

"I mean *really* seedy. Dangerous . . ."

"Yeah, well, ditto. How about height, weight . . . ?"

"How much taller are you in those boots?" She nodded toward Maddy's professional attire, leaning up against the wall of the entry, Bun sleeping on their toes.

"About five-ten, I guess. Add five inches."

"Maddy was five-four, so she'd have been five-nine. One of them was taller, one was shorter. Not a lot either way. One had really bad taste in suits. Well, the other one wasn't wearing a suit so I suppose he had really bad taste in bomber jackets. Right. The taller one had long dirty-blond hair in what I'm afraid I immediately categorised as a greasy pony-tail. It might have been perfectly clean, but he just *looked* greasy. He had an earring, with a blob hanging down that might have been a skull. He had the kind of clothing American kids in rock videos wear, Black kids. But he wasn't Black. He was pasty and spotty. Sort of like Maddy's skin, but worse. The one in the suit was swarthy, Caucasian — and his suit looked pretty greasy as well, but that's subjective too. I think it was one of those shiny fabrics they used to call sharkskin. He was chubby."

"Sounds like you have just described one-third of the population of the city core. Weren't there *any* distinguishing features?"

"You mean like one had a harelip and the other one walked with a limp?"

"Really? Yeah!"

"No."

"Shit."

"Precisely."

21. REGULAR PRICE, FIVE BUCKS, FIVE BUCKS, FIVE BUCKS

Just as I had told Hep, every third person who passed me answered to one of the descriptions she'd given, even ruling out the minor variations — swarthy, chubby guys with greasy ponytails; dirty-blond-haired guys slightly taller than me with shiny Italian suits, etc. I had to assume that Hep's guys had had business on the street, were in the skin game or the drug trade, so that ruled out any guy who looked like he was shopping.

What does a guy who's shopping look like? Uncomfortable, like he hopes his boss won't see him there (as if his boss being there wouldn't be just as incriminating); cocky, like he's trying to convince the world that he usually doesn't have to pay for it; serious, like he thinks everyone will think he has a delivery to make nearby; ingratiating, like he knows he doesn't have quite enough but is prepared to throw his fake Rolex in on the deal . . .

I had several interactions during the early evening which tested my resolve not to take this personally. I decided that the way to fend off potential tricks was to up my rates.

The reaction was uniform:

"*How* much? For *you*? What are you on?"

Gee, thanks, world. "You're right," I told the third one. "You don't *deserve* to have sex that good. Eventually you'll forget you ever met me, and you'll be able to sleep nights again."

He just stared at me blankly, turned to Vicki, and said, "What about you?"

Her rates were in the ballpark. So to speak.

While I was alone on the corner, I decided to retire to my doorway and take a break. I was leaning up against the clinker-brick doorframe, thinking how much a cigarette habit would enhance the image, when a confidential murmur in my ear almost made me jump out of Maddy's boots.

"Maddy? I missed you last week!"

Maddy? Didn't the guy look at the face above the packaged boobs and the fuck-me boots? Guess those bottle-bottom glasses weren't for show. The guy looked like a geek, but by then they all did. Ed Asner would have looked like a geek by then.[2]

He went on, "I waited for you half an hour."

"Oh yeah, when was that?"

The voice didn't bother him either. That really bothered *me*. Until I saw the hearing aid, then it made a devious kind of sense.

"Same time as usual." I looked at the pixel-clock in the drugstore across the street. 11:32 p.m.

"We gotta talk," I said.

"I got our regular room," he said. "Come on. I can't afford any extra time this week."

He really did have a pocket protector, lodged over his heart. I hope it worked. I waited until we got to the room.

"What's your name?" I asked. He looked hurt.

"Norman . . ." he said reluctantly. "You know that."

"Maddy knew that, Norman, but I'm not her."

"What do you mean?"

"I'm . . ." I decided to level. "I'm here dressed like her on purpose. Norman, last week Maddy got killed. When you were waiting for her, some guys were dumping her body on the riverbank like a sack of garbage. Her family wants me to find out who. Will you help me?"

His eyes spilled tears. He pulled off his glasses awkwardly and groped for the edge of the lumpy bed. I helped him sit down, then held him while he wept. When he was calm, I asked him gently, "How long did you know Maddy?"

"Two years," he said, wiping his nose with the back of his hand. This was familiar turf. I reached for the tissue box and handed him several. "I met her two years ago next week. I was

---

2. It's a joke.

saving for an extra two hours. I was going to take her out for our anniversary."

He pulled away from me, blew his nose, and straightened up.

"I know it wouldn't have meant the same thing to her as to me, and I know it's not the kind of situation that people think should be celebrated with anniversaries, but Maddy and I had the closest thing I've come to a relationship, and I appreciated it. I know my brother says I don't have much of a life, but it suits me, and Maddy was a big part of it. I just can't believe she's dead."

"I saw her body. Believe it."

"I didn't know she had family. Except her grandmother. I watched *The African Queen* on video after Maddy told me about her."

If Maddy had trusted him with her real life, I trusted him.

"It's her grandmother, Hep, who wanted me to help her find out what happened. Vicki and I — you know who Vicki is? —" he nodded "— decided I should try to pass as a hooker and see if I came up with any clues. When we got me dressed up I looked a lot like Maddy, which we figured might push some buttons."

He touched my hair. "Your hair's in better shape," he said.

"Yeah, well, I don't go the 'better living through chemistry' route."

"She was quitting, she said."

"Yeah, she was. Stupid, eh? Just when she has a chance for a life, someone snuffs it. Norman, it would help a lot if you could tell me about your routine with Maddy. Times, places, anything she said . . ."

"I work late. I'm a software designer, games actually, and I put in long hours." My lord, he *was* a geek, in the modern sense of the word! "I met Maddy on the way home from work one night. I took a taxi for a change. It had been a terrible day, and I'd had a fight on the telephone with my brother. He was hassling me about my lifestyle. He should talk. He's older than me and still lives in my parents' basement. But he's a lawyer so he thinks that makes him a serious guy, and I design computer games, so that, plus the disability, makes me a nerd, right?"

"Wrong," I said.

"Thanks for the vote of confidence, but I've read *Bimbos of the Death Sun.*"

So had I; I laughed aloud. He went on.

"It was just one of those impulses that get people in trouble. She said, 'Wanna go for a ride?' Only *I* was the one in the car. I laughed, but all of a sudden I just said, 'Sure, hop in.' The next week I was going home at about the same time, and she recognised me. 'Hey, Norman,' she said, 'how's it hanging?' I'd never heard that before. I was embarrassed. But I went with her again the week after. We actually got to know each other pretty well. And on my birthday, she . . ." He sniffed again, overcome.

"She . . . ?"

"It was on the house, she said. A present. For . . . for a friend, she said." Both of us had tears in our eyes.

"What did you know about her life, Norman? What did she tell you?"

"Well . . . she lived with Vicki. They were in love, but Maddy told me one time that Vicki loved her more than she loved Vicki, and it made her feel guilty, so she always was really careful of Vicki's feelings. But that helped her when they decided to get off drugs, because Vicki believed in Maddy and Maddy didn't want to let Vicki down. She said it wouldn't be fair, it would be like kicking a puppy.

"She didn't have a pimp. Sometimes she worked in a co-op, she said, but not for a pimp. That was important to her. She said she had one monkey on her back, she didn't need a whole troop of them. There was some rough stuff a few weeks ago. She had a black eye. I asked her if she wanted to just talk, but we ended up . . . you know . . . anyway. She said it made her feel better to hang out with . . . with a decent human being. She said, 'Men are jerks, you know that, Norman? My face isn't the only place I've got bruises.' And it was true. I could see on one . . . breast, and on her, you know, chest and side . . . and all along one leg, big black-and-blue marks with a funny shape, like cursor arrows. She said, 'Cowboy boots are the pits,' and I figured out they were marks where somebody kicked her."

After a moment he said, "What's your name?" I told him, and he repeated it slowly a couple of times. "Are you a real prostitute?"

"No, I'm afraid not. I was joking about becoming one, because I'm unemployed, but you know what, Norman? The more I learn about Maddy's life, the more I realise how bad I'd be at it. I like sex, but it's not about sex, is it, Norman?"

"She said it wasn't, usually. She said that's why I was fun. She said she enjoyed it with me. I know they say that all prostitutes say that, but Maddy . . ."

"I think she meant it, Norman."

"The thing is," he said, "there are some things that I *am* good at. I figure that anything I learned as a kid I'm bad at. I was always hassled about everything; it was better not to try, and when I tried, the script was that I'd mess it up. But when I moved out, and started learning some new stuff, it was like starting fresh, and I was a lot better at it. Sex was like that. Maddy and I had fun. She relaxed and let me touch her too. She said 'hookers' —" I heard the quotation marks, and the difference in intonation "— don't usually let that happen."

We sat quietly for a moment, then he said, "So you see why I felt bad when I thought she had forgotten my name."

22. HEN HAO MAO

I had to wear the boots home in the subway because Vicki wasn't back from her last trick. On the platform, when I got off, the Asian woman I'd met earlier was reclining on a bench. She wasn't sleeping. She looked at me as if I'd just walked into her living room.

"Ne hao ma," I said.

"Big boots," she said. For a second I thought she said "big boobs", but then I noticed where she was looking. It was definitely the boots. That restored my momentarily shaken faith in her sanity.

Fuckwit was glad to see them too. Bunnywit, I mean. He twined around my legs, but it wasn't me. When I leaned the boots on the wall by the entry, he stayed by them, purring, and even when he heard the scrape of the spoon in the food can he came very slowly. If his entrails were talking to me, I couldn't hear the message. He slept on the boots all night, his toes flexing rhythmically against them in his sleep.

THE BEAR'S BIG MOUTH WAS CRUEL AND CAVERNOUS.

23. THE SUBPLOT?

My feet were killing me.

I'd been too exhausted the night before to care, but in the morning the effects on tendons and muscles of several hours in five-inch heels couldn't be ignored. I hobbled to the bathroom, ran a hot bath into the clawfoot tub, and levered in with many moans and oaths.

Bunnywit, as usual, came to watch. The only thing wet he likes on his own fur is his own tongue, but he has a morbid fascination with human bathing. I was surprised he could leave his boots for so long, but he stayed with me for the half hour it took me to finish my book[3] and the water to get tepid. When I ran more hot in, the splashed droplets rousted him from the toilet lid to the door, which he clawed open (more swearing from me as the cool air poured in) in his escape bid.

---

3. I was rereading *Divine Endurance*, by Gwyneth Jones, about an immortal android cat, of which he seemed to approve.

Without a book to distract my thoughts, there was no avoiding several realities. One was that I was going to be sore-legged all day, no matter how much hot water I applied. Another was that I didn't have much of a life. In a traditional narrative, the subplot would have intervened by now. Another friend with another problem. A kooky, loveable family. A liking for gourmet cooking. A workout habit at a gym with a cute hunk after my ass.

There was no subplot in my life (and wasn't going to be, if I could help it, but that's another story and pretty pitiful in and of itself).

Actually, there was barely any plot either, come to think of it, except this little chore I had undertaken. Pun unintended.

So. I could call Roger and tell him about the bruises. I could call Hep and tell her about Norman. I could call Denis and see if he had any new gossip. I could feed my cat. That was about the limit of my social options. Oh yeah, and I could go downtown and pay my overdue phone bill before the phone got cut off.

By then I was as limber as I'd get that day anyway, and the hot water had definitely run out. I got out and dried off, shivering.

24. THE SUBPLOT, REALLY

I hadn't counted on the universe which, the moment I headed downtown later that afternoon (after making all my calls), decided to show me how badly I'd underestimated it.

The Asian bag lady was on her bench as I limped down into the subway station. The crowds brushed by her as if she were a piece of awkwardly bulky garbage.

"Ne hao ma," I said, grumpily elbowing a businessman who bustled through invisible us, talking self-importantly on a cell phone.

She laughed and pointed at my feet, said something I didn't understand. "I don't understand," I said.

"Bu hao — ow!" she said cheerily, pointing at my feet. "Wo de péngyou Maddy have same boots. She got sore feet also. Very silly boots, Maddy say."

"Maddy Pritchard?" I pulled out the photo and showed her. She nodded.

"You knew Maddy Pritchard?"

"Maddy very good friend. Wo de péngyou." (You understand I looked the spellings of all this up later in the *Chinese at a Glance* phrasebook I used to carry on my travels. I know about five things in any of the Chinese languages, half of those in Puthonhua which was no use here: hello, friend, very good, cat, and "I want to buy that wristwatch." Oh yes, and how to order tea and rice and say I'm sick. Think of me as the Compleat Linguist. Please.)

"When did you see her last?" The train came in, but my priorities had changed. I grabbed her arm and pulled her back to the corner of the platform, away from the Armani-knock-off crowds.

"One week from when you have her big boots."

"Last Sunday? But that's the night she was murdered!"

"What does murr-dur mean?"

"I don't know yet what her mu . . . oh, it means she was killed." I made a graphic gesture.

"Oh, I know 'kill'. Maddy? Someone kill Maddy?"

"Yes. She was found the next day on the riverbank."

The woman, whose name was Jian, which she told me meant Pearl, had seen Maddy in the company of two men and another woman.

"Another one in big boots. Tall, very tall. Red boots. Tall like man dressed as woman for show —"

"Drag queen, you mean?"

"Yes, drag queen — and big hair, fake. But maybe real tits?"

"Real tits? Real woman?"

"Maybe maybe. Maybe half man, on way to be woman.

Maybe guy with good tits. Maybe good fake. I don't know. No chance to squeeze tits, not know." And we laughed, her at her joke and me at the lewd gesture she made.

"Maddy not talk to me. I talk to her, she shake head. 'Old woman, get away,' she say. She know I not old, she know my name Jian. So something wrong? I not know she die. Maybe if I yell at her, she might get away from them then?"

"Three people? You must be joking. They would have thrown you under the train as soon as look at you."

"I know martial arts," she said angrily. "I am no turnover."

"Pushover," I said. "It's pushover. Maddy was no pushover either, but she's dead."

"I see big boots again, working two nights," she said. "If I see those men too, how I tell you? You don't come on subway every day."

"You read English?"

"Some."

"Here's my card. Address. Epi-tome Apartments. You know where that is? This is my phone number. Here's my name." I repeated it until we'd sorted out the consonants. "You see them, you call me."

"No quarter phone. You quarter phone?"

"Here's all the quarters I have. But look, are you going to spend them on booze or dope or something?"

Forget Esperanto. Apparently, the eye roll is the universal language. "No booze. No drug. Just got no house, food."

"Well, since you're working for me in this investigation — this job — you should have a salary too. How much does it cost you to live for a day?"

She named a figure that made me ashamed, it was so low. I gave her four times that without putting much of a dent in a day's wages. "I'll give you this much for every day you work for me, looking for those men."

"Okay." She giggled. "I work for you. Detective." She sobered and grabbed my sleeve. "Maddy — she was my friend. Wo de péngyou."

"Mine too," I said. "Wo-men de péngyou." *Our* friend.

"We find who kill. We find. We find."

"I hope so," I said.

It wasn't a lie, I realised as I rode the train downtown. I was getting kind of personal about Maddy Pritchard, and I think I had liked her, zits and all.

25. MEANWHILE, IN ANOTHER PART OF THE FOREST

The next thing that happened was that Vicki read the mail. She'd been letting anything addressed to Maddy pile up in the week Maddy'd been dead. I guess finally it occurred to her that Maddy wasn't going to stop being dead.

One of the letters was a bulky envelope addressed to Maddy in Maddy's own handwriting. This scared Vicki and she'd waited to open it until Hep or I could be there. I know this because of the messages she left on my answering machine, Denis's answering machine, and Hep's voice mail. Several messages on each. It was Hep who got home first, and she was there when I knocked, panting, on Vicki's door, having run up the stairs despite how my legs felt.

26. OH YEAH, A SUBPLOT

I *had* made it to the phone company on time.

27. WHAT THE POSTMAN . . . ER, LETTER CARRIER . . . SAW

Only problem was, Vicki wasn't there. Door had been unlocked, Hep said, and a letter — a plump brown 9x12-inch envelope — sat on the table unopened, but the apartment was empty.

For various reasons of context, we immediately decided "out for Pringles™" wasn't the answer, and called Roger. Well, it was actually more like fifteen minutes.

I admit it. I'd put on a pair of Vicki's and Maddy's professional-quality nitrile gloves (unpowdered) and opened the letter first.

28. I RECEIVED YOUR POSTCARD TODAY FROM WAIKIKI . . .

2 (two) thousand-dollar bills (they're kind of a magenta purple, with the pine grosbeak on them: they're very, *very* old-style money, as the money design hasn't had a thousand bill for ages now, which I think is a pity) with a hot pink heart-shaped sticky-note reading, *Vikki?*[4]

1 (one) thousand-dollar Hong Kong bill (they're orange) with lime-green sticky-note: *Jan?*[5]

1 (one) clipping from the classifieds of an unknown paper, for escort service

1 (one) clipping from the *Sun* gossip page, with photos of several people at an event in an upmarket art gallery

1 (one) clipping from the *TVTimes*™ television listings

1 (one) photocopy of a business licence for a numbered company, with signature of owner/proprietor

1 (one) Ziploc™ bag (sandwich size) with samples of a white powder

1 (one) Ziploc™ bag (sandwich size) with a used condom

1 (one) Ziploc™ bag (sandwich size) with a cut-up plastic cup

1 (one) brochure for a chi-chi club downtown. Or is it uptown when it's upmarket?

3 (three) round paper clips, which had slipped off whatever they were clipping together and were loose in the bottom of the envelope

---

4. Apparently, I was spelling the girlfriend's name wrong, unless Maddy had, which, though not inconceivable for someone her age, was unlikely.

5. Jian? Quite likely she'd spell that wrong. *She* hadn't been the Compleat Linguist either.

That's all, folks.

29. WHO CALLED ROGER RABBIT?

Rog and Hep sat on the stairs. I stood leaning on the rail, the better to see, through the apartment door, glimpses of the deep-dish-cute constable who was one of the cops going over Vikki[6] and Maddy's flat for clues to Vikki's abrupt departure. Abrupt it had been. Her purse was in the bedroom, contents strewn across the bed, and I couldn't see her animal slippers anywhere.

"Way I see it," I said to Roger, "she's putting together evidence. Fingerprints on the cup? DNA testing on the semen? Test the white stuff . . ."

"Yeah, duh. Obvious. But why not just write us a letter?"

"Look, the kid doesn't have a book in the house. Is she gonna want to write? Does she even know how, as such?"

"Not really," said Hep. "I say so as the recipient of a number of her so-called letters. Besides, it looks to me like it wasn't that easy. Imagine that she wanted to have the evidence but not have it fall into someone's hands. One thing she read and saw around my house, growing up, was mystery stories. So, when the detective posts something to herself . . ."

". . . it's so she can pick it up later, safely. If she wanted somebody else to know, she would have mailed it to them," I finished.

"Just so. Which means . . . which means what?"

"That she expected to be out of danger soon," said Rog. "Then she could give the money to Vikki, and Jan, whoever that was . . ."

"Hong Kong money. How about Jian?" Then I had to explain, and while I was explaining, the obvious occurred to me. "But Jian's homeless, and she's here. How is she going to spend Hong

---

6. See? I'm a fast learner.

Kong money here? So if Maddy changed it for her . . . she'd just have to change it back, or else . . ."

"Maybe there's something about the bill itself," said Hep. "Counterfeit? And what's it doing here, anyway?"

"For that matter," said Roger, "what are the *Canadian* bills doing here? I know this girl was working, but big old bills like this are not easy to come by — they quit making them quite a while ago. We should have a look at them too. I'll take the whole thing down to the lab. Did you both handle everything?"

"No, just me," I said. "And I wore gloves."

"We have your prints on file anyway."

Thanks for reminding me. But Hep wasn't listening.

"I want a receipt," she said.

"Say what?" said Roger.

"A receipt. These things belonged to Maddy, including the money, which she clearly wanted others to have. And as her next of kin, I want a receipt. I don't want this stuff to vanish into an evidence room forever."

She had clearly been reading the right mysteries. Roger wrote out a receipt on a complaint form, right then and there, and gave her one copy. They signed here, and there, and here, with me as a witness.

"And I want both of us to know what you find," said Hep.

"That's police business —"

"That's *my* business too," Hep said.

"Staff, we're finished with the apartment," said the constable I'd been ogling. Roger and Hep got up, Roger groaning and straightening up slowly.

"I'm too old to sit on stairs," he said.

Hep shook her head at him. "Kids these days," she said. "No stamina."

The constable and I stifled our laughter.

"What?" Rog said.

30. CHICKEN OR FISH . . . ?

"Dammit, I can't remember what kind of animals. There's a photo on the mantel," I said impatiently. But there wasn't. "Chickens."

"What?"

"Chickens. They were shaped like chickens. And there should be two pairs, Vikki's and Maddy's. They gave them to each other for Christmas or something."

But there were no chickens, simulated or otherwise, in the apartment.

Only a piece of ID Vikki had stashed in the back of a drawer, which said she was a lot younger than she had told me. Like, fifteen? It could be fake. So which was the lie? Fifteen? Twenty-three?

"Jailbait?" I was still talking to the walls when I got home. "She better not be jailbait. I stood there and let her trick beside me."

But Bunnywit was prowling the hall, looking wistfully for the fuck-me boots which I'd put away in the closet, and didn't have any comfort to offer.

THE BEAR SAID, ISABEL, GLAD TO MEET YOU,

31. SENSIBLE FOOTWEAR

I spent half the next day trying to get out of bed. Bunnywit was with me, but I couldn't be sure he wasn't just guarding the one who could run the can opener. Vikki's disappearance had frightened me — for her, not for myself; that hadn't occurred to me yet — and the clues had me baffled and intimidated. Maddy may have been a bad speller, but she wasn't stupid, and according to Hep she had had a sense of irony. Whatever had caused her to gather evidence had been real, and the evidence meant something.

I was encouraged that Roger thought so too, but like Hep I had too much awareness of police realpolitik. And while Hep's scepticism was based on police-procedural-thriller reading and the movies, mine had a healthy dollop of inside experience to fuel it.

"It's not that I don't trust them," I told Bunnywit. "I mean, Roger ate crackers, or anyway I would have let him had his mouth not been otherwise occupied . . . and I would have let that constable see me naked . . . but . . . they're busy."

Bunnywit looked bored. He tapped my face sharply with a no-claws paw, and turned his head toward the kitchen where his food dish sat. I knew how long the claws-in policy usually lasted, and although I am not a helium-filled gift balloon, I see no point in dicing with death. So, finally, I got up. It was a chilly day. The cold feet on which I padded to the kitchen were real rather than metaphorical.

Cold feet. Why would someone take the chicken slippers and not the envelope of evidence?

If it had been Vikki, it would have been because they were the only thing in the apartment she wanted to save. If she was taking a powder (look who's talking about watching too many old detective flicks) but had wanted us to find the envelope, she'd have left the door open and the envelope in plain view, just like we found it. Say she'd been in a panic: she'd looked around for what she didn't want to live without, and, since I imagined that since she was, under all that pancake, just a kid, she'd seen the slippers and the photographs, now her only tangible connexion to her dead lover, as the only things of value to rescue from a tawdry life.

Setting aside my melodramatic use of the word "tawdry", it was a theory. So, where would she go?

"Where would she go?" I asked Bunnywit, but it was rhetorical. He was prowling the hall and making low cooing noises, as if he could entice the boots out of the closet by sweet-talk.

Sweet-talk. Entice. Between the voicemails and our arrival, something had changed. A human change-agent is always most likely. Who? Who said what to Vikki? What was it that scared her, that attracted her, that distracted her, that pulled her out of that apartment?

32. KISSING COUSINS

I know this woman called Thelma. Because of some combo of

numerology and pyramid marketing, she changed her name to Amleth once, which she thought was pretty clever, but the other women at the insurance office where she types all day just kept calling her Thel so it didn't last. I was glad. I kept spelling it correctly as Amleht and pissing her off mightily.

Okay, actually I'm related to her. Okay, she's my cousin, okay? If there were any more ways in the world to disapprove of each other, we would at least have to try them. But as it is there's enough of a range. I dislike the way she still wears her hair in that lacquered front-quiff arrangement once called satirically The Claw (though Thel hates me to call it that) and now so out of date it doesn't have a name. She dislikes my taste in clothes and my sexual habits. I dislike her runny-eyed little dog, which she claims is a purebred Shih Tzu (appropriate name for what is essentially a yappy little shit machine); she dislikes Bunnywit, which I think is intolerant and short-sighted of her, considering the self-centred similarity of their bitchy characters.

Bunnywit bites her, though, so I guess like and like do not get along whatever.

If I am ever going to have anything like a subplot in my miserable life, I guess Thel is part of it. Thel prays for me. She has a T-shirt with *Soul Patrol* on it, letters curved in a circle around a cross-in-a-medallion design, and she takes "saving souls for the Lord" seriously. More, she feels it her duty to "keep in touch", as we are "the last of the family, no matter what your side has done to disgrace the family name" (kind Christian soul, did I say?), so she comes around at inconvenient times to check on me.

This time it was after work — her work that is. I had gone down to the subway and invited Jian for dinner and a bath. She was having the dinner first, which created a little bit of unavoidable atmosphere.

Thelma sashayed into the kitchen talking nonstop, as usual, but stopped dead in body and voice when she had to take a breath.

"Jian, this is my cousin Thelma," I said. "Cousin, do you know what I mean? Child of my auntie — my mother's sister."

"Hi, cousin Thelma," Jian said. "You come to share our rice?"

Thelma looked in horror at the rice and Chinese food which I'd just made, at Jian wielding her chopsticks with dirty fingers, at Bunnywit trying to sneak up onto the table to steal shrimp, and said, polite with effort, "No, I just dropped by to . . ." She turned to me. "C. . . can I talk to you for a minute?"

"Sure," I said, sitting back at the table, knowing I was pushing her and enjoying it. I pushed Bunnywit, too, and he dropped to the floor, swearing in cat.

"Alone, you moron," she said, and went back through the living room into my bedroom. When I followed her, she was looking around forbiddingly, for other people's shed clothing I suppose, or just not liking the silk-scarf abundancy of the decor.

"Who is that *filthy* person?"

"She's a friend of mine. She was hungry and needed a place to have a bath. I invited her over."

"Doesn't she have a bathroom of her own? Never mind, I'm sure I won't care for the answer. I came here for a reason, you know."

"Yes?"

"You know it spreads disease. And now you're doing it with a street person. Who *knows* what diseases *she* has! You'll get AIDS."

"My dear, Jian is not a lover. But if she were, rest assured I would practise safe sex, as I do with all my lovers." Seeing her face pinch, I couldn't resist adding, "Women, men, *and* otherwise."

She turned away angrily. I was a little sorry for provoking her; she couldn't help being brought up by parents who were evangelical flakes, and besides, finding comfort in the orderliness of a rigid religion is attractive to smarter people than she is.

"Look, Thel," I said, "AIDS isn't spread by gay sex. It's spread by blood and semen. Didn't you listen in school? It's like any other virus. It needs a way out and a way in. Just like the common cold, but a lot less communicable. Sex outside marriage doesn't cause HIV. And when you get it, it's treatable. All that fear is just an urban legend now."

"I don't want to hear this. It's not what I came for anyway."

"I know, but you must stop spreading misinformation. Not just for my sake. For the sake of the people who have HIV, who got it all sorts of ways, who are living with it as best they can, and who don't need to be hated by you. I'm not trying to fight with you, Thel. Just sayin'."

"I came to tell you some good news. I'm sorry I was critical. I wasn't very charitable to that poor woman. Or to you, being Christian enough to give her a meal. I admire that. I really do. I couldn't do it."

I waited.

"I came from the lawyer. They had your phone number wrong so he couldn't get hold of you for this meeting. There's a trust fund. Two thirds of it goes to you. One third is divided between Harold and I."

Harold and me, I thought but didn't say. Thel went on.

"Harold and me, I mean. It won't pay much. But it's a big help for us. I thought you'd like to know. And there are some other things for you, securities or something. I told the lawyer's secretary your right number, and they'll be calling you. It starts from when they died, so there will be a lump sum for the last year. But they need you to sign. *I* need you to sign. Please go."

"Oh, Thelma . . ."

She gave me an awkward little hug. "Hate the sin, love the sinner," she said. "I hope you're all right. You call me if you need anything." She smelled of some kind of perfume that kick-started my allergic reaction: if she didn't back off I'd have a headache in fifteen minutes that, to vanquish, would take an expensive prescription drug I hadn't been able to afford to have refilled.

I hugged her back. It was like hugging an old person: she felt frail and rigid. She was only in her thirties. How did she get so pinched and dried-up? And yet, there was this spark, the reason I hadn't given up on her long ago.

"Thank you, Thelma," I said. "I really appreciate it." I meant it, for a change. And it wasn't the news I appreciated, but the crack in the façade. "Thel, will you do me a favour?"

"What?" She was as suspicious of me as I was of her. What a family.

"I got this book when I did the volunteer course at the AIDS Network. Would you read it? It's about how HIV and AIDS really work, the treatments they use, who gets it around the world, all the history, and also the latest research. Just read it. We don't have to talk about it."

She hesitated, then grabbed it and hid it in her purse. "All right. But it better not be some kind of secular humanist propaganda."

To my credit, I didn't laugh. "Thanks, Thel."

When I got back to the kitchen from seeing Thel out, Jian was grinning. "You social worker, for everybody?" She laughed.

"Yeah," I said. "That's what I used to do. When I had a job, that is."

"Why you lose job?"

"I worked for a place that didn't like homosexuals."

"Homosexels? Oh, that means gaylesbian?"

"Yeah. Or in my case, I swing both ways . . . er, I like both men and women. I'm ambisexual . . . pansexual, it's called now. But when I started working for human rights causes in my own time, they found a reason to fire me. Said it was because of the budget. Couldn't prove otherwise. How about you? Why are you living in a subway station?"

"I come — came — to Canada from Taiwan with new husband. Here, I lived in basement suite, I clean houses for money, no

English, no talk to neighbours. Then, six months after, husband start to hit me. Say Jian too old, too stupid, not sexy kid, all alone, have to take it, too bad. I say, alone no reason to take crap. So I run away. Go shelter, but you can only stay three night. Try English class, but only so many ren — um, people — get funding. Go Legal Aid, go divorce, but he no give money. So finally no place to go. Go subway. Warmer, beg like people do at home. Not so bad life, but I don't like dirt."

"Yeah, I remember from when I was a teenager. I was a street kid for a while. I used to itch."

I took her to the bathroom, dug out the old bottle of Kwellada-P (from the days when my residential-home clients had more to pass on than their feelings via the chairs in my office), explained its use, gave her towels and some clean clothes of mine, showed her my selection of bath oils and soap, and said, "Have a blast, er, a good time. There's no end of hot water in this apartment building." Well, it was *almost* true, that last.

She was an hour and a half in there. I did her laundry meanwhile, and what didn't fall apart, I folded neatly on my bed.

33. SURPRISE PARTY

Out of her layers of dirt and portable wardrobe, and dressed in my T-shirt and sweatpants, Jian proved to be quite a dumpling. She wasn't so old-looking with the dirt soaked off — she was probably in her forties at most — and she had a soft, curvy body. My interest picked up.

"Yum, nice," I said. "Why would that stupid man think you weren't sexy?"

"You got reason — he stupid." I handed her some lotion for her dry hands, and she began to massage it in.

"You ever go with women?"

"Go sex with women? Not really. Not yet. You asking?"

"Maybe. I hardly know you."

She laughed and laughed. "Okay, someday you know me, we talk more. But now is good too."

"Now I have to ask you a question. Maddy sent a letter to herself. It was full of evidence she collected that she wanted to keep safe. In it there was a thousand Hong Kong dollars, one bill, and she put a tag on it with your name."

"Where money?"

"The police have it, but we can look at it if you want to go down there when Roger is on."

"Maybe no need. Maddy ask me look at money once. Hong Kong maybe, but something funny. I tell her, maybe wrong paper, maybe fake money. He tell me that is important."

"He?"

"Maddy. Oh, I mean she. She, he, we don't have this in Chinese."

"Yeah, don't I know. But I still couldn't get laid in Taipei."

She laughed. "That was one week or more before she murder."

"Before she was murdered."

"Yeah. So I say."

She was laughing at me.

"Do you speak better English than you pretend?"

"No, but I could if I talk more. Only say: You got quarter? You got quarter for coffee? No food, you got quarter? I have very small life these days. All in quarters."

"'I have measured out my life with coffee spoons.' It's from a poem."

"I like that. I like you. Where my clothes? Time to go home, I think."

"Oh, for heaven's sake, where's home? That subway bench, with the guards waking you up every hour? Gimme a break. Stay here."

She looked at me.

"On the couch. We'll find you someplace better tomorrow."

"I thought I stay your bed?"

Hmmm. "Maybe after the second Kwellada treatment."

She laughed. "I don't have bugs. I hate bugs. Anyway this city too cold for bugs."

I grinned. "Okay, okay." But I didn't move.

"I got self-respect, you know," Jian said. "I don't have to fuck for bed for night. I don't do for that."

"Yeah, well, I have trouble with my own self-respect. Am I taking advantage of you because you have nowhere to go? And you never had sex with a woman before."

"No, I just kiss her a lot. Chinese, we don't have sex without marry. Girls too shy to have sex together. So we kiss, hug. So now I live a long time, some on street. I learn to ask what I want. I ask now. You not the one to take advantage. Me, I take advantage of you. If you say okay."

34. OKAY

I said okay.

35. HANDS ACROSS THE WATER, HANDS ACROSS THE SKY

She indeed had lovely breasts, full without being pendulous, a nice handful each, and a charmingly puffy belly and hips, like a goddess carving from some unknown history, found in an archaeological dig. She was soft and smooth. Only the skin on her arms and legs was dry, so I rubbed her with more lotion and then grimaced when a kiss behind her knee tasted metallic; she laughed. She laughed a lot in bed, which was nice, because we were clumsy at first. I wasn't surprised how fast she caught on though: there was nothing slow about Jian.

Nothing.

In the midst of things Bunnywit came for a visit, so we slowed down and cuddled with him for a while. Jian talked to him in Cantonese, which I didn't get even more than usual because if I understand anything it's usually Putonghua, and looked sad. I reached for her and tried a few things specific for that. Soon she laughed again, and Bunnywit stalked off, offended at the turmoil.

36. THE SUBPLOT?

Which I guess created another subplot. Or at least a complication. Or at least a change of mind.

HOW DO, ISABEL, NOW I'LL EAT YOU!

37. NOT A CAT THING

Jian and I were wakened by crashing in the other room. I was ready to yell, "Bunnywit, calm down!" when I realised the noise was human-made. At that moment Bunnywit, on the dead run, skittered down the hallway and leapt onto the bed, yowling. He hid his head under my arm. I groped for the telephone while Jian sat up, bedclothes clutched around her fine breasts, breathing quickly in panic but making not a sound.

You know those dreams where you are trying to punch a phone number in an emergency, and the phone keeps changing shape, and the numbers keep fucking up? That's what it was like. Took me three fumbly tries to punch in 911, with the footsteps and crashes coming slowly closer. Sounded like someone was reducing my home to rubble out there.

A piercing whisper: "Fuck, why don't we just —"

"Shhh!"

Clearly at least two someones. Sometwo? The mind is a dark forest; I was terrified and making jokes to myself? It seemed like an age until the 911 operator answered, though it was only a couple of rings, I think. I whispered, "Police" and had to wait again, then heard the comforting beep of the recording machine as the operator answered, so before anything else I said my address — twice — and what was wrong.

"Two of them, at least," I said. "To get in the downstairs door ring the —" but the line went dead. One of the intruders had found the base set of the phone and had pulled it out of the wall. It was weird stereo: the line going dead in one ear while, with the other ear, I distinctly heard the *twang* — *pop* of the cord breaking out of the phone jack in the front room. Maybe Denis was right about the disadvantages of a land line. I *was* almost the last person on the planet to have one as my only phone.

I put my arms around Jian and Bunnywit and yelled, "I called the cops! You better get out of here!"

Jian was horrified. "Shhh!" she said, pulling me down and trying to yank the covers over all of us. Bunnywit couldn't decide what to hate most, the robbers or the airless dark. He howled louder, and gave me one swipe with a claw out before he remembered that I was all that stood between him and skull breakage. He crouched miserably under the covers and began to whine. I thought of Thel's Shih Tzu. Bun would hate to know how much like that little rat he sounded.

The banging died away quickly after the outside door buzzer rang several times in an official and peremptory manner.

"Shit! Get outta here!"

"What about the fish?"

"Later. Come *on!*"

Moments later, the police, in the persons of five constables, were crowding into my bedroom, treating themselves to the sight of two naked women, clinging to each other and the blankets.

"You hurt, ma'am?" said the man who was smirking least.

"Huh?" I looked down to see a drop of blood trickling from Bunnywit's thoughtless swipe.

"Nah," I said. "Cat."

"Say what?" said the worst smirker, so rudely that he had to be elbowed by a colleague. I reached under the covers and withdrew Bunnywit, who was working himself into a hissy fit. "Here, officer," I said. "He needs calming down, and you look like a real kind guy," and I threw the cat into his arms.

It is difficult to say who was the less impressed of the two, but Bunnywit had the cat advantage of always being armed and not having to answer to the Serious Incident Response Team if he used his weapons. I saw the only woman constable in the crowd smother a grin. She herded them all out, and Jian and I put on some clothes.

38. SAATANA PERKELE

My living room and kitchen looked like a bomb site.

"Saatana perkele!" I said fervently. One of the cops looked up. "Lady, that's strong language!" He must have been Finnish.

"Oh yeah?" said the woman cop. "What's it mean?"

The Finn actually blushed. "Er . . . Satan's . . . bum-hole," he said.

"Kakonnen! I've never heard you swear before," she said, and laughed at his stricken look. "First week on the job," she said to me. "Very serious. Degree in comparative literature before he came on the force."

"Finnish-English?" I said.

"No, Finnish-Slavonic. Minor in linguistics," he said. "You Finnish?"

"Nah, I just had a friend used to say that. But he'd never say what it meant. Thanks."

"Yeah, no problem," he said.

Joking helped, but only a little. It was astonishing how much destruction could be wreaked in such a short time. Everything in the living room seemed to be broken. My photograph of my brother who died when we were both teenagers was torn up like kitty litter. All my letters and papers were scattered, some torn, and plantpots had been smashed on them. That was part of what the crashing had been, and the rest was furniture being trashed. Looking for secret compartments? Easy. Just reduce the whole thing to toothpicks. No secret compartments? Pity. Try the next antique.

The only thing that appeared untouched was Bunnywit's litterbox, which he promptly went and used. Books were torn and scattered. Three paintings were slashed, mirrors broken, and though the kitchen seemed to be more spills than breakage, my everyday plates were in shards.

I guess it was a lesson in detachment.

I didn't pass the test. When Roger finally arrived, I was crying.

39. LATER? COME ON

"One of them was gay, or hangs around with gay men," I said.

"You never saw them," Roger said. "How do you know?"

"The misogynist kind of gay man. He said, 'What about the fish?' Who else calls women 'fish'?"

"Point."

"Remember, I told you about the people Jian saw with Maddy."

"You told me no such thing."

I realised that the disappearance of Vikki had prevented me from passing along the description of the "big boots, tall, red boots, maybe man dressed as woman" Jian had seen with two men and Maddy the night of her murder, and then seen twice since.

"Who's this Jian? You say she lives in the subway?"

"Jian!" I gestured toward Jian, sitting wrapped in my long terrycloth robe, looking unhappy. "This is Jian. Yes, she lived in the subway. But last night she moved in with me."

"But the guys said you were . . . you know, in bed together."

"Yeah."

"Naked."

"Well, yeah, of course naked. I don't go in for weird costumes. You know that, Roger."

He actually blushed. It was just cute. But aside from that he was all professional as he turned to Jian and began to make friends with her. Good cop, with no bad cop, unless you count the smirker, whom Rog had sent away immediately. Only Kakonnen and the woman constable, who appeared to be partners (in the job sense), were still there, wearing latex gloves and bunny-suits and searching for evidence in the rubble of the living room while we talked with Roger in the bedroom.

Jian was able to describe the men in more detail for Roger, particularly the gender-ambiguous tall person. The other two men sounded like they could have been — only in different clothes — the two Hep had seen hassling Maddy the last time Hep saw her granddaughter. When Jian was finished, I suggested that Roger talk with Hep about that, but I didn't repeat her descriptions. I didn't want to set up a precondition in his thoughts.

"So you figure the tall one was a drag queen, and he — she, whatever — was one of the ones who broke in here?"

"Sounds too simple. I mean, any one of them could be gay, and the tall one could be trans and lesbian, or a drag queen and gay or straight . . . the permutations are endless. But there's something else bugging me." I picked up Bunnywit, who was busy rubbing up against anything at his level, trying to reassert his control over his territory that had been so rudely trashed.

Roger had to prompt me a couple of times, and Jian came and sat beside me.

"They said, 'Later. Come *on!*' Later means later. Are they coming back, or do they have something else planned for me? And if they did, why didn't it go down tonight? Why didn't they just come in here and hit *me* with whatever they were breaking the place with? After all, they did Maddy in without hesitating . . ."

"We don't know that. Could have been a threat gone too far, could have been an accident during a fight."

"But what about this old thing of once someone has killed once, it's easier to do it again?"

"It's not always true. Depends on the killing. And the killer."

Jian spoke unexpectedly. "Maybe sometimes killing make you sick, very sick, and you never want to be sick like that way again." We both looked at her. "I been many places," she said defensively, "meet many different people."

"She's right," said Rog. "You can't assume anything. You have to go back to the facts."

40. JUST THE FACTS, MA'AM

The facts. The facts were that the cowboy boot bruises had mostly faded by the time Maddy was found dead on the river-bank. She still had the cheque Hep had given her three days before. She had been arguing with two sleazy guys the last time Hep had seen her. Last time Jian had seen her, the night Maddy was killed, she had been in the company of two similar sleazy guys and a drag queen or trans person, and she'd acted strangely to her friend. Sometime before she died (we didn't know what day the envelope had been dropped in a box, how long it had been in the mail: this was, after all, Canada Post), she had mailed herself a tidy envelope full of clues. She was quitting dope. Vikki was missing. Vikki was underage — or not. At least two guys, one either gay or who knew gay men, had trashed my apartment, and it sounded as if they were coming back. Enough

56

facts to confuse you? I was certainly not about to see the light on this thing.

I couldn't relax after the other cops left, so Roger (who stayed around for a while longer in his capacity as a friend), Jian, and I cleaned up the garbage that used to be my life, while Bun crouched in his litterbox and growled if Roger came too near.

The devastation was widespread but not complete, so in the end we rescued a lot. Not the paintings, which were probably beyond restoration, something I resented deeply. Especially as regards my Mendelson Joe, "Going in Opposite Directions", which I'd loved since seeing it on a television show when I was a little kid, and which had taken me a long time to track down and cost me a lot to buy.[7] My few antiques were toast. That part of my collection of glassware which had been on the living room shelves was pretty much in bits, except for three pieces of Bunnykins, which being bone china were pretty tough, and the Japanware porcelain, ditto. My vintage records — yes, vinyl! — weren't even fit to be melted into wavy wall plaques, spray-painted gold, and sold at craft fairs.

I saved the torn-up photos, thinking on the jigsaw principle that maybe I could reassemble them and get them re-photographed. Not surprisingly, only a few of the books (exactly eleven, actually) were ruined: it's hard to trash a book in a hurry — something that the New Right would be wise to remember — and the guys had run off before they could do much in that line. More damage had been done to the books by kitchen staples and the wet soil from the plants I'd watered only the night before, scattered over the previously pristine covers of some first editions.

If I had been the ones hiring these guys to do this to my worst enemy, I wouldn't have had too many criticisms, I thought dourly as I either reshelved or filled trashbag after trashbag (Rog went

---

7. From the estate of Joe Fafard, if you are interested in Joes.

out to get them at the Open-24-Hours corner store) and heaved the bags out onto the back stairs. On the other hand, if I'd been hiring them to find something small, I'd have given them shit, because in the trashing, they had certainly chosen destruction and noise over finesse and time to search.

I said as much to Jian and Roger.

"Trying to scare you," said Roger grimly, sweeping flour and broken pickle-jar fragments (pickles? When did I buy *pickles*? That had to have been years ago, for the last family dinner at my place, well before my parents died. These guys had made it right to the *back* of the refrigerator) into the dustpan.

"It worked," I said.

"No, did not work," said Jian, and again we both looked at her, a little astonished. "You no quitter," she said. "I can tell."

"How?" I said sourly, and then, seeing her clam up, look down and blush, I blushed too. Roger swept busily.

41. SIGN RIGHT HERE ON THE DOTTED LINE

The next thing that happened was to Bunnywit. Oh, don't worry, this is not the part where the beloved household pet is found staked out on the door with four-inch spikes or anything. No, this will not happen to Bunnywit, not in this narrative anyway. No, what happened was that as we were cleaning up, he ate something from the mess on the floor, something which seemed to combine all the worst qualities of elastic bands, string, glass fragments, and emetics, and he started to throw up bloody bile.

He floated right through the vet's room and onto the surgical table on a cloud of money. By the time the next day was over, I had thrown out almost half my belongings, and Bun had become so expensive an investment that I probably could have convinced the insurance company that he was a worthy replacement for my

Mendelson Joe — except that, as I've said, he wasn't gonna get nailed up on any walls. In fact, I faced the truth that he was now too valuable to give away, kill in a fury, use as a plot device, or even call a rude name. He was Bunnywit for good from now on.

If you're the kind of person to whom a pet is just an animated piece of furniture destined to end up in the SPCA if it quits being cute or cozy, you will have to just accept that I considered it money well spent, no matter what I said to Bun afterward. I've known Bunnywit longer than half my friends, and of the ones I've known longer, few have been as consistent. To see him coming out of the anaesthetic moaning, his fur a greasy, patchy mess, his belly shaven and swollen, and leftover bloody spots on his chin fur, didn't disgust me.

It did put the death of Maddy in a line-up, though; likewise my new romance. It was one of those last-straw things. I was supposed to go down to the cop shop with Jian and discuss the case with Roger et al., but for a few days after Bunnywit's bowel resection I only left the apartment to pick up baby food (for him) and fish sticks (for me — a regression, I agree. As an aside, I also realised his entrails would be no use in divination hereafter, their natural configuration having been seriously altered forever.)

Jian was around a good deal, but by the time I'd had a day's worth of strongly-worded discussions with the little Fu . . . er, with Bun about dressing changes, stitch removal schedules, and the necessity for regular pills and injections, I was too tired to fool around. She was patient, but we didn't know each other well enough for her to have to exercise this much patience.

"I suppose at home you mostly ate 'em, which sounds about right," I said grouchily on the third evening. I wasn't sure it was clear to everyone that I was grouchy at Bun, not Jian, and that my remark was a threat to him, not an ethnic slur. I was going to have to fix that, later. Bun whined.

"Nah, only sometimes," Jian said, too cheerily. "This one not so good taste anyway, too much drugs in meat. Probably we eat, we go to sleep too. Not that sleeping any different than now . . ."

"I really am sorry," I said. "That was a crap thing to say. We'll go downtown tomorrow. We'll come back and go directly to bed. Really."

Jian gave me a sharp look. "I got a better idea. We go to bed now, we sleep, we wake up early and stay in bed all morning, we go downtown afternoon. Roger know you not morning person?"

"Works for me," I said, and that's how we did it. Making up, if that's what it was, felt great.

While we were making love the next morning, Bunnywit hopped onto the bed with only a medium-sized groan, and licked both our heads in a generous way. I would have been more touched if later that morning he hadn't knocked over the new shampoo and tried to eat it, puking all over the bathroom thereafter and proving that his interest in our hair was not kindly nor thankful so much as just the real Bunnywit returning at last. After making sure the vomiting hadn't hurt him (the stitches seemed intact, there was nothing in the puke but Pinkly Grapefruit Shampoo, and he was waiting by the food bowl five minutes later), I went downtown with Jian without a qualm.

ISABEL, ISABEL, DIDN'T WORRY,

42. NOT A VIRGIN . . .

Roger was in a bitchy mood. All his cases were like this one, he'd told us: stupid destruction for no discernable reason. "I'm gonna quit and open a 7-Eleven," he'd said by way of greeting.

"No results?"

"No, fingerprints haven't gotten any matches yet. Takes a while, you know."

"You try Hong Kong fingerprint place?" said Jian. Roger looked at her. "She have Hong Kong money," Jian explained over-patiently. "Hong Kong money come from Hong Kong people. Many Hong Kong people come to Canada. Sometimes not honest people, sometimes gang people. Not everybody Hong Kong good, you know."

"Yeah?" Roger was doing a good imitation of me the last few days, and Jian was getting irritated at both of us.

"Chill," I said. "Roger, you and I have got to get over being grouchy, or we'll never see Jian again. I don't know about you, but

I would mind that. And besides, you'd hate running a 7-Eleven. When you got robbed you wouldn't be able to arrest the perps."

"Okay, okay. Let's look at the list," said Roger.

43. LOOKING AT THE LIST

2 (two) thousand-dollar bills (magenta purple, pine grosbeak) with a hot pink heart-shaped sticky-note reading *Vikki?* [unidentified-as-yet prints. not counterfeit. no other info.]

1 (one) thousand-dollar Hong Kong bill (orange) with lime-green sticky-note: *Jan?* [unidentified-as-yet prints. counterfeit?]

1 (one) clipping from the classifieds of an unknown paper, for escort service

"It's from *Intro Deluxe*," said Roger. "The July first edition. *Tammy's Perfect Dates. Boys and bi's our specialty.* That apostrophe you see? Buyer of the ad insisted on it. Tammy is about six-four and prides himself on never having turned a trick himself, but we never could get him on pandering because it's a co-op which pays him to do the administration, and he pays his taxes. They all do. They even have a dental plan. If there really were Grammar Police, we could get him on the apostrophe, but that's it."

"Poor Rog," I said. "Vice ain't what it useta be."

"Yeah, why do you think I transferred? It's a different state of mind than when I was pounding the pavement. Community policing. What did we know from community policing? My first partner taught me the right way to hit somebody with a night-stick for maximum effect, minimum bruising. Twenty-five years later, I have to teach recruits how to manage diversity. It keeps me awake nights, let me tell you. On a good day, I might be one step ahead of 'em."

"Must never show belly," said Jian. "Young ones, they will tear your throat out and eat all food themselves."

She laughed like a cat, a silent yawn. Roger grinned.

1 (one) clipping from the *Sun* gossip page, with photos of several people at an event in an upmarket art gallery

"Now this clipping is interesting," said Roger. "It's from the May twenty-third edition. Fundraiser at the art gallery. That —" he pointed to a grizzled — er, I mean distinguished — and expensively-groomed man on the left "— is Lazslo Stinchko, *not* pronounced Stinko thanks very much says the columnist but it probably is, and one of the *richest* men in the *country*, don't you know? And this ravishing creature is his trophy wife Panda. If I were them I'd change their names. But I guess it's worth her while to be known as Panda Stinko. This —" pointing to the handsome young man smiling down at her and holding her elbow confidently "— is a paid escort from Tammy's Boys and Bi's. He says his name is Kurt Amor. He is on retainer to Lotsi, as she calls him, and Panda, on a weekly salary. Tammy is in hog heaven, and so is Studly Amour here. He's been in two porn videos and had a bit part in the remake of *Road to Avonlea*.

"Tammy disavows any knowledge of Madeline Pritchard or Vikki whoever or Vikki Melville or any of the Vikkis. The Stinchkos are on a cruise, pun unintended, on Stinky's yacht."

1 (one) clipping from the *TVTimes*™ television listings

"*Road to Avonlea* reruns. Hah! So Kurt is our target?"

"Maybe, but he's with the Stinkos floating around the Côte d'Azur."

"Nice work if you can get it."

"We'll interview him when they get back, which is supposed to be in a few weeks . . ."

1 (one) photocopy of a business licence for a numbered company, with
    signature of owner/proprietor [No information yet.]

1 (one) Ziploc™ bag (sandwich size) with samples of a white powder

At the lab. No results back. I asked Roger why he hadn't put a little on his little finger and tasted it like the cops in the movies, and knowingly pronounced it heroin, cocaine, or icing sugar.

"I don't have much of a life," said Roger, "but I'm kinda attached to it. I'd hate to lose it on a stunt like that."[8]

1 (one) Ziploc bag (sandwich size) with a used condom

At the lab for DNA analysis and blood testing. I asked Roger why he didn't . . . . He gave me a look.

1 (one) Ziploc bag (sandwich size) with a cut-up plastic cup [At the lab.
    Fingerprints not matched. Saliva DNA tests not complete.]

1 (one) brochure for a chi-chi club downtown

"It's a private club advertising live sex shows," I said to Roger. "Do you suppose they really are?"

"Not only live, but one-on-one," he said. "We used to bust it once a week for a while, then all of a sudden it changed owners. The new owners were a numbered company, it got even more private and redecorated all chi-chi, and suddenly, no busts. Suspicious? We thought so. But that was then. I'm in Homicide now."

"Numbered company?"

"Yeah, I'll check on it."

---

8. Joking aside, it takes very little fentanyl to kill you. About as much as you would get if you licked your finger and touched it to some white stuff that was in a tiny little Ziploc™ bag inside a sandwich-size Ziploc™ bag. So.

3 (three) round paper clips, which had slipped off whatever they were
clipping together and were loose in the bottom of the envelope

"Those are cute," I said. "Where would you get round paper clips?"

"Lawyers office use them," said Jian. We looked at her. "I see on desk when talking about my husband divorce. Very pretty."

44. THE DOUBLE SHUFFLE

"You haven't asked me about Vikki," Rog said when we had quit unproductively kicking around these so-called clues.

"Okay, what about Vikki?" I said obediently.

"Vikki. Now, Vikki is the most interesting part of my week to date. Remember how pissed off you were that she might be underage, when we found that ID?" He actually waited for my nod. I hate that guy's way of breaking news. "Remember you were all ticked off about how you believed her line about college?" Another nod was required. "Well, you can restore your faith in your own instincts. The ID is what's fake, not the story."

"You mean she's not junior jail-bait?"

"Well, we don't know, because we don't know who she is, but who she *ain't* is Vikki Melville, aged fifteen-and-a-half, runaway from suburban Toronto, Ontario."

"If I live in suburban Toronto, Ontario, I run away too," said Jian, taking a turn at sourpuss.

"Listen up. It's a pretty good fake — a real one scanned in on a good scanner and nicely computer-altered — but when you get it out of the lamination, it *is* fake."

"She really was serious about her jailbait schtick. It must have been lucrative. Did somebody run her? Somebody who needed proof to show clients? Tammy?"

"If so, he's branching out from boys."

"Boys and 'bi's', remember," I said reprovingly, making the illicit apostrophe with my finger.

He glared at me. "We're checking on it."

"Besides, that customer of hers said she never had a pimp, but she worked for a co-op sometimes. How many hooker co-ops could there be in this town?"

"Twenty-six that we've found so far," Roger said in an unbecomingly triumphant way.

"Shit, I really *should* have taken up prostitution. Then I wouldn't have had my Mendelson Joe slashed."

"Maybe you find her college, you find her with same name," said Jian. "If I get fake name, I keep part of own name so I will not get confused."

"And she said she gave up a kid, remember."

"Well, I thought of that, as a matter of fact. Got that officer you —" turning to me "— thought was so cute working on that. You want to co-operate with Constable Sloan on that investigation?"

I glared, Jian laughed. "Sure, she like to co-operate pretty good with cute cops. Like on TV, bend over the car and spread 'em, yes?" She laughed more as we turned to look at her, both blushing and both shocked for different reasons. "You got any cute cops I co-operate with?"

"You might think about just what on that birth certificate got changed," I said, doing a number on the subject of the conversation. "Maybe the rest of the data is correct, and just the last name and year are different."

"I'm 'way ahead of you, kiddo," said Roger. "I'm waiting for Vital Statistics to get back to me. These things are harder to track down now that registries have been privatised, but if all goes as it should, we should find out a lot more about Vikki not-Melville this afternoon."

45. SOMEWHERE OVER THE RAINBOW

There was no point cluttering up Rog's office (which was cluttered enough already) waiting for the lab, the fingerprint department, or Vital Stats to maybe-or-maybe-not call that afternoon. (Yeah, despite my tendency to cling to the archaic, I split the infinitive. I do it a lot. It's the post-"to boldly go" era now: call it a style thing and let's move on.) The next move, for a change, was almost obvious.

"Drag queens," I said. "The thread kinda recurs, doesn't it? And it's Friday."

"So?" Roger was straight, didn't know the club nights, but Jian got it.

"We go look for drag queen I saw. Yes?"

"Yeah. And I know just where to go for help. He got me into this, and it's his turn to do something helpful."

ISABEL DIDN'T SCREAM OR SCURRY.

46. LITTLE BOXES MADE OF TICKY-TACKY

Denis was gardening, clearing out summer growth, putting the beds to sleep for the winter. It's a melancholy thing for me: it always seems so destructive. Real gardeners like Denis don't seem to mind. They lay about themselves with a ferocious glee, and the compost pile grows.

Denis threw a few more armfuls of blooms on the discard heap, peeled off his bright lavender gardening gloves, and took us inside.

"Me for the shower, girlfriend," he said. "Make tea. Pour cocktails. Whatever . . ." He traipsed off down the hall of the bungalow he inherited when his father died.

Someday I'll further emulate Sherlock Holmes and write a monograph: in this case, called "The Tyranny of Architecture", about the way house and apartment designs just assume their residents will come in a certain family shape and lifestyle, and in it I'll cite the people I know who have managed to subvert the tyranny of the suburban bungalow. One case study will be the family of artists who put their studio in the big room with the picture window and the good light, and the "living room" in the putative master bedroom, where the door can be closed on the family turmoil so they can read or listen to music in peace. The other will be Denis, who keeps his dressing room in the big front room with the window and the hardwood, because there isn't another room big enough for the wig shelf.

In fact, the whole house is upholstered with the layers of Denis's busy and seemingly pointless — but very flashy — social life as a stalwart of the drag community. I say seemingly pointless only because although he is a powerhouse as a fundraiser for charities, he never brings anyone home, almost never takes anyone up on a proposition, and never accepts the crown in the yearly pageant. As a social life on that level, it sucks.

However, there are layers of meaning here. As a political expression of the fallacy of gender constructs in defining personal lifestyle, Denis is a brilliant success, and the many friends he allows into his life, and who have the run of his suburban paradise, love him for his wit, his generosity, his kindness — and know his secret: that he is kind, smart, sweet . . . and terrified of intimacy. His work as a crisis intervention worker with teenagers is brilliant, and we know how many lives he has saved by caring and by being smart enough to say the right thing at the right time.

But we also know how much he *loves* costume.

Denis had dyed his hair again. Some of his hair. The Titian locks were now streaked with purple to match a really appalling 1969-vintage bell-bottomed-pantsuit in which he appeared after his shower, his slender hips girdled with a belt of linked lime-green plastic circles and tin medallions. He sat down to paint his toenails with stylised daisies to match the fabric, and the cork-soled platform sandals were waiting.

"I forgot how glad I was not to belong to the sixties," I said. "Once around was bad enough for those clothes. My mother always looked like a space alien in those photos."

"Disco lives," he said.

"Disco was later, you infant. You're back in the Summer of Love, or at least the half-decade of lust."

"Retro lives, then."

"Retrograde, you mean. Honestly."

"Calm yourself, honey, it washes out," said Denis. "At least, so they say. So, this is Jian? How's Fuckwit — I mean Bunnywit? Still detecting? You, not the cat. Anything I can do?" A characteristic question, that last.

"Yes, and fine, and yes, and as a matter of fact yes. We need to be in drag tonight. As something else."

I explained to him that last time Jian had seen the villains of the piece, she was a street-dwelling and rather grimy person. Now she was clean and differently dressed, but they had looked at her face when she greeted Maddy, and her face hadn't changed. She needed to be unrecognisable.

"The best way to do that is not to play with disguises, but to assume some other kind of attitude, and the costume to go with it. Wouldn't have to be much," Denis said. "Make-up, mostly, and don't smile. Smiling is fatal to Attitude."

He sat Jian down in front of the picture window, tilted her head so her face would catch the late afternoon light, and started to work. "Clothes later," he said. "And what about you, girlfriend?"

Me, I had to decide whether to look like Maddy again, or as different from her as possible. The former might heat things up or completely scare off the opposition; the latter was perhaps the better part of valour. As if that ever stopped me.

I chose Maddy. That meant getting the fuck-me boots from home. Denis lent me his car for the round-trip downtown, so I brought Bunnywit back with me for a visit, as I sometimes do.

Bunnywit loves the car. It's almost a reason to get one of my own, so we can cruise off into the country, to catch mice or look at landscape as our natures take us. Bun was happy enough to be riding again, though because of his sutures he lay quietly on the shelf behind the back seat instead of bracing his front paws on the dash and his rear paws on the front passenger seat and miaowing instructions as he supervised the city flowing by outside.

At Denis's, Bun chose a fetching pose under a familiar-to-him late-blooming cluster of hibiscus (Denis's triumph, being rare in this climate, but it grew in full sun in a sheltered nook on the south side of the house) and roses (Granada). I went inside.

In Denis's living room sat two women. One was an elegant "Oriental-beauty"-style confection in high heels, a short dress, saucy red lipstick, and a rich array of astonishing jewellery. If I hadn't expected Jian to be somewhere in the house, I'd never have recognised her. She looked frighteningly good in the lowcut sheath dress, her make-up flamboyant and the black hair (some of it was actually Denis's hair, from his large collection of wigs and hairpieces) cascading past her shoulders in a rush of curls. She looked like she would have her photo in the society pages tomorrow: she was the very image of a rich, plush-hipped, sexy socialite dressed to go slumming among the queens in the Queer Village.

She also made my mouth water.

She stood up to greet me, smiling remotely. (Denis had clearly also instilled Attitude.) I went over and started to kiss her, thinking of the lipstick at the last moment and kissing the nape of her neck instead. "Can I undress you later?" I murmured.

"If you give best offer," growled Jian, up to the hilt in her new rôle, but she spoiled it by grinning and spinning around so I could get the 360° view.

The other woman was a small black-leather-jacketed dyke with a bleached-white crew cut and severe black eyebrows. She wore black cowboy boots, black stovepipe jeans, an embroidered vest and white silk shirt, and a bolo tie with a turquoise slide.

She took off her mirrorshades. It still took me a double take to recognise her as Hep.

"Hep, your hair!" I said, aghast. Hep had had beautiful, butt-length hair when she let it down from its Hepburn-trademark braided crown. Now it was cropped short and spiked up a quarter-inch from her head, and her natural white I had taken for a bleach job in the modern style. "Your beautiful hair!"

"Thanks, honey," she said, diesel-dyke rough. "You like it?" and she ruffled her hand across the velvet top of her head.

I looked from Jian to Denis, who had stood in the archway to what had been the dining room when the house was inhabited by suburbanites. Now it was office, studio, and sewing room. Denis raised an eyebrow. "She changed her mind about an active rôle," he said. "The haircut she already had when she showed up here."

There were tears in my eyes. Hep came over to me, shedding adopted Attitude in favour of her own warmth. She put her arms around me. "Honey, it'll grow back," she said. "You don't have to get all tragic about it. Besides, I donated it to breast cancer patients. Hairdresser told me it should make two wigs, it was so long and thick."

"Yeah, sure. Sorry," I said. Bun scratched at the door, and I took advantage of the diversion of letting him in to compose myself from that uncharacteristic lapse.

"Actually, you guys look great," I said. "Incredible."

Bun advanced into the room, looked at Hep and Jian, and hissed in fear, backing up against my legs. The others laughed as I picked him up, and hearing their voices, he seemed to relax, but he really had been frightened by these half-strangers. "It's okay, Bun," I said. "They scare the hell out of me too."

There was something wrong with a process of enquiry that changed its initiators beyond recognition, but what could I say?

It had been my idea to come here; I was going to have to bear the symbolic weight of it alone — or at least, in silence.

47. "YMCA, I WANNA HEAR IT FOR THE YMCA . . ."

Silence was not the prevailing mode at the clubs. I regretted not having earplugs. Bun had stayed at Denis's, Jian and Hep went in as a team, and Denis and I ran interference with a girlfriend act I drew mainly from *The Adventures of Priscilla, Queen of the Desert* and its bad Hollywood movie rip-offs. Denis had changed his mind at the last minute and opted for evening drag (adding only half an hour to our prep time, a miracle of economy) and wore a platinum-blonde big-hair wig, a gold strapless floor-length sheath dress, and spaghetti strap gold sandals with elevator soles and six-inch stiletto heels (I should mention that Denis is over six feet tall barefoot). I was back in the fuck-me boots, feet already killing me, but in a silver lamé-and-chain-mail minidress and a matching silver wig. We looked like a kitsch Marilyn Monroe salt and pepper set. Several gay men had to check twice to see that I wasn't a drag queen, which pleased me, as I certainly felt I was a drag sensation.

Over the course of the night we covered every club on the strip — twice. The last time we took taxis between them because my feet hurt so much. The taxi drivers were used to queens, I guess, because not one complained about the half-block trips even before they got the outrageous tips.

In a traditional narrative, or a movie, there'd be at least a montage of drag club scenes, if not an unbalanced amount of time devoted to a semi-prurient, semi-anthropological survey of the scene for the armchair voyeurs. I can't supply it. I knew most of the queens from their other activities: civil rights advocacy work and volunteer work with gay youth; hours helping others in alcoholism treatment; police liaison work; weeknights at the AIDS agencies where in the past the older ones gave unpaid palliative care and now all ages did fundraising and safe-sex workshops and educated new volunteers.

My main problem was trying to stay unrecognised. The silver hair and makeup, and an all-over treatment of Body Shop tanning lotion to darken significantly all the skin I had showing, had helped some. For the rest, I didn't talk much, and Denis spoke to me exclusively in CBC French, which, like many Canadians not born near Québec, I understand fluently, though I can't speak it well. (His joual, we'd established years ago, I could hardly deal with, as my French, although learned in Canadian schools, was more Parisian than Québécois. Tabernac.)

48. TABERNAC

We struck pay-dirt at Rod's, a crowded after-hours bar with the usual excuse for a Live Sex Show (leather queens dancing crotch to crotch, erections sometimes obvious and sometimes obviously absent, choreography by MuchMusic out of Gypsy Rose Lee — "she can't sing, she can't dance, and she won't strip"). Never mind. I got over the worst of my Live Sex Show disillusionment years ago. I suppose to see the real thing, I have to either get the bucks together to join a club like the one in the ad we'd found in Maddy's envelope of clues or leave Canada, but even at my most well-paid, I hadn't ever accumulated enough bucks to invest in coming of age sexually in private, in Amsterdam or even in San Francisco. Maybe now, depending on what the lawyers said when I got around to visiting them, but I preferred not to think about that yet.

So the leather lads were dry-humping to headbanger tunes and video screens were showing the action in close-up colourized slo-mo when a little leather dyke came up behind me where I stood on the edge of the dance pit. Without stepping down, she grabbed my hipbones and pulled my butt against her crotch. Thank goodness for the makeup or my blush would have lit the place up like day.

"Hep!" I whispered, "don't!"

"Girlfriend," she said in a normal tone, "is it only the guys who have a chance with you?" Then in a whisper, "He's here. She's here. Whatever. Play along, for goodness' sake!"

"Sweet thang, anybody with the price of admission, I'll admit," I growled.

"That is *so* tacky!" she whispered, then, aloud, "Meet me at the door, silver streak, and I'll show you a good time too." Two can play at tacky, it seemed.

I wiggled through the crowd, catching eye contact with Denis as I did, and the four of us converged at the door. Hep and Jian were playing a game of argument-in-a-whisper into which they drew me. Clearly, Jian was Hep's date who hadn't been consulted about a threesome. Denis was the nosy drag queen who couldn't help getting involved in her friend the hooker's business. But the content of the whispers was something else.

"Right over there, by the pillar. In the red," said Hep.

The queen was tall, wearing a black miniskirt, a red shirt tied under tits so spectacularly ill-sited that they had to be fake, not implants, and thigh-high fuck-me boots like mine — I mean Maddy's — except red and about size thirteen. The hair was black bouffant, à la early sixties TV, and the face was already showing beard shadow through the makeup. Mind you, it *was* almost 4:00 a.m. now.

"That's what he wore when he was with Maddy," hissed Jian. "Just like that, but with black leather short coat with long stuff down off arms, what you call it?"

"Fringe?"

"Yes, fr-inge. Leather fr-inge. Very cool coat, awesome, but bad face, yes?"

Bad face for sure. I'm afraid that after seeing this character, I wouldn't have been able to laugh as easily at phrenologists and Victorian-era proponents of theories of criminal physiognomy. I don't know if I would have recognised the man beneath the make-up if I'd seen him on the street, but the queen made an impression on me in a few seconds. She had an expression of such condensed badness that her whole face looked like a death mask. How to describe the way an attitude can alter a face, the features of which could belong as easily to a librarian or a mild-mannered shoe salesperson, but which, infused by anger or fury, could double for a horror-movie villain? I'd never had the experience before, and it frightened me existentially as well as practically.

Two frissons of fear created interference patterns within me: the first at the face, the second — immediately after, and immensely greater, causing me to look away from the group by the pillar without seeing clearly any of the others there, and feeling my back prickle with cold sweat — when I realised s/he was staring right at me. Denis realised it at the same time, and I saw him reflexively place his body between me and the big queen as his voice rose.

"Well, honey, if you think that turning a trick with these sluts is a better deal than a night out with me, you can take your little silver butt out of my face right now, and don't call me, either, cuz I won't be home." He swivelled dramatically and started to stiletto away, turning back to shout, "Bitch!" He walked directly up to the queen in the red-and-black and I could hear him begin to rant, the only audible word being "fish."

I stared after him, jaw open.

"You're catching flies, girl," said Hep. "Come on," and she and Jian linked arms with me and started to pull me away.

"We can't leave him with her," I said. "She — he probably killed Maddy!"

"Shhh," hissed Jian. "What you do, all silver-wrapped like big shiny fish? Show up like big light. Come on. We hide outside, follow. Get proper shoes from car."

"But Denis has —"

"I have key here. Come, come! You want that big fuck to see us, figure out something wrong, hurt Denis?"

Given that argument, with which I had to agree, I turned, got back into our rôle-play, and we oozed out through the crowd. I hated the moment when I turned at the door and saw the big queen move around Denis, cutting him off from my view, looming over him.

He *was* a big fuck.

49. INTO THE JAWS OF DEATH, INTO THE MOUTH OF HELL, RODE THE SIX HUNDRED

Outside the bar, a group of suburban teenaged boys were gathered, shouting and screaming. All of them had short haircuts. With them were a few older guys, one of whom, a tall guy with a pony-tail, wore a T-shirt on which the words *Soul Patrol* encircled a medallion with a cross on it. The kids wore high-school team jackets and baseball caps on forwards and backwards. Some of them had sticks and bats. One had a tire iron.

Just as we came out the door, they began shouting about "fucking faggots" and "cornholers" and "fucking perverts" and "dykes" (whassa matter, you stupid little gits, don't dykes fuck? since you're so uneducated you only know one adjective?) and closed on the crowd of men and women leaving the club — and on us.

My silver hair and dress were like the Olympic flame, attracting cheers and jeers and an amazing amount of the action from the gay-bashers. Pushing Hep behind me, I waded out into the crowd, hoping she and Jian at least could get away. Being taken for a drag queen had developed a down side.

My way was blocked by two older men, who seemed less noisy, more intent. One was the tall guy, and the other also wore the Soul Patrol colours, stretched across a Michelin-Man™ set of bulges under a beige windbreaker.

"Pervert!" the chubby, hard-looking man whose face was six inches from mine was shouting, but for some reason he seemed insincere about it, though the fist which thudded into my belly was sincere enough.

"Grab her," the taller, thinner one said. "Come on, let's *go!*" but someone in the mob had other ideas. I saw the movement coming at my head only out of the corner of my eye, turned and raised my arms in defence, fell off the damn high heels, and began to fall in slo-mo as the stick struck my head.

"Grab *her?*" Italics mine, fleetingly. Then blackness . . .

50. LOST, UP IN NO-MAN'S LAND . . .

Which is why we didn't guard Denis — but also why I didn't get kidnapped, why I woke up in hospital, and why Roger was there when I woke, waiting to talk with me.

SHE WASHED HER HANDS AND SHE STRAIGHTENED HER HAIR UP,

51. DOES IT HURT WHEN I DO THIS?

Once they were satisfied that I wouldn't fall into a coma from the concussion, the doctor said, I would be allowed to go home. So Roger figured that since I had to be kept awake for the first few hours after my injury anyway, he might as well take my statement. He listened to my whispered descriptions of the two older guys without surprise.

He had a scrape on his cheek too — from one of the gay-bashers who resisted arrest, he said. I didn't have the energy to ask him why he'd been so near by. He went away with his notebook to talk with the others, and eventually came back to tell me, while the nurse was checking my pupils yet again, what the night's score was.

Denis was missing and so was the big drag queen, I had a concussion and black bruising on my belly (alliterative perhaps, but not a pretty sight, and not too pleasant to be feeling either), Jian had twelve stitches on her arm — she'd waded into the fray when she saw the stick hit my skull — and Hep had a sprained wrist and little finger from fending off a punch in a proactive manner, and a cracked toe bone from kicking a skinhead on the shin, manner ditto.

However, Hep had been right behind me, so in addition to fingering (so to speak) the gay-basher with the religious T-shirt, she had also been able to identify the man who punched me and his buddy who tried to grab me as the two who had been talking threateningly to Maddy the last time Hep saw her. As if any of us had any doubts by that time.

Did that mean we were further ahead, further behind, or just hurting more? All of the above, I suppose. I was too exhausted and aching to care, and they wouldn't give me strong painkillers because of the concussion. Hep and Jian had already left the hospital, together I assumed, though Roger didn't say and I was too tired to ask. By morning, when they let me go home in a taxi, I was staggering with pain and fatigue (and the need to walk on feet which last night had spent eight hours standing in Maddy's five-inch heels).

I fell into bed, Bun came and sat on my concussion, we had words and compromised on him leaning on my face instead, and I passed out for twelve hours.

52. SET THE CONTROLS FOR THE HEART OF THE SUN

When I got up and staggered out to the kitchen the next evening, the voice mail indicator on the phone base was blinking furiously. Ouch, strobe, too bright. Seven messages, which I turned down in volume to a whisper. Three were from the lawyer's office to whom Thelma had given my number, two were from Thelma, one was a hang-up, and the last one was from Denis.

Now picture this. Last time I had seen Denis, he'd been sashaying up to the meanest looking Queen of the Night that I'd seen in my life, someone who gave me existential terror with one glance, and who was suspected of murder.

Since then I'd almost been kidnapped by two men who likely were also murderers, my friends and I had been attacked by a brawling mob of gay-bashers, and I had sustained a concussion. I had almost decided last night, as the nurses kept me awake, that Denis was already dead like Maddy, and that I'd be going back to the morgue. That's the state in which I heard Denis start to speak — and this is what he said:

"Hi, girlfriend, how are ya? Listen, honey, I've found out something about our big queen, which I must say puts a spin on things, and you don't have to worry about *her* for a while, I fixed *that*. I'm off to work now, as soon as I have a quick shower. I have to work the *whole* weekend — I traded some shifts to get my garden done — so don't worry if I don't call. You didn't answer! Hope you guys got home all right. We went out the back way. Oh, everything turned out fine, by the way. I talked to Roger, that big cop you told me about? How come in all these years of police liaison — and I don't mean liaisons, unfortunately — I never met this one? *Oooh*, what a hunk. Did you do him? I bet you did. Is he pan? I *almost* broke my ban and invited him home, but I had a better idea! Ta ta for now!" The time on the message was 6:45 a.m. — I'd still been at the hospital.

Discovering in this manner that Denis was not dead — in fact, had apparently had a completely uneventful time while we'd been assaulted — made me feel like I could kill him myself, or so I said to Bun and the empty air of the kitchen. Then I began to cry with relief. Crying hurt. I stopped.

I called him and got voice mail. "You bugger. Pun unintended. Dammit, I thought you were dead! Where the hell did you meet Rog? Call me."

I called Roger, but he wasn't at home. The office said he was on duty but out of the office. He wasn't answering when called. My head was into a country of agony beyond sensibility. I fed Bun, groaning as I bent over and the pain peaked, then started to rummage around for something non-threatening for me to eat. The refrigerator light burned out the back of my retinas like a tiny sun, leaving a dazzling afterimage when I squeezed my eyes shut. Ow. Carefully closing the fridge before I opened my eyes, I realised that I had been operating this far in a twilight lit only by streetlight glare and the clock on the microwave oven.

That's about right, I thought, and looking in the freezer, which has no light, found something to thaw out. The annoying little buzzer which accompanies programming the microwave was headsplitting. Microwaves have lights too — there should be a law. I was in technohell, and some eighteen-year-old suburban bigot was to blame.

I put the meat back in the freezer and instead put frozen mini-waffles into the toaster, a nice old-fashioned device with no son et lumière. I could find the maple syrup in the fridge with my eyes shut, and did.

It had already obsessed me for the hours I spent in the hospital cubicle that I hadn't even seen which one of the little psychos — it's a technical term we helping professionals use — got me, so I wouldn't be able to testify. I'd been concentrating on the guys in front of me — if concentrating is what you call reacting to a sucker punch.

"Grab her." But everyone else in the crowd of bashers thought I was one of the drag queens. *Pervert*, yes, *fucking homo*, yes, but every one of the kids had said "Get *him*!" or "Kill *him*!" The two in front of me had had no doubt I was a woman.

I had to interpret their pronoun that way, because I couldn't believe the other option, that they were politically aware of the gender-critiquing diorama played out in the choice of high-camp female tropes to create a topos of female construct confounding actual genetic sex and backgrounded against issues of orientation politics, and had chosen to use the semantic signifier to indicate recognition of the radical linguosocial statement inherent in the transvestism of queer/drag.

No. They just didn't seem that complex; they seemed like old-fashioned thugs, not at all postmodern. Given that, I had to assume they knew just exactly who I was, despite the silver wig, the Body Shop tanning lotion, and the Diana Ross dress.

Thinking hurt. I decided to stop. But I didn't want to lose the memory of this, as I had when I first talked with Roger. After taking one of the painkillers the hospital had given me to take after a certain number of hours which had definitely passed, I left another message on his voice mail, and lay down on the couch, my throbbing head propped up with pillows, to eat the frozen mini-waffles.

Bun tried to sit on my stomach bruises to lick my empty plate. I managed not to scream, knowing that the noise would hurt, nor did I throw him across the room. Instead, I used his own weaknesses as strengths, put the plate on the floor, and of course he chose it over me. This is a cat I'm talking about here. He has his limitations.

53. BETTER LIVING THROUGH CHEMISTRY

As do we all. The painkiller finally took effect, and I drifted off into an uneasy state of wakefulness-without-consciousness, where the pain stood ten feet to the side and made comments about the state of my health, fitness, and sanity, and my brain simply gave up and went away.

It was rather peaceful, actually, once I realised that pain was only a kind of sensory Muzak and began to ignore it.

54. "I'M A SOUL MAN . . ."

Soul Patrol? It woke me up.

Groaning, I reached for the phone and, wincing at the dial tone and sharp little beeps of numbers as I dialed — how come we still say that? — Thelma's number. As it rang, I dry-swallowed the next scheduled painkiller.

For that matter, how come I know her number by heart?

"Thelma? . . . Yes, I got your messages, but that's not why . . . Thelma, hang on a second . . . Thelma, please be quiet, you're hurting me. Thank you. Thelma, I need your help."

Silence from the other end of the line. I was pretty surprised too. I need your help: the four words I never thought I'd hear go from my lips to her ears.

Finally she said in a small voice, "Are you all right?"

From her, four others of equal shock-value. Gracious. We were acting like family.

"No. Yes. Sort of. I got beat up. Can you come over?"

Goodness, it *was* four-word surprise time. As we discussed a time, the call waiting beeped. On the other line was Roger.

"Great, Roger! Can you come over? Soon?"

I went back to the haze for a while. Shocked awake again by another thought, I called Hep. Yes, Jian was with her, as I'd thought; and yes, they'd come over; and yes, she knew Denis's new work number; and yes, she'd see if he could take a break.

"And please don't call me back," I said. "If the phone rings, I think I'll die." I turned the ringer down, just in case, told them to use the key Jian had, and lay back in the twilight.

It wasn't until long afterward that I wondered how I managed to convince Thelma to come over to my house at almost midnight — and then realised she hadn't even protested. I must have sounded worse than I knew. That, or it was truly a night of miracles between us.

55. "IT'S ME, IT'S ME, O LORD, STANDING IN THE NEED OF PRAYER"

Have I mentioned that Thelma is a Christian? She has me on her prayer chain. People I don't know pray for me to have lives like theirs instead of like mine. Usually it irritates me, being prayed about without my consent, but tonight I thought I might ask her to mention my headache to them. I felt that I wouldn't mind some healing energy going into the universe on my behalf, if I got to pick what was meant to be healed.

When Thelma arrived, before Jian and Hep so I was forced to creep to the door to let her in, another miracle occurred. She neither fussed nor prayed. She capably and quietly found a towel, wrapped it around a bag of ice cubes, and arranged it on my head so it almost felt soft. Then she made similar ice packs for my bruises. She tucked a blanket around my shoulders with strong, minimal motions, and made me lie down on the couch with a pillow under my back and another under my knees. Intensely grateful, I mentioned the possibility of switching the focus of the prayer group, and a little smile tugged at the corner of her mouth. Not an "I knew she'd come around" smile, but a wry little "from each according to her ability" recognition smile.

We had done the best we could do for one night. The others arrived as I was getting used to a limited amount of light from the hall fixture (indirect, also Thel's idea).

The Soul Patrol T-shirts were the issue, of course. Those things aren't sold in stores. They're given out to people who volunteer for community service in evangelical and fundamentalist church circles. Thelma had been very proud when she got hers; she had showed it to me last spring at her Easter Forced Family Event.

Now, Christians may hassle prostitutes about turning to Jesus instead of turning tricks, but "holier than thou" is usually their watchword, emphasis on the "holier" part. I needed to know how a guy who hassles homosexuals and prostitutes gets Soul Patrol endorsement — well, okay, how a guy who hassles them *criminally* rather than as a hate crime.

To find out, I needed a local guide. I'd have to convince Thelma to take me there. She knew the lingo. I began to tell her what I'd been up to.

She was surprisingly resilient about it. She only *tsk*ed about a dozen times and only said, "Disgusting!" twice (and once was about Denis's sixties outfit). It helped that Hep had her pictures of Maddy. The kid's pitiful looks even got to Thelma.

56. "THEN I GOT THROWN OUT OF CHU'CH FO' TALKIN' 'BOUT DITTY-WAH-DITTIE TOO MUCH . . ."

"We can pray for her," she said.

"With all due respect, Thelma," I said, "she's dead."

"She may suffer in Purgatory. Maybe our prayers can help shorten her time in the Lake of Fire."

"We had something more like catching her killers in mind," Roger said.

"You said *we*," I said. "Thanks, Roger."

"I was talking about we the police," he said.

"So what are you doing *here*, then?"

"I'm in a terrible conflict of interest position," he said.

"Think of it as civilian liaison work, looking for relevant information," said Hep. "Which it is. We *are* civilians, aren't we?" and she glared at us all as if she expected us to develop undercover cop credentials on the spot.

Thelma was charmed. Did I mention she watches a lot of TV? Not all of it is the gospel channel, I guess.

Then she came through in style — Thelma's inimitable style. "You could never go there," she said. "Even if you could see straight, which you can't, or walk straight, which you can't, you could never look straight. I have to go for you."

"Thel, you're a doll," Denis started to say.

"It may be dangerous." Roger, of course.

"Besides, do you think I want everyone at church to know my cousin is a homo? That's worse than anything some hoodlum could do to me."

We all looked at her, struck silent.

"And I won't go unless you promise me something," she said, turning to me a little faster than my eyes could track, which made for a fetching if vertiginous "traces" effect, like a bad acid-trip sequence in an early-seventies movie.

"What?" My momentary glow of liking had worn off with the homo remark.

"You have to go see the lawyers. I'm sick of them calling and calling, as if *I* could make *you* do anything you didn't want to."

"Except now you think you can."

"I never had anything you wanted before," she said with devastating truth and simplicity.

"Oh, Thelma . . ." I said, feeling hit while down.

"Just promise," she said. "You don't have to like it."

"I promise," I said.

"This week," she said relentlessly.

My head was throbbing. She gently took the ice-pack-filled towel and refolded the package so that it felt cold against the lump. "This week," I mumbled, "as soon as I can walk again."

If I were to say they were all there when I went back to sleep, that wouldn't be saying much, since immediately after I saw her nod with satisfaction, I passed out again before I finished the agenda of the midnight meeting I'd called.

Or should I say, "and then, I knew no more . . ."? Especially since that was the net effect?

57. STOP ME IF YOU'VE HEARD THIS ONE

When I regained consciousness . . . okay, you've heard that one too. Never mind. The next three days weren't pretty. I couldn't keep solid food down at first, and discovering that by experience hurt more than I believed possible. As soon as I awoke, I realised that Denis hadn't told us what he had discovered about the big queen, but as I had already passed out in the middle of one arbitrarily-summoned team meeting, as Hep and Jian reminded me, I shouldn't call another one until I was sure it wouldn't happen again.

The meeting had been late Saturday, so I had hoped Thelma could get results the next day, but when I phoned her between bouts of nausea, she told me sharply that Moses wandered in the desert for forty years. I managed not to reply that we didn't want to spend that long on this little problem.

After that, Hep and Jian took the phone away from me and I couldn't convince them that calling Denis would make me rest better. Or that calling Roger first thing Monday morning to see if the lab tests were back *yet* would set my mind at ease.

"You have to stop, think," said Jian. "Let that head relax, or head can't heal."

"Good point," said Hep.

Stupid point, I thought grumpily, but to contest it took too much effort. Hell, lifting my hand took too much effort. I got as far as making them promise to call Denis and make him promise to call Roger.

I spent three days lying on the couch, sipping ginger ale, comfrey tea, ginseng broth, chicken soup, and other time-honoured remedies through a straw, and gradually getting to the point where standing up didn't make me consider suicide as a viable analgesic.

Hep had called the doctor, who said, "Watch her. Call me if she gets weird." Did I mention that my doctor ran a storefront clinic in his spare time? So Hep and Jian took turns staying awake watching me while the other crashed on the bed.

I drifted in and out of dreams where Hep's face became Maddy's became Jian's became the Soul Man's became Bun's became mist.

Bun came by occasionally to lick my hairline consolingly, but he soon figured out who was filling his food bowl now, and spent time reminding Hep and Jian that he was a Good Cat. I couldn't decide whether I applauded his pragmatism or despised his lack of solicitude and loyalty.

Every time I considered the question, though, I'd drift sideways into the dream twilight and Bun would become Hep would become Jian would become Roger would become the big queen would become the Soul Man would wake me sweating.

It seemed like forever before I woke up with a clear head, but when I asked, Jian said it was only Wednesday morning.

THEN ISABEL QUIETLY ATE THE BEAR UP.

58. DON'T MAKE PROMISES YOU CAN'T KEEP

A promise is a promise, I thought unhappily that morning as Hep helped me wash my hair. Feeling her hands tenderly avoid the concussion site reminded me of her erstwhile long hair, and such was my state of fragility that a few tears of grief leaked out before I realised it. Gee, I thought grumpily, next I would be crying about the three inches of gut Bun lost to the vet during *his* recent health crisis. Hep and Jian were going out shopping, and then to Hep's house. Hep being the same sort of fanatical suburban gardener Denis was, it bothered her that she hadn't yet cleared out her raspberry canes or something.

I said that sounded to me like a Christmas project, and Hep looked at me.

"Sounds to *me* like you're fit to be left alone, at last," she said.

As soon as they were gone I called the lawyers' office.

"Kirk, Spak, and Lennie," said the receptionist.

I said, "I bet you get a lot of Star Trek jokes."

She said, "Huh?"

"Never mind," I said, and she put me through to the extension of Mr. Spak, whose whispery voice had left three messages that I associated with twilight, pain, and the taste of frozen waffles. Mr. Spak was tied up, said his secretary. He does that at work? I asked. Huh? she said. Never mind, I said.

I was disappointed to hear from the secretary that Mr. Spak was eager to see me and could "fit me in" that afternoon. I said that made me sound like a dental prosthesis.

"Huh?" she said.

"Never mind," I said. I got her to spell Mr. Spak's name.

After I hung up I looked at Bun. He'd understood all three jokes, I could tell by the way he miaowed when I looked at him. He miaowed again, and then nodded three times.

"You could be right," I said to him, and went to find something suitable to wear to a lawyer's office. I chose one of the outfits I used to wear to work last year, although after my recent experiences I would never again be able to think of it as anything but "social work drag". It was comforting to think I was wearing armour that would keep Mr. Spak from knowing anything about me.

I discarded the idea that Maddy's boots might set the right tone. With my head in this state, I said to Bun, I couldn't take the altitude. When I opened the hall closet door to get my coat, he gave a little *prrrt* of pleasure and made a beeline for the boots, curling up on them and purring.

I'd successfully put off this moment for months. It occurred to me that but for Maddy Pritchard, whom I'd never met alive, and Thelma, whom I was beginning to think I'd underestimated, I could have put it off forever. I didn't know whether to wish I'd never heard of Maddy at all, or be secretly glad. It was sort of like going to the dentist to have an abscess lanced. Even to those who don't like it, pain can become an old friend, and you can be sorry to see it go, even if you enjoy the new sense of freedom from pressure.

"Ha," said Bun from behind me, and I spun around (vertigo ensued) to see him spitting out a bit of fur.

"No comments from the gallery," I said, and he stared at me coldly, then went back to licking the base of the little ducktail he has instead of a real cat tail. It was a hint. I left him and the boots alone.

59. EARS PIERCED WHILE YOU WAIT

Kirk, Spak, and Lennie camped in one of those beautiful glass towers whose surface of reflective panels, called "curtain walls", reflects a crazy-quilt of sky and nearby architecture. I sat on the edge of a planter outside the building and held my head together with one hand as I tilted it back to look up — 'way up, as Friendly would have said.

As I tipped my head back to level, my involuntary groan earned a glance from a couple of suits passing by. One of them had long sandy hair in a pony-tail, the other was a little chubby, and they both wore Italian suits, but unless our villains had had plastic surgery since the riot to turn them into stockbrokers, these guys were in a different class. They eyed my outfit and me with a sideways glance. Since my suit was upmarket leather, I felt I had won the encounter, despite my groan, and I grinned at them. One blushed and the other one frowned. As they walked away, one chaffed the other, the words "dyke bitch" floating back in the breeze. Goodness, it was everywhere. Clearly clothes did not make the man.

Or, in my case, the heterosexual.

The receptionist at Kirk, Spak, and Lennie looked just like she sounded. Despite that, I would rather have been stuck in an elevator with her for eight hours than spend a minute in the company of Mr. Spak, lovely though he was when he came out to the reception area to meet me. Tall, with naturally marcelling hair, and with gently-brown colouring to match his cashmere suit and turtleneck sweater, he looked like a certain kind of high-class, faded-tortoiseshell cat, perhaps a Rex. He didn't have big ears, though: his were delicate and shell-like and hugged his nicely-shaped skull. In fact, he was very cute, and in another life I would have done him in a New York minute, after checking with the co-owner of his wedding ring.

In this life, he terrified me.

"I'm Spak," he said. *No*, I thought, *I've already established that your ears aren't pointy enough*. "Come this way," and I thought, *No, when I come, it's not nearly that quiet and calm*, but I followed him without speaking.

60. A GREAT LORD'S KITCHEN WITHOUT FIRE IN'T ...

His office was large, almost empty, and law books were stacked in the corners. There were several good pieces of art (paintings, prints, a collage, and one sculpture) leaning against or sitting near the longest wall. One desk and two chairs were the sum of furniture. "Just moving in," he said. "Sorry. Have a seat?"

I sat, feeling emptier than the office. I looked vaguely at the corner of his desk, waiting for him to start. The silence got longer, and finally I noticed, woke up, and looked up at him. He was smiling at me.

"Not easy to come here, was it?" he said gently. I liked him for that, through the protective cloud of hatred I was trying to generate.

"Not a bit. I was bribed to get me here at all."

"What kind of a bribe would do what a year of my effort couldn't?"

"Information. Recognition."

"Thelma called me. She said you were doing something hare-brained and almost got yourself killed. I wouldn't have liked that."

"You don't even know me."

He pulled open a drawer of his desk and out of it he wrestled a four-inch binder and a filing folder almost three inches thick and plunked them down on the desk. "I know you," he said.

"What the fuck is *that*?" I said, involuntarily. I would have said *I ejaculated*, but one bad cum joke is enough for this scene.

"All the paperwork. The private detective's reports. The photographs."

"Photographs? Of me?"

"Um, no. Of the crime scene."

"Crime scene? You mean, my parents' house?"

"Yes, sorry."

"Can I see them?"

"Um . . . are you sure you want to?"

"Yes."

The digital colour glossies showed a house in as serious a state of disarray as my living room had been after the Soul Patrol had been there. I hadn't remembered it as quite this horrible. The bodies of my parents showed as huddled, barely human shapes with black pools of drying blood around their heads — what was left of their heads. The shotgun lay beside my father's hand. The thieves who had tossed the place around their dead bodies in the week before they had been discovered had taken almost everything else of value, but left the gun. I shuddered.

I didn't notice him move, but he was beside me, taking the photos out of my hand and handing me a gigantic cotton handkerchief. Beige, with thin darker brown border lines. I wiped my eyes. Crying still hurt.

"Not easy for you to see it again," he said.

"I see it in my dreams," I said. "Literally, cliché or not. In colour."

"Yes, you would. So you didn't want to get any closer."

"No, I just didn't want to profit from it."

"I can understand that, but they were your parents and you are their only child. Only *living* child," he corrected before I could do more than open my mouth.

"I don't understand why they did it," I said. "They weren't weird people. They didn't even shoot things. He had to go out and buy the damned thing."

"Yes, I know, I read the report."

"The gun shop owner was kind of funny in a black-humour way. He was just so — nonplussed. He kept saying, 'The guy was, like, a professor.' I kept wanting to jump up in the inquest and say, 'No, he wasn't *like* a professor, he *was* a professor.'"

"No terminal illness diagnosis, no family violence history, no history of depression, no new medications with potential psychotropic effect . . ."

"No reason for a suicide pact . . ."

"And certainly no evidence of murder was found, either by the police investigation or by ours."

"Why did *you* do an investigation?"

"Well, there is a great deal of money involved."

"Come on. I know what they had in the bank."

"Then there's the insurance, as well as the investments. And the trust fund of course."

"Insurance? Trust fund?"

"Of course. I wouldn't have been this thorough for a simple bank account. Their wills far more than have to go to probate."

"Trust fund?"

I thought about my father's salary from his tenured position at the uni. I thought about my mother's "little hobby" of writing romance novels, and her modest inheritance of $12,000 from her mother's estate.

Trust fund?

Wincing at the light from the huge plate glass windows behind his head, I got up and slowly moved the chair around until it was beside the desk and in the background, instead of the entire lumen-power of the sun, was only an ivory linen-finish panelled wall.

"Let me put it another way," I said. "Trust fund?"

"Probably seven hundred a month interest for you, half that for Thelma and her family. She intimated that she had told you about it."

"Not in that much detail. But still." I thought for a minute. Arithmetic hurt too. "That's gotta be from a sum of maybe a quarter of a million to half a million. I hate to say it this way, but that's not much."

"Unless you add the insurance, which was half a million on each of them, and no suicide clause. Acts of God, yes, but not of violence. The agent says they got it because they travelled a lot, wanted protection from terrorism and tourist victimisation. The suicide thing was just a side effect. It was expensive."

"I had no idea it was for that much. They argued about the premiums."

"Yes, I know. In addition to the insurance, there are the mutual funds, the GICs, and the other RRSPs. Then there is the stock portfolio."

"Stocks? My folks had *stocks*?"

"High-, medium-, and low-risk investments. Their broker actually *made* money on Bre-X for them, by selling before the crash. And there was some gold, and then commodities, of course. It was a diversified portfolio."

"And this all equals . . . ?"

"After death duties and other relevant taxes, about one and three-quarter million dollars. *Not* including the trust fund."

"What?" Ouch. *What?*

"Yes. You see why we wanted to be absolutely sure that you were not in any way implicated." It wasn't a question.

I did see, but it didn't help my reaction.

"You investigated *me?*" I would classify my tone as a squeak. Bun would have been ashamed of me.

"Indeed." He steepled his fingers, and for a moment looked a lot like the TV character: thoughtful, inscrutable, and detached.

"And what did you find?"

"Sexually active, but bondable."

I looked twice. The twitch around his lips was indeed a smile trying to get out. Or a laugh? When I laughed, so did he, which settled that.

When we were done laughing, I sat there, feeling emotionally numb. Also laughing had made my headache into something potent and malevolent again. I breathed quietly until it calmed down. It was rather peaceful, actually.

"Now what?" I asked.

Mr. Spak leaned back and arranged his lovely hands on the blotter beside my file. "Well, we give you the money and you retire."

"I already got retired. Without my consent."

"Yes, that was terrible."

"Terrible?" I mimicked his suburban tones, but he replied quite seriously.

"Yes, that kind of discrimination: terrible. You could have sued, you know."

"Not in this province."

"Civil suit. I could have done something with it, I'm sure. Human rights. Charter challenge. Well, never mind that now, it's water under the bridge." He tapped the file, probably indicating that he had a copy of the waiver I had signed in exchange for the severance package. "But I want to say that I think it was shameful."

"Do you know anything about Baptists?" I asked.

"Yes, my father was one," he said.

"Was? I'm sorry."

"So am I," he said. "Now he's going to some born-again evangelical church that makes the Baptists look liberal."

"Well, so is Thelma, so I guess we have something in common. My folks were Baptists. I guess you know that already. I had just come out to them. I didn't do it very well. There were words. When they didn't answer my calls, at first I thought, well, fuck it, if you're going to not speak to me again, I can live with that. If your right-wing religion is more important than your only remaining child. My brother suicided, you know, when he was fifteen. With pills."

"Yes, I know. Often one suicide breaks the family taboo, and other family members feel they have permission to consider it an option."

"Yes. I know."

"I suppose you do. Sorry."

"So when Thelma called and said they hadn't been to *church*, that was when I got worried. There was nothing I could have done, but I always felt guilty about leaving them lying there for so many days . . ."

"But that's not all."

"No," I said, surprised. "But why do you want to hear it all?"

He had his fingertips steepled again, and this time he bent his fingers and straightened them like the spider-on-the-mirror trick of childhood. Noticing me noticing, he folded his hands in his lap. "I have been living with this file for over a year," he said, "and I made some guesses."

"Well, you're probably right," I said, "if you guessed that I felt guilty because I thought they couldn't live with their daughter being ambisexual. You see, my brother left a note that I think said he was killing himself because God hates pervs. Two in one family?"

"I didn't know that there was a note," he said. "But you didn't know, it seems, that your brother was sexually active with a girl he'd gotten pregnant, and had given her money to help her pay for her abortion so she could carry on at school. That was a mortal sin, as they saw it. So if he thought he was gay, that muddies the water."

"I never saw the note. My folks told me. They said that he wrote he 'couldn't live with his sexual behaviour' and that he had done something abhorrent to God. I was so worried about whether I might be a dyke that I must have misread it."

"I think you did. If that helps. But there were a few other things. The university had offered your father early retirement —"

"He said he chose that!"

"Well, he didn't. And they had asked him to write fewer letters to the editor signed 'Professor of ——'. And your mother —"

"What. This is some kinda show-and-tell?"

"— wanted to leave him. She was running out of endurance."

"So he killed her and then himself?"

"No, it's as the police told you. Each one pulled their own trigger."

"Who went first?"

"Your father."

After that, we sat quietly for a few moments. He re-steepled his fingers unconsciously twice, noticed and undid the steeple once.

"Mr. Spak," I said. "Do you have a first name?"

"Dafydd," he said.

"Davis?" It had a short *a*, and what was that sound at the end?

"No, Dafydd," and he spelled it and sounded it out. "It's Welsh. My mother is Welsh."

"Do you sing in a choir?"

"Yes."

I shook my head. "I don't want their money," I said. "They were people I wouldn't cross the street to greet if I weren't related to them. They made my life miserable for years, and my brother's too. I blame them for his death. They killed themselves without thinking of how the rest of us would feel. I blamed their deaths on my sexuality and made stupid promises about never getting laid again, which of course I broke, which added to the guilt. I was tired of them alive, and I'm tired of them dead. What good will all that money do?"

"Feed you and your cat for the rest of your life. Make you independent of the kind of people who fired you. Allow you to help your friends as you are helping Mrs. Pritchard, without worrying about fees — once you get a licence, so you won't skate on the edge of legality as you are doing now."

"How do you know about that?"

"Thelma told me."

"I don't want the fruits of their parsimonious suburban lives."

"You own them whether you want them or not. Besides the considerable personal legacy that helped form you into a rather good person, you have been left a tangible legacy of goods and funds. They are yours by law. Even without their very explicit wills, the laws of inheritance are clear."

I ignored the compliment. "What would you do?"

"Me?" He was clearly surprised, though it can't have been the first time that question was asked of him by a client.

"Yes, you. Dafydd Spak, multiculturalism poster lawyer."

He smiled. This guy didn't grin, he smiled. He was a cultured fellow.

"What I would do: I would take the money and spend it doing things my parents would hate. Helping people my parents would hate. Also, I would give more of it to Thelma, who stood by them through the church controversies and the letter-writing business. I wouldn't be surprised if there had been an organic cause for that, by the way. Personality change comes with several illnesses, not just Alzheimer's. But the autopsy was concerned with the mechanics of death and the possibility of foul play. They didn't waste, as they saw it, any time on routine organic stuff, and cremation put an end to investigation. Anyway, I would give some to Thelma. The amniocentesis results weren't good, and she doesn't believe in abortion."

"She's — they're — pregnant?"

"Yes. Diagnosis of Down's syndrome, I believe."

"Fine," I said. "I'll think about it. Start by giving her a bunch of cash, then increase her monthly income — give her the whole income from the trust. Don't tell her why. Make up something. As for the rest, keep it wherever it is. I have to think about this. And Dafydd . . ." I used Roger's technique: paused and made him ask.

"What?"

"Don't call me."

"I can't just leave it! I have my code of ethics . . ." And his curious possessiveness, I thought.

"Don't call me for six months. If I call you before then, fine."

"Three months."

"Six."

"Three. And you sign these. Or I won't promise."

My head was aching. "All *right*! Fine." But it wasn't fine — bending over his desk to affix my signatures to some pages whose blurry writing I pretended to read was excruciating. As long as I only pretended to read them, I could pretend I didn't know I'd just given in, which wasn't fine either.

Before I signed, I stood looking at the paperwork spread across the desk, and the financial statements on the side, for a long minute.

"All I said before was true," I said finally.

"I know," he said.

"Still, I'd rather have my parents," I said.

"I know," he said. "But."

Leaning over to sign woke my head up and I had to plunk down into the chair to finish, which put an end to any more Moments.

"Fine," I said again when I was done and he had given me copies. I stuffed them in my pocket. "*Now*, can I go home?"

He called a taxi for me, and escorted me down in the elevator.

61. EVERY SILVER LINING HAS A CLOUD

I guess that qualifies as an excellent subplot. Come to think of it. Which I hated doing; it made my head hurt. Clichés abound, and I wanted to refuse the rags-to-riches one. Yet again, from beyond the grave, my parents were making my life difficult in yet another weird way.

I tried not to blame them for it. I tried to rise above it.

When I got home, I threw up. That *really* hurt. You have no idea how much hurling moves the head around, until you have to do it while concussed.

Bunnywit watched me and purred. To him, throwing up was normal. Bulimic little turd.

ISABEL MET A HIDEOUS GIANT,

62. GALACTIC HERO OR NOT, SOMEBODY HAS TO FEED THE CAT

After taking two painkillers and lying down for three hours —
no, let me be honest, after doubling the recommended dose of
painkiller, then lying down and conking out for three hours of
remarkably unpleasant semi-oblivion — I wakened to lie on the
couch and try to think.

I wasn't quite managing to think about the mysteries with
which I was surrounded. Instead I thought about Roman
numerals, specifically the Xs. After the concussion, I had for days
felt like those cartoon characters with Xs for eyes. I was considerably better, but still found that when I closed my eyes the galaxy
wheeled its spiral bulk in a monochromatic, pixillated slant across
the canvas inside my eyelids. It was vertiginous, nauseous, and
left me feeling like I was in flight, abducted by the concussion
aliens, never to return to my home planet.

Which wouldn't matter except for three things.

The least important of the three to anyone except Bunnywit
was who would feed the cat if I got stuck out in the Oort Cloud.

(Bun miaowed enough to make *his* priority clear: his nagging was what brought me out of my stuporous reverie to open a can of Seafood Medley, a.k.a. gross tuna spare-parts.)

The other two were tied for first place: who'd see that Jian got back where she belonged in life, and who'd find Maddy's killer? Aside from the obsessive edge the latter quest was gaining in my thoughts, I also felt it was far less dangerous than facing my parents' legacy.

Others, apparently, didn't think so, which I was about to find out.

63. ONCE MORE UNTO THE BREACH, DEAR FRIENDS . . .

I began again in self-defence. I started with Denis and replayed the message that was still on the answering machine. When he came by to bring me a cunning little casserole of lamb and artichoke hearts with hot walnut vinaigrette over basmati rice, I asked him what it was that I wouldn't have believed, four days ago (four years? An aeon of galaxy-whirling and Roman numerals? Whatever).

He pretended innocent, and straightened the white silky five-inch fringe on the yoke and sleeves of his turquoise satin Western shirt.

"Just queen gossip, honey. It's nothing."

I got up and walked over to the machine, played back the message. We listened to the breathless voice: "Hi, girlfriend, how are ya? Listen, honey, I've found out something about our big queen, which I must say puts a spin on things, and you don't have to worry about *her* for a while, I fixed *that*. I'm off to work now, as soon as I have a quick shower. I have to work the *whole* weekend — I traded some shifts to get my garden done — so don't worry if I don't call. You didn't answer! Hope you guys got home all right. We went out the back way. Oh, everything turned out fine, by the way. I talked to Roger, that big cop you told me about? How come in all these years of police liaison — and I don't mean liaisons, unfortunately — I never met this one? *Oooh,* what a hunk. Did you do him? I bet you did. Is he pan? I *almost* broke my ban and invited him home, but I have a better idea! Ta ta for now!" Denis avoided my gaze, got up, and started fluffing up pillows. Since I only had two, it was quite a performance.

I hit the *save* button at the same time I snapped, "Will you *stop* that?"

His hands stilled, hugging a pillow.

"I can't tell you."

"What?"

Stubbornly, he turned away, tossing the pillow aside and picking up his shoulder bag: today, a tooled leather 1950s special with leather lacing holding together two roughly-circular slabs with ponies' heads as their motif. Along the strap were tooled letters: *Raven Rodeo 1952.*

"Sorry, sweetie. My lips are sealed. And it's not just the cheap lip gloss."

"What are you talking about?"

"Hep made me promise."

"Promise . . . ?"

"She doesn't want you on the case any more."

"I saw her this morning. She said nothing to me about that!"

"She said nothing to you about the case at all, did she?"

I had to admit that was true. In fact, thinking back, the soothing caregiver noises I'd heard from her all week seemed to have been at triple intensity whenever I talked about when I'd feel ready to get back at it.

"She was horrified by the violence. She feels it was her fault."

"Gay-bashers are not her fault!"

"Come on, don't play stupid. Gay-bashers who knew who you were? Who went for you? After trashing your apartment? Get real, girl. Why do you think there has been someone here with you all so much of the time? Why do you think Roger has one of his baby cops stationed across the street all night every night, watching the door and the fire escape?"

"But I haven't seen anybody." As I said it, it sounded stupid, and Denis knew it too.

"Face it, girlfriend. If you had been able to stagger over to the windows, what could you see? It's only been in the last thirty-six hours that you could focus your eyes!"

"Okay, so what?"

"Hep loves you, in case you haven't noticed. Jian loves you. Even I love you, though you are a stubborn little diva and your cat is nuts. It's even possible that in his odd way Roger loves you. We are interested in keeping you around!"

His vehemence was too loud. I winced.

"Sorry," he said more moderately.

"But what about Maddy?"

"Maddy's dead. There's nothing more anyone can do for Maddy," he said brutally. *And besides, the wench is dead*, I thought, and shivered.

"And Vikki? She needs to be found. She could be dead too, for that matter. I can't stop — we can't stop."

"I agree with you. *We* won't stop. We haven't. But *you* will. We had a meeting. We agreed."

"I don't remember any meeting."

"Not us and you *we*. We *we*. The rest of us *we*. You weren't invited, chérie."

"Then your decision isn't binding. I wasn't consulted."

"You need to get better and get back to looking for a real job before you run out of cat food again."

Suddenly I was defiantly glad that I'd signed the Rex-cat lawyer's paperwork. I told Denis about the lawyer, my parents' money, and the fact that I never needed to work at my puta-tive *profession* ever again; nor would I need to take Hep's money. Between joy on my behalf, amazement that I had tried to refuse a fortune, and reaction to me giving him Attitude, Denis took quite a while to simmer down, but at the end, I got what I thought was a pretty good last word.

"Which means, all the rest of the stuff aside, that I don't have to take the advice of your nasty little *meeting*. I'll be carrying on with my questions, and if you people block me, I'll go back out on the street."

Unfortunately he's a drag queen. They *never* allow anybody else the last word. "If you can't walk across the room without staggering, how will you be able to walk in Bunnywit's fuck-me boots?" And he went out, heedless of me following him to the hall, and left, slamming the door resoundingly behind him.

Ow.

When the reverberations of that had died down enough that I stopped seeing the whirling galaxy even with my eyes open, I saw that indeed the closet door was slightly ajar and Bunnywit was still making the boots his home. He had begun sucking on the zipper pull like an unweaned kitten. Around his mouth the supple leather was wet with besotted-cat drool. Annoyed, I yanked the boots out from under him. He tumbled to the floor, gave an outraged yowl, and swiped a set of naked claws at me with intent. I barely escaped with my life.

Clearly I was oh-and-three today. And I still didn't know what Denis had found out the night of the drag show.

"Oh, fine, ruin the damn boots," I said crossly. "What else are they good for?" I threw them back down. Bun skittered away. "And don't act like I beat you," I admonished him. "I'm the one who gets beat up around here." I went to put peroxide on the scratches on my arm.

64. EPIPHANY: NOT A HOLIDAY IN DECEMBER

When I called Hep, figuring I may as well while I was on a streak, she said she could come over in about an hour.

"Is Jian with you?"

"No, Denis just called and she went somewhere to meet him. He sounded upset."

"Ah. Well, I wish she would come with you. I miss her." She'd been gone all of eight hours. What a stupid thing to say.

"She worries about disturbing you."

That was even stupider. Why were these people I loved suddenly forming their exclusive cabal with me on the outside? I had a good mind to give them a talking-to — but at that moment I fell asleep again and didn't wake until I heard Bunnywit greeting Hep as she used Jian's key to get in. She was carrying some freshly-baked rolls. Between Denis's casserole and the rolls, it was the first time food had smelled good to me for days.

Hep looked particularly fetching, if several decades out of date, in a summer-weight tea-gown with a wide skirt and a fitted waist. Ah well, I'd seen the same type of outfit on the cover of *Vogue* magazine last month, so clearly what goes around comes around — as she soon found out. As soon as the inevitable flutterings of concern died down, I tackled her about what Denis had told me.

Hep was adamant. "Look at you," she said. "That's my fault."

"A skinhead with a baseball bat," I said. "Remember? I'll admit the abdominal bruising is more relevant — but I chose to be there. So let's not have the touching scene where you say I wouldn't have been there if not for the investigation and I say gay-bashers are everywhere and you say your conscience won't allow yada yada yada and we go on in that vein for a while. My head won't take it. Let me just say that I made this my problem as well as yours a long time ago and I am not giving up. Furthermore, you cut your hair for this. So get over this bullshit and let's get on with it. Denis won't tell me what he found out, and Roger is on assignment and his office mates won't say where. I need you to take the muzzle off Denis, and I need to get working again."

I was quiet for a moment, then admitted: "Besides, I have things I want to get my mind off. Off which I want to get my mind. Whatever."

I found myself telling her about the money, and about my parents. Hep was not only a good listener, but she was smart. As she listened, she had such a sympathetic look that her first words surprised the hell out of me.

"They're dead," she said. "You're not. When are you going to stop letting them control your life?"

For a change, the blazing light that dawned as I heard her words didn't hurt my head. In fact, for a second, I felt no pain at all. How simple! She was perfectly right. I was reacting as if they were around to see me get even by rejecting them the way they'd rejected me.

I won't say that the scales fell from my eyes. It was more like part of the nausea was gone instantly, leaving only the part related to the concussion. Which, I had to admit, also wasn't as much as it had been earlier.

After that we shared Denis's casserole. It tasted pretty good. Hep was still adamant that we should cool off the investigation, but although I was prepared to argue the matter, I had a little perspective now, courtesy the epiphany she had forced, and I figured we had plenty of time to talk about it. Like at least until after the dishes were done.

Bunnywit liked the casserole too. I gave him a bit with his cat food and he left the cat food until later — amazing. Usually he scarfs down those pig guts and tuna veins like there's no tomorrow. (Of course, I eat wieners, so there's not much moral high ground there, come to think of it.)

After dinner Hep washed the plates while I lay on the couch with Bunnywit trying to warm my head. For the first time since I had been hurt, Bun actually achieved a balance where his weight wasn't on my skull but on the sofa cushion, and yet his furry warmth gave comfort. It was peaceful and comfortable.

Until the doorbell rang, and Bun used my skull to launch his startled leap.

Thanks, animal friend, I thought, as the world reeled. Hep went to let in Jian and Denis.

65. MR. BIG & TALL

Jian and I settled down on the couch in a position more comforting than Bun's cuddle, and more vertical than my usual in the past week. I was feeling better, and I had had an epiphany. Two good reasons to start acting like I walked the land of the living. The third good reason was that if I lay down I couldn't have my lover by my side, her arm around me and our legs casually entangled, her curvy thigh against mine.

Denis had changed his clothes. He now wore the straightest clothes I'd seen on him in weeks: a white Lindbergh shirt with ragged pleats down the front under pale blue embroidered flowers, loose over 7Diamonds low-rise dress jeans.

"Nice rags," I said.

"You like? The cutest little boy in Urban talked me into it. Said it looked great even if I *was* an old guy." He sprawled in the armchair and, after she handed him a cup of tea in one of my best cups, Hep stood over him with a stern face and said, "Denis, little flower, what have you done?"

"It's so obvious?" Denis was plaintive, playing the child.

Jian laughed. "You read him like teleprompter," she said, and I looked at her. She couldn't suppress a grin. Denis had outfitted her in something draped and slinky, not a brand that

I recognised but clearly quality, which accentuated her cleavage without making her look slutty. Available, but cool. She wasn't acting cool though. She was acting like a kid waiting for Christmas to dawn. I got the impression she knew Denis had a secret and was aching for him to tell us.

"Something's going on for sure," I said, "and I'm not sure who gets to make trouble first."

"Me," said Denis at the same time Jian said, "Den-*ny*."

Hep glared at Denis. Denis stifled the smile that had just begun and swallowed nervously. "Okay, Hep, I'm sorry. I know I promised," he began, "but —"

"But I told him he must do what he thinks is best thing to do," said Jian to me, "and also that you will not like to stop."

Hep said dangerously, "I quite have my mind made up —" and the doorbell rang again.

Out in the hall closet Bun, startled again off his nest of boots, chirped in annoyance. Denis leapt up and sidled (there's no other word for it) past a still angry Hep (she *hadn't* had an epiphany) and down to the door. I heard the rumble of deep voices mixed with Denis's high trill. Roger? and who else?

Hep clearly knew. She threw down the dishtowel she'd been twisting into a garrotte, and swore.

"Fine," she said then. "I give up. Get yourself killed if you like. Get all of us killed," and she stomped out to the kitchen, recapturing the towel on the way in one swift balletic swoop.

Clearly, she knew who was coming up the stairs. Jian turned to me and kissed me. "You too smart to get killed," she said. "I told Denis to trust her friend."

The doorway was suddenly filled with tall men: Denis, tall and willowy; Roger, tall and sturdy — and, tallest of all, a well-dressed man with that cop physique that comes from all the time they spend working out in copshop weight-rooms: wide muscular shoulders, slim waist, bulging biceps: a Denis special, for sure (and indeed, Denis's eyes were on him). He wore a Joseph Abboud suit in dark grey, cashmere I'd bet, with a light blue linen shirt that looked like it could be a Gretzky. It was designer day in my flat, I thought. He had the cleanest tie I'd seen outside an Armani ad.

I couldn't see his face at first as he was half-turned in the doorway and looking down at Bunnywit, who was twining uncharacteristically around his legs in a complex entanglement of purr and cheek-rub. I half-rose to grab the damned cat, and the man turned to me.

He had one of those beau-laid faces that some say are so ugly they're beautiful, but which I have always found tremendously attractive without qualification. High cheekbones and a long jawbone, a long hooked nose, maybe First-Nations except his cropped black hair was curly. He smiled at me as if he knew me. His teeth were almost too perfect, almost spoiled the overall Marlboro-Man effect. Except of course this guy would never have let a cigarette near his healthy physique —

66. BEAU LAD

— except in a long glittery cigarette holder, in a drag bar, in red fuck-me boots, men's size about thirteen, in backcombed wig and Elvira makeup.

This was the evil drag queen.

Beside me, Jian gasped, while I simply sat back down on the couch feeling sandbagged.

"Hi," said Roger. "Guess you recognised Lance. He's one of us. On the job. Undercover."

"Yeah," I said. *Lance?*

"Hi, Lance," said Jian. "You clean up nice." Explained her gasp, I guess.

Lance bent to pick up Bun. The damned cat rubbed its face on his, both sides. He hardly ever does that to *me*, let alone total strangers.

"So that's it," I said to Denis. He nodded, not taking his eyes off Lance's butt as Lance bent again to deposit Bun on the rug.

The room seemed very full of cops, though there were only two of them. Tall, big, fit, macho cops.

The room seemed full of drag queens — tall, big, fit drag queens — though there were only two of them. Unless, as Hep came back in and stood glaring by the kitchen door, you add the three of us temporary pretenders.

"You'd better come in and tell me about it," I said resignedly. I was beginning to distinguish between headaches. This time I was getting the kind that had nothing to do with baseball bats.

ISABEL CONTINUED SELF-RELIANT.

67. A TRULY CANADIAN FIGHT

Lance was really his name. Not only that, he was one of twins. His brother's name was Arthur. His only sister's name was Gwen, short for . . . you guessed it. He sat on one of my dining room chairs, which he had brought into the circle of conversation, leaning back with his legs crossed elegantly. "My parents were hippies," he said resignedly. "I'm just as glad for Lancelot. At least I could shorten it. I could have been called Windstar, like my best friend in home-school. Now *he* had trouble when we went into regular high school, for being named after a van. He was on the basketball team with me. They called him Windy and made fart jokes."

This had nothing to do with why Lance had been undercover as a drag queen, but it's necessary to keep up the civilised rituals — or at least, that's what Hep always says, and why not, really?

Roger had the armchair, which left Denis to collect his teacup and perch cozily beside Lance on the Belle-Epoque demi-lune canapé — which was a little shakier than it used to be since being repaired after the break-in, but seemed to be supporting them both okay. Denis didn't seem to mind the proximity — he sat on the edge of it like an expectant job applicant, looking around brightly. It didn't fool me one bit. He was nervous as hell.

Once we were all settled with cups of tea — in more of my mostly-surviving collection of porcelain (porcelain is *tough*) Japanware teacups, thanks to Hep, who knew enough to wash the dust of ages as well as the shards of recent violence out of them first — Roger cleared his throat.

"I want to make it clear that Lance was not implicated in Maddy's death. I know Jian IDed him as with the suspects, but he was undercover and being monitored. We won't be talking about that because it's another case, so let's go on to the lab reports," he said, "and if anyone asks you, nobody but Lance has seen these."

"No, let's not," said Hep. "Let's go on to how our prize amateur detective here can't stand up without reeling because she got bashed on the head and punched in the gut by the low-life pair with whom your lad Lance is apparently cheek-by-jowl. Let's talk about how real friends would back her away from this investigation, especially as it now seems to have enough cops in it to do the job. Let's talk about getting back to our lives and trying to forget about being heroes. Let's all talk about that."

"Temper, temper," said Roger.

"I'm the only person in this room who has any goddamn sense," said Hep. Bun squeaked in protest. She glared at him too. "The only being," she said. "And I forgot to add to the list a slashed art collection, and a cat with intestinal repairs."

"Look," I said, just as Roger said, "Maybe you think we —"

"Me first," I overbore him. "You think this is like returning something to the store? Get your money back, no more substandard goods? Well, stopping now won't take away my headache, or take me off Soul Man's radar, and it sure as hell won't get my Mendelson Joe back in one piece."

"I tried to stop them," said Lance.

"You were *there?*" squeaked Denis.

"Undercover," Lance said, and shrugged, as if it all made sense.

I squeaked in my turn — perhaps Bun was a virus, rather than a cat. "You were *there*, and let some guys *trash my place* and try to *kill my cat?*"

"I was the lookout. Bottom of the fire escape. I didn't realise they were going to trash the place until I heard all the noise. I thought it was a burglary. I came up, but I couldn't stop them quick enough. Sorry."

"Sorry? Sorry?" My howl hurt even my ears, and I noticed Bun freeze and start backing away, his eyes on my face, like he does when he's hoping I won't notice the lick marks on the butter that I've just surprised him in the middle of making.

Roger intervened. "He got them out of there before they trashed *you*, and that's the main thing."

"But they got her at the club," said Hep, "so what's the difference? You haven't been much help."

"Hard to run in high heels," murmured Lance just as Jian said to Hep, "First you said cops could finish, now you say cops no good. Sound like we better solve this case after all."

Hep started to glare, then sighed, then, after a moment, laughed ruefully. "All right. All *right*. I give up. We're back on the case. Just don't say I didn't *try* to save our fool heads."

Roger started to speak, but Hep wasn't done with him. "And I don't want to hear *you* complain about civilians in police business. My granddaughter is dead. If she was involved with this *under-cover operation* —" her tone was withering "— then I want to know why, when you were with them before, you didn't prevent them from going on to kill her. You owe her. And us."

"The prosecution rests," said Denis campily, then, deflated, "and don't glare at me like that, girlfriend. I'm-a on *you* side!" The fake Italian accent was the last straw.

"Oh, shut up, all of you," I said, the edge still on my voice, "until you can play nice with each other." *Including me*, I thought, and breathed in and out until I could look again at the tall young cop without wanting to tear his perfect shirt the way his criminal buddies had torn apart my living room.

He lifted his teacup. "Hey, they didn't get these," he said. I had to obey my own rule and not growl. It took a minute, but finally I got my tone in order.

"Thank you, Lance, for stopping them before they killed me or broke *all* of my grandmother's Nippon-ware. Thank you, Lance, for confession to complicity in the destruction of much that was emotionally significant to me in the world, including an original painting called 'Going in Opposite Directions' that took me fifteen years to track down and for which I had to get a five-figure bankloan to buy. I will endeavour to treat you as well as I expect us all to treat each other. And —" noticing that Bunnywit had gone to him for comfort "— at least half as well as my goddamned cat is treating you already." Oops. Blew it.

There was a moment's silence, during which everyone looked guiltily at everyone else. I broke that up too. "Okay, enough Canadian guilt. Shit, that was the *nicest* fight I've ever seen."

"Yeah," said Lance. "In my house, nobody would have looked up from their spaghetti." He carefully pushed Bunnywit to the floor, looking to see if I noticed his rejection of the unconditional positive regard Bun had offered him. I nodded stiffly. It was a start.

"So, that's that," I said. "And I don't want to hear any more about it. Makes my head ache." The others made Scout's-honour signs. I had to grin, though I shook my head doing it. "So, now what?"

Roger opened his gym bag and pulled out a folder. From it he spread out photos of some of Vikki's clues.

"Maybe the lab results? And an update on the rest of the stuff?" said Rog.

"Sound good," said Jian.

"Not really," said Roger. "What I have is something that will only help *after* we have a bad guy. Corroborative rather than indicative, you might say. But here we go anyway."

THE GIANT WAS HAIRY, THE GIANT WAS HORRID,

68. PIECES OF SKY

I reached over to the table under the lamp, grabbed the legal pad I'd used to make my notes, and flipped back to the original list. Remember?

> 2 (two) thousand-dollar bills (magenta purple, pine grosbeak) with a hot
>   pink heart-shaped sticky-note reading *Vikki?*

They looked a lot less magenta covered with all that fingerprint crud they use at the lab for enhancing prints under the glowlights.

"The prints," said Roger, "have been put through the computer. There are not enough characteristics to get a complete match. However, we have a short list of three hundred and twelve possibilities. I don't want anybody to get their hopes up, but on that list is one Stanley Kowalski, alias Stan Walski, alias studly Kurt Amor, and one Madeline Pritchard — the younger, that is — and three hundred and ten others whose names may or may not come up later."

He looked up at me. "You did not contribute a print as such, you understand. The smears you kindly left only on each side of one corner with your gloved thumb and forefinger did not obscure the others. But the rest are jumbled, and there are lots of people with similar whorls as each other has. That doesn't sound right. With whorls like . . . oh, you know what I mean. So unless it's Kurt Amor or one of the others — useless."

"'Similar to each other's', you mean. Why do you have Amor's prints?" I asked.

"Soliciting. Sucking dick in the park. The usual."

1 (one) thousand-dollar Hong Kong bill (orange) with lime-green sticky-note: *Jan?*

"The Hong Kong bill is definitely counterfeit. It was also under something that was written on by someone who had a dentist appointment at ten-thirty Wednesday. What Wednesday we don't know, but it's in English, and not in that distinctive Hong-Kong-British handwriting so many people from there use, either. The prints? No more than the other — less in fact — no overlaps with the database. Nothing useful yet."

"Fewer," I said, but very quietly.

1 (one) clipping from the classifieds of an unknown paper, for escort service

"Remember *Intro Deluxe* and their dental plan?" I said. "Do they go to one particular dentist? You could check on their appointments for the last dozen or so Wednesdays."

"On it already," said Rog. "But it's the usual — dentist of your choice. So we have to go back on each claim and check the appointment schedule. And since I just have one guy on it, and I find out that he's been spending the other half his time seconded to some goddamned undercover investigation that I never knew about until Sunday, we haven't got very far."

Lance said, "Sorry, boss."

"You're both in Homicide," said Den. "How come you didn't know?"

Lance sighed. "Look, IA opens a file like that, they keep it quiet. Need-to-know basis. Some other cop might have some connection you don't know — some friend or neighbour — and if you tell 'em the story, they tip off the bad guys, and there you are."

"Don't think much of your colleagues, then, do you?" said Hep drily.

"It's a rule," said Roger. "Trust no-one — except when they're your backup, of course." Lance snorted. I guess it was cop humour.

1 (one) clipping from the *Sun* gossip page, with photos of several people at an event in an upmarket art gallery

"Revisiting Lotsi Stinchko and Panda," said Roger, "we find that they too have records. Panda's is, strangely enough, for fraud. Used to work for a charitable organisation in town which shall remain nameless. Diverted several hundred thousand dollars of facility funding before the inevitable moment of truth."

"Wait! I was on that board," said Hep, jumping up to lean over the photo. "But her name wasn't . . . and she didn't look like *that* . . ."

"Certainly wasn't 'Panda', and she wasn't blonde, and she wasn't skinny, and she didn't have the best tits money can buy. Right. But the rap sheet does not lie."

"I was the one who initiated the investigation," said Hep. "I was doing the board-member audit, you know, two members sign the financials, and something looked off. It all balanced, but when I looked back in the minutes, it didn't jibe with the statement two years before. I was the only one who'd been on the board that long. I had parallel files at home."

"*I* remember that too," said Denis in surprise. "Didn't she threaten you in court?"

"Yes, she seemed to think that she would be looking for me when she got out. You know, she used to babysit Madeline now and again back then . . . you don't think she could have planned it to get back at me?"

"She only served just over three years, and she got out of jail two years ago. If she really meant it, I suspect she would have done something right away — assuming she knew the right bad guys," said Lance. "But I'd say she was busy hitching up with the beautiful people, namely Lotsa Stinky."

Roger made a few notes in his little book. Those little books look so unthreatening. That's probably why cops have them. But they're kept as evidence, and guarded like the doors of the Mint. "Still, I didn't realise the connexion. I'll have a few more questions to ask them when they come home.

"Now, Laszlo's record is for something a little more interesting. Especially given all the news stories about the millionaire playboy —"

Denis groaned. "Oh, for fuck's sake. He's a park fag, right?"

Roger looked up, startled. "How did you know?"

"Stands to reason."

"If he's bi, and maybe she is too, it does explain Twiggy's Guys and Dolls or whatever it was called." I picked up the clipping. "*Tammy's Perfect Dates: Boys and bi's*. With the questionably placed apostrophe. Right."

"He has been picked up three times in three different cities for cruising a little too — shall we say enthusiastically? One time the charge was dropped — he groped an undercover cop, and there were accusations of entrapment — but in Cawthra Square in Toronto he was busted with his pants down and his cock in some boy's face, and in Victoria Park he was fucking a hooker who turned out to be underage."

"So he advances to chief suspect," said Denis brightly.

"Don't be a fool," said Roger. "Some of our best friends — not to speak of colleagues — are queer."

"I wasn't talking about queer," said Den. "I was talking about underage. I bet you five dollars the creep knew he had chicken."

"Between you and me, you'd win. But he had good lawyers, and the chicken . . . ? Ended up working for Tammy."

"And lived happily ever after," said Denis bitterly.

"No, and died two years later. At the age of seventeen, HIV-positive and with hep-C."

"No relation," said Hep. I was the only one who got it. The rest just looked at her.

1 (one) clipping from the *TVTimes*™ television listings

I shuffled through until I had the *TVTimes*™ listing. "What about Mr. *Road-to-Avonlea*-comeback?"

"None of them are back from Greece yet, so no interview. But I did note that besides his Vice convictions, he has one for attempted extortion."

"Try to blackmail fine citizen?" asked Jian. "Hey, you fuck boy, so you have to give me money? Maybe even, hey, I only fifteen, so pay me?"

"You got it in one. Except he wasn't fifteen any more, and the fine citizen was out of the closet. So. Convicted in adult court, suspended sentence, spoken for by his foster father, who happened to be — Tammy's accountant."

1 (one) photocopy of a business licence for a numbered company, with signature of owner/proprietor

"The numbered company is indeed the one that owns the club. They call it the Kitty Kat Klub now, but the Vice guys call it the Pussy Pause Motel. They own some other places too — a health spa, holistic clinic, some kinda beauty salon, that kind of thing. This signature?" He pointed his pen at the plastic bag. "Lazslo Stinchko."

1 (one) Ziploc™ bag (sandwich size) with samples of a white powder (not present, no photo)

"The white powder?" I asked. "Where is it?"

"In the evidence locker where all the confiscated drugs are kept."

"What was it? Heroin?" asked Hep.

"Oh, come now. Fentanyl is the ruin of choice, these days."

Lance leaned forward and grinned. "Luckily, there's something else . . . it was cut with rice flour. Hong Kong counterfeit money, rice flour . . . an Asian theme, perhaps."

"It might help if we find the bad guys with a stash of opiates cut with rice flour," I said, "but I can't see what else is relevant. For goodness sake, every second gang in this city peddling drugs is Asian since the Vietnamese boat people in 1980-whenever and the Hong Kong takeover in 1997. The African gangs are just starting to muscle in. One hesitates to mention it because it is so annoyingly stereotypical —"

"But is true," said Jian. "Last thing I say my husband, 'Your mother know you are a drug dealer?' He broke my nose."

"Your husband was a drug dealer?" I said at the same time Hep said, "Your husband broke your nose?" Jian answered me.

"For sure. Because he had lots of money, lots of cash, bought a fancy car last month before I go. You know, I forgot this? One time told her, his I mean, little Viet friends I was his ma. I look old, with bruised eyes, look like old tired woman."

"Well, honey," said Lance, sounding uncomfortably Denis-esque but baritone, "you look like a million bucks now, so fuck 'im, right?"

She shivered. "Never again," she said, and her eyes closed for a moment. "Like a million dollars," she repeated.

"Canadian dollars, not Hong Kong," Lance said, and though it sounded to me a bit dodgy as comfort, Jian laughed.

1 (one) Ziploc™ bag (sandwich size) with a used condom (not present, no photo)

"Wasn't there a condom in that stuff?" said Denis.

"In cold storage at the lab. Sure, the DNA can be compared, but to whom, and why? Why the hell did she have to be so illiterate?"

"She knew what it was about," I said. "She didn't have to write herself a note. She didn't expect to be dead."

"Ten feet tall and bulletproof," Denis said, tugging his lank scarlet hair over his face with an impatient hand. "They all think they are, at that age, even the street kids. Whereas we old men know we are brittle."

Surprisingly, it was Lance who snorted and said, "Don't be such a wanker."

Denis blushed. Blushed? I thought he was an unblushing, shameless strutter. What else had he discovered about Lance that night? His gaze hadn't been off the hunk for more than ten seconds tonight.

1 (one) Ziploc™ bag (sandwich size) with a cut-up plastic cup (not present, no photo)

"Same again with that cup," said Roger. "It's with the condom at the lab. Traces of saliva. Different DNA. Again, if we had the guy, and the provenance of the cup, maybe it would mean something. As it is, it's a piece of the sky."

"Sky?" Jian said.

"In the jigsaw puzzle," he said. He looked at her uncomprehending stare. "Picture cut in little pieces? You fit it together? Sky has no clues? Never mind."

After he looked away, Jian winked at me. She knew *jigsaw puzzle*, all right. I didn't laugh, for the sake of my skull, but I felt like it.

1 (one) brochure for a chi-chi club downtown

"So Stinko owns the sex club," I said. "What does that mean? It's not illegal, not if nobody pays, right?"

"More or less right. It's not public sex, it's not prostitution . . ."

"In fact, I have often yearned for such a venue where a woman could go to get what gay men get in bathhouses," I said. "Anonymous yet respectful sex in a safe and yet neutral environment.

"Preferably non-smoking," I added.

There was a general cop-chuckle at that, though I didn't think it was an unreasonable addition. Does one have to choke down toxins in order to get laid? Bun, however, hopped up onto my lap and reached up to lick my nose, clearly agreeing with me.

"The lack of busts I told you about doesn't have as suspicious a source as I thought," said Roger. "It results from a couple of new readings of the law and a shift in the priorities and mission statement of the police department."

"Which means that we're all grown up now and sick of hassling people who just want to get laid?" I said.

"You might say that," said Roger.

"Or not," said Lance, but very quietly.

3 (three) round paper clips, which had slipped off whatever they were
clipping together and were loose in the bottom of the envelope (not
present)

"Where the pretty paper clips?" asked Jian.

"At the lab," said Roger. "They prove to have some trace
substances on them. Saliva with some interesting drug traces.
Also male, not Maddy's. We thought she might have sucked on
one or pulled it off some papers with her teeth, but somebody
else did that. Somebody who'd be in the frame if we knew where
the hell they came from, and why."

69. YOU WERE WAITING FOR THIS NUMBER, WEREN'T YOU?

Saving some rude jokes too, I bet. Hah. Sucks to you.

70. I'M THE SNAIL WITH THE MAIL . . .

There was a small silence after the last item of the list. Jian broke
it. "Where Vikki?"

"Not found yet. We're looking, but —"

"Who Vikki?" Jian interrupted him sharply.

"Don't know yet," said Roger just as brusquely. "Wish I did."

"She not dead?"

"Not that we can find. If she's outside town in a field somewhere . . ."

"You found Maddy. Nobody hid her. Same killer wouldn't
hide Vikki. Why hide? So if not dead, then I have question.

"Did anybody ask if Vikki get any other mail that day?"

HE HAD ONE EYE IN THE MIDDLE OF HIS FOREHEAD.

71. SILENCE IN THE COURT

You don't realise how much noise a purring cat makes until all human noise in a room has stopped. Bun was the only one who didn't stop talking, moving or even breathing loudly when Jian dropped that bombshell.

After a moment of something between shock and respect, the profound silence was broken by five people starting a word at the same time, then stopping, then looking at each other, then trying again, then looking at each other again, then waiting for someone else to talk first, then noticing that everyone was waiting, then trying to talk again, all in remarkable, if unintentional, synchronicity. It was kinda like a Marx Brothers movie, except not all that funny. We all understood the significance of the question so really, why were we rushing into speech? To break the eerie silence, I suppose.

Finally we got ourselves sorted into a kind of pecking order, Lance waiting for senior-cop Roger to speak, me waiting for Hep, and Hep, Jian, and Denis waiting, strangely in my opinion, for me. That meant that Roger won, not that he did it any justice. They don't give rhetoric lessons in cop training, apparently.

"Well." Clearly a placeholder. He might as well have been clearing his throat. He tried again with a little more resilience. "I'll look into it. Well, I mean, I'll have someone look into it. Um, letter carrier, mail sorter . . ."

"I'll get on it, boss," said Lance gently. We all watched Roger shake his head.

We all turned to Jian and applauded. She stood, and gave a Chinese Opera bow. Then she bent backward and put her hands on the floor behind her heels. Then she slowly turned herself inside out in a complicated way and stood up slowly, grinning.

"Pretty obvious question, but — I like applause. I ever tell how I met that husband? I was extra in opera. Too fat to be star. But I was Madame White Snake understudy. On world tour."

That was another conversation stopper. When we recovered, a little more swiftly this time, it was Hep who shook herself like an untidy Pomeranian and said, "Well. I'll make us some tea, shall I?"

72. AN ASIDE

I've read in books about people who think tea is the cure-all. Now I know why. It tasted pretty good, especially out of those delicate and beautiful Japanese porcelain cups, which, like the Bunnykins, had had the quality to bounce not shatter.

The cups were like Jian. They'd been through a lot too, and kept their beauty and purpose through it all.

The thought I'd had earlier that day came back. Jian needed to be where she belonged. Though I didn't know where that was yet, I was pretty sure it would involve going away from me, even if only physically. The thought gave me a pang, but hey.

I may not be able to do those contortionist moves, but I'm pretty flexible in my own way.

After we had sipped tea and said "Mmmm" — Hep having broken into my store of Kwan Yin and mixed it with some gunpowder (gunpowder tea, of course) — I said, "Okay. Clues are ongoing. Jian has been brilliant, and now for the next act. Lance was our sinister drag queen. Why?"

Lance stood up and took off his immaculate suit-jacket, folded it carefully over the back of one of my dining room chairs, and sat back down.

73. LANCE'S STORY

Okay, well, it starts with a file we opened in March. Well, okay, it starts before that. It starts with some shootings at a wedding. Rival gangs. I was the detective on Homicide that night. My Staff — that's Roger here — had me liaising with the Gang Unit guys, well, actually, I ended up sorta seconded to Narcotics — well, anyway, it's a long story. But I ended up being the only one who hadn't had my picture in the paper or been in the news footage.

So, the staff sergeant in Narcotics opened the file, but when he put me in the field, basically it was my ass on the line, right? So I started going into the clubs, making the odd buy, getting the stuff to the lab, but none of it had the rice flour component in it, so I sent Tsang — that's my partner — into the Asian clubs, but not much of it was being moved there either. It just kinda happened that I was in Denim and Fairy Dust downtown when I saw a buy going down, so I thought so what if I'm off duty, and I kinda tracked it down to the tranny in the toilet who had a couple dime bags of the stuff, and bingo! there it was. So I went down to Leather Ranch the next weekend and scored some more of the same stuff.

So I went to Staff, not this Staff but the other one, in

Narcotics, and we set up this thing, well, I didn't actually like it much but I had to admit I know the club scene, even though I thought Tsang would be better because he's smaller, but there's the Asian factor, so I decided to hide in plain sight, sort of. And of course it was hush-hush in case there was any leak, that's how it always goes, so I didn't tell *my* Staff because I had orders, so until the stuff he sent to the lab came in and the results were cc'd to me, I had no idea we had an overlap.

74. NOW, DOES THAT MAKE SENSE TO YOU?

Roger looked at our faces and laughed. "Let me translate," he said. "Sir Lancelot here is our first out gay man in this police service. With his name, this has been harder to weather than Windstar Angel, who's on the basketball team, but some of us have gotten used to it. However, Cummings, who is a staff sergeant in Narcotics and the one who opened this file, is a little bit — how do you say it   heterocentric, and he immediately figures that a fag is the best guy to go into the fag clubs. You may have noticed that Lance here is not exactly inconspicuous, so Lance decided if he was stuck with the assignment, which he was, because Cummings basically threatened to, and I quote, 'boot his pansy ass back out on patrol if he didn't take it like a man', he would try the flamboyant move of going in drag. If you can't be inconspicuous, they teach us in undercover school, be audacious."

"You have undercover school?" said Denis. "Cool!"

"Of course we don't," said Roger. "For Chrissake."

"Oops," said Denis, and tried to look cowed, but I noticed Lance stifling a smile.

"It's called Advanced Training in Investigative Procedures," murmured Lance aside. Maybe the Lindbergh shirt was going to get Denis somewhere after all. If, of course, he didn't chicken out like he usually does. And if Lance was single, or slutty — or if we all wrapped this meeting up before my painkillers finished wearing off . . .

"And they didn't tell me . . ." Rog went on.

". . . because it's a *rule!*" we all chorused. Ow, I thought, too late to not participate.

"And because Cummings is an asshole," said Roger, "but you never heard me say that."

"An insult to assholes everywhere," muttered Lance.

"What's that, Constable?" Roger said with a sharp look.

"Nothing, sir," said Lance, ignoring Denis, who was now the one grinning.

75. À NOS MOUTONS

"So, what did you find?" I said.

"The two guys who beat you up," Lance said, "are minions of a guy called Dominic Matrice. Of course he gets called the Matrix, or Do Matrix." He pronounced it "Dah Matrix", as if in a B-grade Mafia movie. "Former plastic surgeon, got in trouble with the AMA, still has a toney health and rehab clinic facade, rich ladies and gents go there to get thin, get botoxed, get their habits under control — as if. Matrix ran coke out of a place called Wing's, which was basically a bar of last resort, until it was shut down by the health department a couple of weeks ago. Until then I was working up the connexions between these low-lifes —" ("low-lives"? I couldn't help wondering, but I bit my tongue) "— and the big bad guy, but the bar closed and everything destabilised. Now, the two guys who tossed your place are regulars at Leather Ranch. They do the whole leather scene, actually, but they don't seem to have much time for it since they started moving this Asian product. Which we have no idea where it comes from. So when they said they had a little job and needed a lookout, I went along. But I had no idea they were tossing the place, like I said, and I had no idea you were mixed up with Sarge here, because —"

"—Yeah," I interrupted. "Because you hadn't compared notes yet because you all keep secrets like they were love letters, there in the cop shop."

"Well, yeah," Lance admitted. "Look, I came up and tried to stop them. When you yelled that you'd called the cops it was great. But I still don't know what the fuck, sorry, ma'am —" to Hep, not me or Jian, I noticed "— they were doing there. And when I saw the Matrix's guys at the club, beating you up, and then I saw Staff, I mean Roger, there cleaning up after, I managed to lip him off enough to get arrested, along with Denis here, and we finally got our scenes together."

He looked dubious, and smoothed the sleeve of his shirt. It *was* a Gretzky. I foresaw an elegant designer-conscious period in Denis's future, and hoped it didn't last long. I like him as the queen of tacky.

Lance's posture wasn't exactly the most comforting, though.

"Let me get this straight," I said, "well, not straight, but let me be sure I understand this. Some drug guys trashed my place, but you don't know what they were supposed to scare me away from, and they may or may not be the same drug guys who probably killed Maddy Pritchard and who beat me up. The former guys are missing because you haven't found their new place of business yet, the latter are missing because they got away from the Basher's Ball, and nobody knows why either of them, unless they are two and the same — which by Occam's Razor is likely — thought it was important to nail Maddy — or me. All the clues Maddy left point to some people with no visible ties to Asian dope, who just like to have sex a lot. Vikki is the only person who might possibly have a connexion, and she's so missing that there's no hope. Is this correct?"

"Hey!" said Roger. "I'm sure we . . . don't look at me that way."

I looked at him that way some more.

"Okay," he said. "I give. That is correct. Sorry."

"Sorry don't get you no cookies," I said, and got up to go find the painkiller that had been due half an hour ago, leaving my living room full of detectives, not one of them with a fucking clue. Not that I was any better. My clues weren't fucking either.

Bunnywit came to the kitchen with me. I gave him a dab of ice cream and got myself a whole scoop, with chocolate syrup, to wash down the pills, which I am supposed to take with food. The fact that I couldn't before, because I couldn't eat, was probably about one-quarter of my returning stomach problem. Another quarter was the concussion. About half was the return of the anxiety. What the hell were we going to do now?

I know what I wanted to do. I wanted to go to bed. Preferably with Jian, preferably right now. I told the room so, and they all got up and milled around interminably, making dates and murmuring about future activities. Bun howled at me for more ice cream. Jian asked, "You sure that head okay?" and I nodded, which was a bit of a mistake, but not as much as before.

Hep tried to flutter, but her innate honesty wouldn't let her, so she hugged me, kissed me as if there was going to be a later for her and me too someday, and left, skilfully cutting Roger out of the pack and taking him along with her, her hand tucked under his arm. I hope he was prepared: she looked like she was loaded for bear, and he's the cutest bear *I* know.

That left Lance to offer Denis a ride home, and Denis to accept in a frighteningly normal way. As I hugged him goodbye, I whispered, "Just be yourself! It'll be all right," and he whispered back, "Yeah, but who *am* I?"

I shook hands with Lance. "I almost forgive you for everything else," I said, "but the Mendelson Joe is going to take a while. Nice to meet you, anyway, and I hope we'll enjoy working together." He looked slightly horrified at the thought that this relationship might be described as "working together", and I smiled to myself as he and Denis went off at the same time, pun unintended. I figured Denis would have a better chance with Lance a little off balance.

Let Denis never say I haven't done anything for him.

Jian and I went to bed.

76. GRAVITY SWITCHBACK RAILWAY (69 REDUX)

My head was fine. Just fine. So was hers.

We went to sleep after only a couple of hours though. For me, it had been one hell of a roller-coaster day.

GOOD MORNING, ISABEL, THE GIANT SAID,

77. WHAT THE POSTMAN SAW, REDUX

My head was so fine, in fact, that when the telephone rang the next morning, it hardly hurt at all.

"Yo," I said into the wrong end of the receiver, then turned it around and heard Roger saying, "Put Jian on! She deserves to hear this first."

"No way," I said. "You'll just tell her that there was another brown envelope that day. From . . . ?"

"No idea, but the letter carrier thinks it might have been the same writing."

"So Maddy told Vikki something that made her grab her slippers and flee."

"She had a flea?"

"Shut up. Here's Jian."

I buried my head under the covers while Jian heard that she was brilliant and Bunnywit howled for his breakfast. Jian hung up and dived under to find me. She had ways of making me wake up happily . . .

78. . . . ALTHOUGH . . .

. . . it did occur to me later that while we now knew how Vikki had got the word to leave, we still didn't know why or where she'd gone, so why were we celebrating? I didn't bother to mention it. After all, Jian *is* brilliant, why deny it? Worth celebrating.

It was a warm day and Jian threw the windows open wide, admitting some city air and more show tunes. I fed Bun, who jumped up on the window sill just as the volume went up on "You say *po-tah-to* . . .". Bun hissed and ran away to hide under the edge of the couch.

"No kidding," I muttered.

79. "YOU . . . TURN ME UPSIDE DOWN . . ."

Jian, dressed in a T-shirt and leggings of mine, and with a scarf wrapping up her hair, was standing on one hand on the back rail of a kitchen chair turning herself inside out slowly. When Bun ran past her, she lost her concentration and fell off, flipping to land on her feet with barely a thump.

"Stupid song," she said, and exaggerated her accent to sing: "'I say "gerd molning", you say "good morning", ret's carr the whore thing off . . .'"

"No thanks," I said. "You say 'potato' fine for me."

"Stupid song," she repeated. "How you say things doesn't matter." She snorted and picked up another chair. Within moments she was standing on her right hand on one chair-back, her ribcage curved alarmingly backward and her pelvis above her collarblades, and with the other hand reaching up through her legs to balance a second chair, which wavered too close to the newly-repaired glass cupboard doors to suit me.

"If I take this top chair away will you fall?" I said.

"Not usury," panted Jian.

"Usually," I said. "Usury is charging interest on a loan."

After I removed the deadly weapon, I turned it right-side-up, sat down, and watched Jian do her compact exercises. Even I could see that she wasn't as flexible as the child acrobats in the Chinese circus, but she was more flexible than Nadia Comăneci (I'm old enough, just barely, to remember the shadow of Nadia and her Cult of Personality), so I figured she didn't have far to go to get back in shape. But when she uncurled after half an hour, she was sweating and she stood at the counter stretching and swearing — I assumed swearing, anyway — in Mandarin.

"I thought you were from Hong Kong? But you speak Mandarin?"

"Hong Kong, yes, just studied in Beijing. Came to Chinese Opera festival in Singapore. Flew to Taiwan later that week, after I sang Madame White Snake one performance. Stupid young girl. Free to fleedom. Joke intended. Got to stay Taiwan, but fell for stupid man. It's same old story, yes? Except I dance away at the end. Monkey queen. And he . . ."

"And he . . . ?"

"Don't wish to know," she said. "You still like me if I tell you I did something bad to him?"

"Depends. I'd have a hard time if you said you killed him, but if you turned him in to the cops or burned out his sports car, I'd be able to live with it."

"No, just called a guy who used to call him, some guy with a very bad voice, and I said, hey, this guy beats me and he has a lot of money in the attic. I figure maybe if this guy is drug guy, he figure the money might be partly his, and would want it back."

"*Did* he have a lot of money in the attic?"

"No, just two guns and some gold. Nothing big. But money was somewhere, because of the car and stuff. So if something happen to him, I don't feel too sorry. Am I bad?"

"I've seen those scars where his ring cut your breast," I said.

"I find it hard to make a negative moral judgment in this case. I have a conflict of interest."

"Huh?" She came up behind me, but before I could answer her, assuming she meant it, she had done a handstand on the back of my chair and was lowering herself, upside down, to kiss me.

"You gonna show me up like this all the time?" I said when my mouth was free.

"'Show me up'?"

"Idiom, means make me look bad by comparison. I can't do that stuff, and I'm too old to start trying."

"Was doing in bathroom or when you sleep. But enough back in shape to show off a little. You don't like?"

"On the contrary, I like it immensely. And I have a really good idea. But for later. When we find out who killed Maddy, and find Vikki, and everyone's safe. A surprise."

"Okay, let's go find out today so surprise comes fast. I like surprises."

And all this was *before* breakfast. Ours, naturally. Bunnywit, of course, had dined luxuriously.

80. SOUL SEARCHING

After breakfast I called Thelma. When she heard my voice she said, "Oh, praise God, and thank you!"

"What?"

"You went to see Mr. Spak."

Stifling Trekkie remarks, I waited.

"He said that while the estate was frozen he was not able to fully assess the trust fund, but now you had signed the papers, and he found the income from it was substantially more. He couriered over a cheque for a lump sum that he said was a legacy, plus the retroactive adjustment. I've never seen so much money in my life! Harold was flabbergasted!"

She paused, but I was too embarrassed to say anything. I heard her chuckle. Not laugh, not giggle, not tinkle like a little bell, but actually chuckle like a real person.

"I bet you're blushing," she said.

"Yeah, I mean, yes, I am," I admitted.

Then she said something that took my breath away. "When you're poor," she said slowly, "and you see something bad coming toward you, God is all you have. When you get one hundred and ten thousand dollars in the mail, you have a choice."

I hesitated, but I had to ask. "What did you choose?" I said.

"God," she said, "but maybe I don't have to hang on to Him so hard."

Wow.

And I had better get humble, I thought. If even *Thelma* could do it, then *I* wasn't one to get holier-than-thou. Pardon the expression.

But meanwhile, I had to change the subject before she said something else and wrecked the moment. "Soul Patrol?"

"Huh? Oh, right. Yeah, um, yes, actually, I think I do have something."

81. SOUL ON PATROL

But Thelma too was hesitating, uncharacteristically in fact. "Um, can I say something else first?"

"Sure." I braced myself for more dreaded thanks, or, more acceptable, recriminations for not going to the Starship *Enterprise* sooner, but she had something else in mind.

"I know you mock my faith," she said, "and sometimes I have nights of doubt too, but I really do believe in the things I believe."

Again, a silence so long I felt forced to break it.

"I know you do, Thel."

She sighed. "But I know there are people . . . who make a mockery of the faith from inside it. They give us Christians a bad name."

I waited.

"I've decided," she said, "that I am going to make a change in the way I profess."

She couldn't see my wrinkled forehead. I made a minimal-encourager noise — I was on social worker full alert by now — and waited.

"It was Christians who beat you up," she said. "Because they believed."

"Skinheads," I said.

"Christian skinheads," she said. "Soul Patrol. Active wing. They do it *on purpose!*"

"Thel, what's wrong? Where is this going?"

"Jesus," said Thel furiously, "talked to prostitutes and Samaritans and lepers and everybody. He didn't hit them with baseball bats. He didn't post a website that said God hates *anybody*. I'm taking that . . . that . . . that darned . . . no, that *damned* T-shirt right back to the Reverend and telling him a few things about the Soul Patrol!"

"Calm yourself! Just tell me."

"The inner council of the Soul Patrol," she said bitterly, "dedicates itself to patrolling for sinners and *punishing them*. Homosexuals. Jews. Jesus was a Jew, for Heaven's sake. Prostitutes. Sexual deviants, as they call them — people who live together outside wedlock, people who go to those clubs —. Anyway, they find them, and they beat them up. They don't preach, or minister, or profess — they *beat them up*! And they take what they call 'holy joy' in it!

"Christians! They call themselves *Christians!*"

"Thelma," I said. "You are a marvel. Thank you."

"What? For what?"

"Well, I'm not sure," I said, "but whatever it is . . . let's call it a breakthrough."

"Well, maybe it is if you think they were the ones to kill Maddy," she said, "but according to them, they want their victims alive to 'suffer and repent'." I could hear the quotation marks from here, knew that she was making little hooks in the air with her manicured fingers.

I wasn't going to strike her when she was down, but I figured that next time she came over I'd lend her *What the Bible Really Says about Homosexuality.* I'd have to get it back from Denis. He borrowed it to read up while he was deprogramming a kid whose parents had him kidnapped and given some bogus religious "therapy" for being gay. Its sleep deprivation and electric shock protocol had only made the kid scared, broken, runaway, and determined to stay gay. He'd been troubled by fear of God, though, so Denis had worked more on that than on coming-out issues.

Right now, though, this was about Thelma's detective work.

"That's great, Thelma. Did you call Roger?"

"I was just about to. But I was so *mad . . .* !"

"Yeah, I mean yes, I can see why."

"But now what?" she said.

One of the existential questions. *I* certainly didn't know the answer.

I'LL GRIND YOUR BONES TO MAKE MY BREAD.

82. BREAKING THE FOURTH WALL: A MEDITATION

Not that I meditate as such. But I must mention this: you realise of course, dear Reader, that when people write books about the things that happen to them, we leave a lot out. You didn't realise that? Sorry. Santa Claus isn't real either.

You may have noticed that in a previous section I gave you the chance to discover I'd left out stuff like the repair people coming to fix the glass in the kitchen cupboard doors, and that was supposed to have helped, subliminally, to acquaint you with this disillusioning reality.

It's mostly for the reader's own good. Habitual actions are often boring even when we are doing them. Why bore you all over again by telling you about us doing them? We put in what's necessary to build character (well, actually I mean build characterisation, but I'll let the double meaning stand, including the ambiguity about whose character), create mood, and advance action.

Sometimes in books writers also leave things out to fool the reader. Withholding clues in mysteries and all that. Building up to the trick ending. I want to tell you right now that I will never knowingly do that to you. Accidentally, maybe — it's not easy getting all this stuff in order, especially the stuff that doesn't do me any credit — but not on purpose. I hate those Jeffrey Archer twist-in-the-tail things.

But if I forget to let you in on the Activities of Daily Living (as the social work trade calls 'em), it's mostly because it's not germane to the issue. "That way is rump of skunk and madness"[9] — in literary terms. So I've left out big chunks of the next week or so. Stuff got done, more china got replaced, phone calls got made, and Denis got laid — but to avoid an unsightly slump in the book, I'll stick with hitting the high points.

I *am* saving some stuff for later, but it's not clues. Trust me.

Besides, nothing much happened until the second murder was attempted.

83. AND AGAIN, WITH FEELING

And don't ask me who Germaine is. I've heard all those jokes before.

84. FOURTH WALL REDUX

The other problem with telling my own story is stuff that happened when I wasn't around. The way I found out about it was that somebody told me, but in a book that's called "talking heads" and too much of it gets annoying. I had to decide here how I'd handle the fact that the next breakthroughs weren't mine. Third-person narration, here we come — real soon now, I promise.

---

9. As R. A. Lafferty wrote (in "Thus We Frustrate Charlemagne", a story published in *Galaxy* magazine in February 1967, and reprinted in his collection *Nine Hundred Grandmothers*). (TMI, right?)

85. WHAT HAPPENED WAS . . .

Vikki went back to her old workplace, Thelma went to church, and I went downtown. These all happened at the same time, but I'll start with me.

86. FINDING MENDELSON JOE ISN'T EASY

Unless you count a technological breakthrough: I did have one of those. I figured that I could now afford, literally, to join the twentieth century. So what if it's already the twenty-first? Better late than never. So I went out with my newfound wealth and bought a cellular telephone.

I spent the morning squinting at the small print of the manual and setting the phone up to ring not-*too*-annoyingly. I admit, I did once pick it up and, even though it wasn't, alas, a flip-phone, say, "Beam me up, Scotty!" Kirk, Spak, and Lennie move over. Then I call-forwarded my land line to the cell, pocketed the new tech, and packed a bulky but surprisingly light canvas shoulder bag to go downtown.

Through a steadily darkening day, I rode a trolley bus down The Long Street of Increasing Pretension until I got to the gallery district, and got off near the gallery of the marvellous woman who'd tracked down the Mendelson Joe painting for me.

I ducked into her classy teak door just as wind hurled the first huge splattering precursors to torrential rain. I shook the drops off my head like Bun does when he drinks from the drip in the bathroom sink. Then I headed back to Marta's inner sanctum.

Marta employed me in one of her galleries back when I was in social work school. That was some time ago, and I've changed a fair bit, but she looks just the same: beautiful, sensually-rounded, and well-dressed; and she acts just the same: genial in a refined-genuine-Austrian-accented way, kind, knowledgeable, and with a vast memory for faces and art and money. She was sitting at her desk in the back room amid several lush floral canvases in vivid reds, rusts, and creams, her blonde hair fluffed around her smiling face, wearing a red cashmere sweater set, and looking like a high-class photographic portrait, a Roloff Beny maybe, only in colour, so maybe an early Peter Sutherland, 'way back when he was using Ilford Cibachrome. When I told her so, she laughed.

"Zo, how is ze Mendelson Joe?" she said, which was her standard greeting.

I had to tell her.

I swear tears came to her expressive eyes. "Zat is terrible."(You get the accent, right? So enough with the zeds already.)

"Yes," I said. I peeled the canvas bag from the victim it had carried to her. "Can it be restored?"

My heart broke again as I watched her fingers explore the damage.

"I think so," she said finally, "but it will not be cheap."

"Oddly enough, I can afford it," I said. "Should we get in touch with Joe himself?"

"I have lost touch with him since we got this," Marta said, tapping the frame, "and finding him isn't easy. But anyway I am not sure it is good for an artist to hear that one of his works has been — raped. Murdered."

"Does that mean if I restore it, I'm into zombie territory?"

She laughed again. "No, more like resurrection. Pray to God if you like, and meanwhile I will take it and see what I can find out. You will trust me to do this right for you?"

"As I always do," I said, and something invisible nudged my hip. I jumped about three feet. My pocket rang. I must have looked completely blank for a moment.

"It's your cell," she said.

I jumped again, then rummaged in my pocket as the ringing went on and on.

146

"Telephone?" she said as it rang again and vibrated its little heart out.

Finally I fumbled the quivering thing out, with none of my earlier beam-me-up-Scotty nonchalance, figured out how to swipe it on, and managed, " . . . um . . . .hello?"

"Roger here," he said.

"Roger that," I said.

"I've heard all those jokes," he said. "From you mostly. I found Vikki. Or she found me."

"Where is she?"

"Sitting in my office," he said. "Asking for you."

"I can be there in fifteen. I'm at Lamb Gallery," I said.

"I thought I called you at home?"

"Duh. Cell phone."

"Welcome to the future." He had my number in more than one way. He went on to prove it again. "Pretty chi-chi address. Getting the joe on the Joe, are you?"

"I don't need to hear *those* jokes either," I said. "I'll come right over. Is she right in front of you?"

"No, I'm huddled in the john talking on my cell. Of course she is."

"How does she look?"

"She's not wearing bunny slippers, but she's fine."

"Chickens," I heard a voice from his background say at the exact moment I did.

"Yeah, whatever," he said, and hung up.

87. HOW DID YOU FIND MISS VIKKI? HEY, I WALKED IN AND THERE SHE SAT . . .

I got to Roger's office about four-fifteen in the afternoon, shivering and damp and not pleased with the change in the weather.

"Hi," Vikki said nervously, looking up from the straight chair by his desk. She looked like shit. Her skin was zitty and she was parchment-pale. Her hair, however, was cut better, and her skirt almost covered her ass. A red vinyl jacket draped over, and dripped from, the back of her chair. Her legs and feet were muddy, and she was swabbing at them ineffectually with a wet paper towel.

"You took off," I said. I found a plastic hanger on Roger's coat-tree and hung up my dripping leather jacket beside his dry one.

"No shit, Sherlock," she said. Then, after a beat, "Sorry."

"No you aren't." I ran my hands through wet hair then shook hands and head. Roger grimaced as cold microdrops sprayed him.

"No, I'm not. Fucking letter comes that says if you get this I must be dead, what the fuck would *you* do?" She threw the paper towel at Rog's wastebasket, missed. "Fuck it," she said, sotto voce.

"I'd call the cavalry."

"Whaddya think I'm doing here? Duh. Just . . . later. Besides, I left the other stuff for you guys."

"So why now?"

"Disclosure," she said. "Action. Conscience. Getting on with things."

"And where were you until you figured it was *later* enough?"

"Going back to college," she said. "They have deadlines, you know."

"Give me a fucking break," I said. "We're busy finding out who killed your girlfriend and getting bashed up, and you're back in fucking suburbia signing up for some fucking grad school?"

"Undergrad at the downtown campus," she said, "but basically right. Who bit *your* ass this morning?"

"It's afternoon," I said, "and I've spent the day with a sick friend of the painted variety. Which is basically your and Maddy's fault. Not to speak of one tall undercover cop's," I asided to Rog.

"Roger told me about your place and your pictures and shit," she said. "But would you rather it'd been me or you?"

"No," I conceded. "Not even you. So why'd you and your slippers shuffle off?"

"I guess that was pretty chicken of me," she said.

At this point, despite our Alpha-dog duelling, we both broke up laughing.

"I will *never* get women," said Roger.

"Not with an attitude like that," Vikki said.

88. GOIN' DOWNTOWN WITH MY HAT IN MY HAND /. . . MIGHT AS WELL BE LOOKIN' FOR A NEEDLE IN THE SAND . . .

While I was replacing or repairing dishes and furniture, Vikki was re-emerging from self-imposed exile. About noon, around when I was asking to be beamed up, she swaggered onto the drag where she did her best work, on a mission, wearing a chip on her shoulder and platform fuck-me sandals inappropriate for any other workplace — or a rainy day. Between shoulder and shoes her clothing was suitably abbreviated.

It was windy on the drag, and soon started raining again. Vikki swung open her short vinyl jacket perfunctorily at a few of the cars that slithered over bleakly glistening asphalt. Drivers ignored Vikki's enhanced cleavage while their cars' tires clove the puddles, sheeting mud in passive-aggressive CSI spatter-patterns onto her legs. Soon her shoes would never be the same again, which, considering their cost, pissed her off no end, and made her reflect bitterly that no good deed goes unpunished. Under her microskirt, her legs reddened and goosebumped, and her ears hummed from the crossplay of icy wind gusts.

Finally, giving the finger to a carful of yobbos whose driver had swung close to the curb to deliberately splash her, she unsteadily shouted "Fuck it!" to the uncaring grey sky and tottered off to

Wing's Sports Bar, which — despite the health department closure notices still pasted to the door — was open for business as usual. Outside the door, a potbellied guy with a bald head and big beard, illustrated by tattoos on every inch of his arms, neck, and parts of his skull, competed for a wet T-shirt prize while scraping at the glued-on notices with a razor-blade knife. He paused ill-humouredly to wipe his streaming pate and let Vikki in.

There are no sports in Wing's Sports Bar unless you count the genetic kind. Wing's is the Bar of Last Resort for a neighbour-hood where the norm at the run-down bars of ancient fleabag hotels like the York and the Royal is not an elevated clientele in the first place. Wing's will, and does, serve anyone, and at one-thirty a.m. the streets radiating from it are staggering with its ejected patrons, fighting and fucking and fumbling their way to rooming houses, warm grates, hollows in caragana hedges, the one shelter that will take the stoned-and-drunk, and cheaper-than-cheap hotels.

But at one-thirty in the afternoon, only the regulars, busi-nessmen (read "dope dealers"), and working women are there. Vikki pulled the door open against the wind, tripped extrava-gantly over the flat lintel, and stumbled into the fuggy warmth created by the combination of a roaring space heater hanging in the upper corner of the room, the steamy stench of beer, eau-de-piss-and-vomit, rancid deep-fat-fryer oil, and the stink of unwashed bodies — uncharacteristically cut with a dash of industrial cleanser, which probably had to do with earning the ability to reopen.

Over by the bar, a couple of dealers with cell phones were having a non-literal pissing contest while one of the daytime regulars stumbling toward the men's room already had his dick out of his zipper and was on the verge of the real thing before he even hit the tattered plywood door separating the pisspot without from the urinal within.

At a booth by the window, a few of the daytime girls were warming their hands around cups of coffee which also could have been described as pissy. It was a very urinary day, Vikki thought as she weaved over to them, trying not to overdo it, but making it real clear that she was back, and back on the stuff.

Sammy, Serena, and Bonnie-Rae watched her coming, then nodded to the other two girls, who craned their rumpled heads around, then hiked over on the Naugahyde™ bench until there was room for one more skinny ho.

"Hey," Vikki said. "Shakin'?"

Bonnie-Rae laughed. "If it ain't the skinny little moniyâw muff-diver!"

Vikki riposted "You just want some. Pay for the lay, girl!" and things went on like that for a while. The dealers were pissing standing up, Vik thought, but girls piss sitting down. The two beside her were new. One of them looked about twelve. Old enough, on this street. Sammy wasn't much older.

"Hey," Sammy said, "we was thinkin' that you was serial-killed like them other girls, you been gone so long."

"Couple, three weeks," Vik said.

"Forever down here," said Serena.

"Yeah. Well," Vikki said. "Got freaked when Maddy got offed. But I run out of money, hadda come back and make some. And I gotta score. You seen Rabbit around?"

She tugged her skirt down. A fresh, wet draught from the opening door shivered her and she used the move of pulling her jacket around her to throw a glance at the mirror behind the bar, check out the newcomer. Good. She was hoping he'd show up, just didn't expect it to be on cue.

Pink Rabbit was her former connexion, and she pretended she hadn't seen him swagger in through a door held open for too long so that everyone in the bar would get a chill down their back. Vikki despised him for the cheap effects he affected, but he had a good pipeline to Do Matrix's good product, so in the past she'd put up with him.

"He just come in, girl. You blind?" Bonnie-Rae said.

Vikki heaved up out of the booth and minced over to the bar on the tiptoes of her platform shoes.

"Fuckin rainin' cats and dogs," said Pink, a short, skinny crackhead with a long black braid, who was shaking rain off his wet leather jacket and his wispy facial hair. "Fuck."

"Hey, Pink," she said, and leaned closer.

Pink Rabbit was called that 'cause one time when he was stoned he went to the wrong house to make his connection, and decided if it wasn't his connection's place it must be his. When the granny-looking white woman who answered the door couldn't get rid of him, she said, "Look, you don't live here, fella. *We* live here, just us and our rabbit," and she thrust toward his face a huge and grotesque stuffed toy she'd been holding when she answered the door.

From below, his friends watched the cheap stuffed rabbit advance on their swaying pal. It was as tall as a ten-year-old child, hot pink with a white bulgy belly, its head bigger than that of the confused crackhead and bracketed by eerily flopping ears, and the gang on the sidewalk hooted when their buddy leapt back in terror and retreated down the stairs. Against their laughter, he'd managed to regain enough composure to mutter, "She's fuckin' crazy, man!" but it was too late. He'd been called Pink Rabbit now so long most of his customers didn't even know his name was Leonard.

"Don' fuckin' call me that," he muttered reflexively. "What you wan', bitch?" His Siksika accent made it "bitss".

"Same old same old," said Vikki with desperate jauntiness. "Come on, baby, let's sit down and talk about old times . . ."

89. VIKKI'S STORY

So, like, the thing is, I promised Mad if anything ever happened I'd take our nest egg and go back to school. It was supposed to be next year, but what am I saving for now? Also detox is a bitch, I'll have you know. I've missed a bunch of classes.

Not that it's hard. School, that is. I'll catch up. I got my profs to cut me some slack. Death in the family. All that. Can you believe I'm living in residence? Seven blocks away from the drag and it might as well be a hunnerd miles.

Old Pink's just the same. Thinks with his dick. 'Course that's 'cause most of his actual brain cells is fried. He was a fuckin' pushover today.

All right, don't get your thong in a twist. There's the letter, on the desk. Like, 'If you read this, something went wrong with Matrix and his fucking goons'. Duh. Like she was gonna win a standoff with him. Stupid fucking bitch, even if I did love her tits off. Go up against Do Matrix without backup? Duh. If I'd'a knew, I'd'a kicked her ass. And then made her go see her fancy granny for money instead. *Before* she got herself killed, Maddy I mean, not the gran.

She was shaking him down, Matrix himself, can you believe it? Because she did a trick or two for some of his guys and saw something go down. Something with this chick she said she saw at her grandma's house when she was younger, but she had better tits now, the chick I mean, that's what she said, anyhow, not the chick, Maddy I mean, and wasn't so fat. The chick I mean. Also something about a rich dude. That Matrix wasn't gonna want screwed up.

Well, I guess it didn't get screwed up, because they just offed her instead.

Fuck, I hate cryin', makes my fuckin' head hurt like a sonuvabitch. So I did what she said. Got out, kept my promises, detox, tuition. And now it's revenge time. Except I learned something from her. Don't do it alone. So here I am.

Also except, I don't know all she knew. So even if I was gonna do it alone, I couldn't, because she left out a few things. Like what it all means.

She thought she was gonna live forever. Happily ever fucking after.

Fuck, so did I.

90. TRANSLATION

Dear Vikki ♥ —

If you get this I'm probly somewere warmer and I don't mean San Fransicso. I been hitting up Doctor Matrix for our retirement fund because I done a few tricks on his club there, the sex one where the rich fucks come, and I seen somebody who ain't who she used to be. I used to see her around Gran's place but she was fatter then, some kinda cherity comitee queen. She got thin and bouht some tits and has a rich dude maybe he bouht them for her but I dont think so he didn't look like a ~~filan pilantrop~~ the kind of guy who dos favers for chaep sluts. So tonight Matrix is delliverring the cash and me + you can get out of town. But jst in case I'm doing what they do on mystery tv they send leters and hide the evvidance just in case. Becuase you never know if hes gone be a jerk or not so I will tell him to watch out I sent all the evvidance. Tell Gran it was the chick who come arond with finanshel statmunts that time when I was playing my Barbie and her head came off. Gran will remmember cuase I went bulistick. I luv you ☺ <u>so do what we prommised or I'll cum back and huant you!!!</u>

Xoxoxoxoxoxoxox yuor own

Maddi ♥

91. SHOCKING NEGLECT OF THE SUBJUNCTIVE

"We useta do that thing with the hearts," said Vikki. "We were gonna get matching tattoos." Which explained why the girl hadn't even spelled her own name the same as her grandmother had.

After a moment I cleared my throat and blinked. "'If you *were* gonna do it alone'," I said, then sniffed.

"Yeah, what if?" Vikki's voice was as shaky as mine.

"I mean, you said 'If I *was* gonna do it alone' and one says 'were' not 'was' in that case. Subjunctive. What do they teach people today in schools?" I shook the scrawled letter. "Look at the appalling spelling and usage in this thing."

"Whole language," she said. "It's why I can't spell for shit either. According to my writing teacher."

"You're taking writing?"

"Business writing. Part of the commerce courses."

I imagined a business memo as written by Vikki, and winced. She glared at me. Recovered, I saw. I didn't fold.

"Enough bullshit," I said. "Isn't it about time we mutherfucking solved this mutherfucking murder?" (Okay, I watched *Snakes on a Plane*. Sue me.)

"We know all this," chimed in Roger. She transferred the glare. He didn't fold either. "We IDed the Bride of Stinko right away as a convicted embezzler. So . . . ?"

"You mean, what's my 'value-added'?" With the air quotes scratched by her new, long, decorated fake fingernails.

I have a friend who says the air is getting too cluttered with air quotes and we should erase 'em if we use 'em. But Vikki and my cousin were both air-quote graffiti artists. Make 'em big and make 'em often . . .

Rog said, "Fucking right, chicken-feet."

"Well, this tape, I guess," Vikki said, shaking a little answering-machine-sized tape out of her sleeve. "It's Pink and me talkin'. I wish I hadda had a digital recorder. I thought he'd hear this one, but I guess he was too whacked out. Oh, yeah, and I saw who her trick was. That night. I can give you a positive ID, if he's ever been booked."

Roger was up out of his chair and leaning over her almost before I could react. "You saw her trick, and you didn't tell me? How the fuck could you have delayed the investigation more?"

I backed up a bit and watched.

Vikki tipped her head up and sideways and I suddenly understood why "chick" was a popular idiom. And maybe why the appeal of the slippers.

She said, very quietly, "I got no idea what her scam was. Or who the trick was. But when he does hits, Matrix uses low-rent people from out of town. I went and got where, who, names, on that fuckin' tape, and I done it on the drag, talk to my friends what never woulda give you nothing. So you have your answers, Mr. Cop, answers I got without 'muddying the water'." Even with more air quotes, she sounded almost grown up.

Roger didn't care. He made a winding hurry-up gesture. She sniffed, swiped a hand under her nose.

"I'm getting there," she said. "Fucking impatient pig."

All right, I said *almost*.

"Hey," said Roger. "I don't call you a fucking annoying six-times-an-hour douchebag whore, now, do I?"

"Ex-douchebag-whore," she said.

"Fine," I said. "Now everyone knows where they stand."

They ignored me.

"I talked to Rabbit, you know, Pink. Leonard Over-the-Mountain."

Roger nodded.

Vikki proceeded to give us the story I put up above. All the details are hers, though the language is mine, because if you had to wade through the *being as how*s and the *on account of because*s, you'd be as wound up as Rog and I were by the end.

Finally she got to the point. "So then he says the hit was two goons from Saskatoon. Name of Edouard and Darryl. Known as Spot and Puff. Because one has real bad skin and the other is a poofter. They're comin' back right away because there's some kinda big score set up down at the gravel plant. Basically Pink was sayin' that I should keep my skinny ass, which it is not skinny, it is very nicely formed, just not large like some of them bitches down there, out of Matrix's way 'cause I prob'ly remind him of Maddy and that is not a good idea right now if I want to keep shaking said ass. So I told him I was outta there and if I can help it he'd never see me again, which is nothing but the fuckin' truth. And by the way, here is the dope and somebody owes me some cash."

"Why would they come back?" asked Roger. "Another hit?"

"Pink didn't know. All he knew was Matrix is moving his stuff through his skinhead Soul Patrol. The religious dipshits."

"We know about them, sort of," I said. "See this?" and I bent over and pointed to the shaved patch and stitches on my head.

"No shit?" she said reverently, and reached toward my noggin.

I reared back, then relaxed as all she did was tip my chin down so she could see better. "The fucker had a Soul Patrol T-shirt," I said.

"Yeah, they are not supposed to be sinners, right? Like, as if. My stepdad was in the Soul Patrol and it didn't do *him* no good. Rabbit says Matrix has a brother-in-law or something in there, who has some of them playing both sides of the fence. Fuckin' hypocrites."

She shook her head, then I could see her pick up her chip and balance it back on her shoulder as she turned to Roger. He didn't seem to notice that she'd ever removed it.

She minced up to him on her wretched, tottery, sodden little platform fuck-me sandals and went on, "Is that enough value-added for you, Mister Not-so-polite Policeman?"

She put one finger on Roger's breastbone and pushed, then wheeled, grabbed her coat, and tottered toward the door. She looked like a spottier, sluttier version of Reese Witherspoon in *Legally Blonde*. Actually, she looked pretty cute, too, if bedraggled, like a Barbie™ (speaking of Barbie™) doll that's been dressed up in the Disco Barbie™ outfit and then left out in the rain.

"Don't go *anywhere*," said Roger with menace.

"Charge me," she said, and stared him down.

After a long moment, he crumpled the piece of paper he'd been holding and threw it aside.

"I thought so," she said.

"I'll get Lance to break out the photo IDs," said Rog. "And after, you wait up. I'll need a statement before you go."

"Lance?" she said. "Typical cop name — sounds like a bath-house alias." But she stayed where she was, tapping her tiny foot.

Afterward, I told myself she deserved it, though I'm still not sure whether Rog should get credit for bringing her down a peg or reproach for kicking an innocent (if annoyingly-barking) puppy.

Because when Lance walked in and she recognised him as the big drag queen, she stepped back all the way to the bookshelf, almost spraining an ankle in her scrambling haste, and turned even paler, if that was possible.

It was almost worth the price of admission.

Or maybe it *was* the price of admission.

ISABEL, ISABEL, DIDN'T WORRY, ISABEL DIDN'T SCREAM OR SCURRY.

92. LANCE A LOT

Vikki wasn't as easy to convince as Denis, or me for that matter, that Lance was on the side of the angels. There was a certain amount of loud, strong language that hurt my ears. I went out to the cop-shop cafeteria (no vending machines or doughnuts for the modern police: I even saw alfalfa sprouts in a sandwich there) for hot chocolate while the three of them settled it. A couple of acquaintances hailed me to their table, but they weren't Germaine either. When I wandered back to Rog's office with my ecologically-sensitive ceramic cup, sipping the too-hot beverage and getting whipped cream on my upper lip, things were calmer, and Vikki was agreeing to go off and look at mug shots.

"I'll come by and get Maddy's boots," she said to me. *To get?* I thought.

"I'll drive you," said Lance.

"No fucking way I'm gettin' in a car with that goon," she said, again to me. "I'd rather ride the fucking bus than get in a car with him after what I seen him do down on the corner."

I give up, I thought. *Let the Grammar Police get her.* I said, "Roger says he's okay."

She made a moue. Really. "So does Denis," I added irrationally.

Instead of "Who?" she said, "Denis is a fucking limp-dick do-gooder. They always think the best of people. I still think Boyfriend sucks."

"Well, he sort of does," I said. "Sucks Denis, for one. So I guess Denis is biased. But I have some ideas how we can use him and his boots and me and my boots to do a little investigation . . ."

"No fucking way," said Roger and Lance in chorus.

"Aren't they cute? They're trying out for the police choir," I said. "Let Lance drive you 'cause we need a car."

"Forget it," said Roger, and Lance, who was looking slightly interested despite himself, did a fast fade. Roger winced as the door slammed, then snarled at me. "If you're going to do this shit, get a private investigator's licence and get the fuck out of my office. Not in that order."

"Are you going to play the tape, Roger?" I asked him sweetly.

"It's a confidential part of a police investigation, and I'll deal with it as such," he said, and tossed it into the file box on his desk. "So fuck off."

"I have never heard so much untrammelled profanity," I said primly, "as in this fucking office today. I am bloody well sick of the whole of the bunch of you, and I'm going the fuck home. See you later, Vikki."

"Later," she said.

"Not," said Roger, but I ignored him.

I went home. In a taxi.

93. IS THAT ANYTHING LIKE GOING HOME IN A HUFF?

Yes. But more expensive.

On the other hand, what did I care about expensive? I could afford taxis now.

I had been thinking about money all day, one way and another.

SHE NIBBLED THE ZWIEBACK THAT SHE ALWAYS FED OFF,

94. BETTY CROCKER IS DEAD

Jian and I went out for supper to the Double Greeting, the great Chinese restaurant around the corner.

"Anything like Mum used to make?" I asked her as we shovelled the meat-and-pickled-mustard soup into our hungry mouths.

"Wo de ma-ma a very bad cook," she said. "If it's like she make, health board close down right away." Soup done, she pincered some steamed cold cut chicken into her rice bowl and heaped onion and ginger dip over it. "I too am not good cook, very much," she said. "I can make this. And cooked lettuce. Fish ball and seaweed soup. Not much else."

I refrained from the obvious insinuendos about where she *did* cook, but I think she got some of it from my lascivious grin.

"Someday," she said serenely, "I go to Ramen Museum in Yokohama, Japan, make a pilgrimage for my mama. Lucky I am born after 1958 or I starve to death as child and never meet you."

95. FLOW MY (CHARTS), THE (AMATEUR) POLICE(WO)MEN SAID

When our feeding frenzy slowed, I got out my pen and turned the Chinese Zodiac placemat over.

Look," I said, "it doesn't make sense. Maddy might have got hassled by those jerks because she wouldn't pay, but why kill her? Far as they were concerned, she had a nice little habit going, and a good clientele to maintain it. And even if she quit and they lose a customer, there's a sucker born every minute."

After I explained the expression to Jian's satisfaction, I started making a chart.

"Okay, here is Maddy. Maddy buys dope off Pink Rabbit who buys off a connection who buys off Do Matrix. Maddy argues with Bad Guys, neither of whom is Rabbit, but who are minions of Matrix."

I stopped to explain *minions*, gave up when I had to go all the way back to Henri the Whateverth of France (Catherine de' Medici's son), changed the word to *henchmen*, and had to explain that.

Another set of circles and arrows.

"Maddy gets knocked off by Alphonse and Gaston or whoever, from Saskatoon. Spot and Puff. Hired by Matrix. Why? If it's a drug thing, why not have the slimy henchmen beat her up as per usual? A dead hooker can't earn away her debt. And even low-rent hits cost money. So . . . ?"

I started a new group. "The evidence Maddy sends home 'just in case' brings in Lazslo Stinchko and trophy wife Panda."

"Pandas are not bears," said Jian, reading my add-on. "Joke doesn't work."

"Never mind," I said. "She's a bare-faced liar in the other sense of the word. Two sources now have IDed her as an embezzler. Does Lotsi know? Unknown."

More scribbling.

"They hire Studly Amor to be their boy-toy, and end up adopting him into their little love-nest. Tammy's Boys and Bi's, with that abominable apostrophe, is a co-op, independent. *Not* working for Matrix."

So what did this all prove? What connexions were we missing? I was staring at the chart when Jian reached for my pen and said, "Don't forget cops." She added in her elegant script Lance, Lance's boss, and a mystery subject under suspicion. I added Cummings — the Narcotics staff sergeant's name.

"Why 'mystery bad cop'?" I said. "Lance's thing was supposed to be investigating Matrix's drug operation." I added the dotted line to Matrix.

"He say AI. I know from TV."

"You mean IA?"

"Whatever. AI, IA: there is always bad cop," said Jian.

"In the movies," I said. I added a dotted line to the arguing guys who were probably also the guys who trashed my apartment.

Why had they bothered?

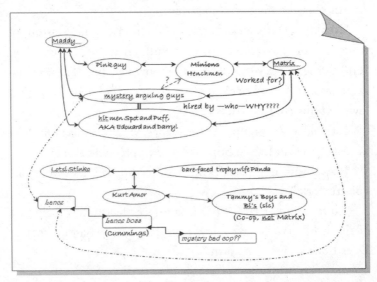

96. SCHRÖDINGER'S COPS

Then I thought about the description of the arguing guys[10] and
the description of the hit guys,[11] and I drew a double-line/equals-
sign between them. Same description, a team of one gay man
(or man who could be gay) and one guy definitely with bad skin.
Same guys? Duh.

"Bad cop also happen in real life," Jian persisted. "Remember,
I am not from this place, where all police supposed to have
ee-thics. Places I know, some cops good, many bad."

"*Eh*-thics," I said absently. Po-*tay*-to.

"Also, even if good, cops change things. Go under cover in
big boots, stomping new path. Schrödinger cops. Looking in
box. Killing cat."

I looked at her.

"What?" she said. "I take physics in school; don't you?"

---

10. Reprise (so you needn't flip back): Hep: "Maddy was five-four, so she'd
have been five-nine. One of them was taller, one was shorter. Not a
lot either way. One had really bad taste in suits. Well, the other one
wasn't wearing a suit so I suppose he had really bad taste in bomber
jackets. Right. The taller one had long dirty-blond hair in what I'm
afraid I immediately categorised as a greasy pony-tail. It might have
been perfectly clean, but he just looked greasy. He had an earring, with
a blob hanging down that might have been a skull. He had the kind of
clothing American kids in rock videos wear, Black kids. But he wasn't
Black. He was pasty and spotty. Sort of like Maddy's skin, but worse.
The one in the suit was swarthy but Caucasian — and his suit looked
pretty greasy as well, but that's subjective too. I think it was one of
those shiny fabrics they used to call sharkskin. He was chubby."

11. Pink Rabbit, via Vikki: "So then he says the hit was two goons from
Saskatoon. Name of Edouard and Darryl. Known as Spot and Puff.
Because one has real bad skin and the other is a poofter."

AND WHEN IT WAS GONE, SHE CUT THE GIANT'S HEAD OFF.

97. KISSING COUSINS REDUX

As you recall, I said I had to relate two breakthroughs (breaksthrough?) in the third person. Here's the second.

Thelma didn't have to get tricked out (pun intended) quite as distinctively as Vikki had in order to go to church, but I know she made an effort because I saw her after we got home and she was wearing a blouse with a ruffle down the front and a Peter Pan collar, and a pencil skirt that hugged a rounded belly too slim to be considered *showing* yet.

Thelma spends time on her appearance because, as she sees it but in my words, make-up and fashion are armour protecting a tender heart from the vagaries of the world. (I was beginning to believe in that tender heart for the first time in my life, but I wasn't there to discuss it with her as she got ready, nor to let her in on my secret: that a black leather jacket, a spiked choker, and some strategic body piercings sometimes work just as well.)

Her heels were almost as punishing as Vikki's, though not platform because at a thin five-nine, Thel already thought she was plenty tall enough. Just as she got off the bus, the heavens opened and rain came down so fast that the sidewalk couldn't drain itself, which meant that long before she arrived at the church, her shoes, also like Vikki's, were on the way to ruination. Thelma always carried her umbrella, so higher up, her body shaded from drenched to dry like the cheap ombre dresses in the Added Touch™ catalogue. She had also had the foresight to put the sheaf of paper she carried into a transparent pink plastic shoulder-tote she got as a freebie with a perfume purchase.

The Right Reverend Andrew Cutter (I've sometimes, I admit, infuriated Thel by calling him the Far-Right-Reverend) met her at the door as she was shaking rain from her umbrella and hanging her sensible beige car coat on the rack inside the church annex door, right beside the Reverend's lamb-leather overcoat. "Sister Thelma," he said. "What brings you here on such a foul day?"

"Rain is part of God's plan too," said Thelma. She later regretted it, but she was still steamed up. About the shoes, now, too. She liked those shoes.

"Of course, of course," he said. She tapped up the stairs in her soaked open-toe pumps, trying not to wince as she heard the excess water squishing from their soles, and he followed her closely. She didn't realise it until afterward — when she regretted that too as unfair, since she knew the Reverend's weak points — but she'd probably worn the pencil skirt on purpose.

In his office, Thelma settled herself with a flounce in the before-the-desk Naugahyde™-upholstered (another parallel with Vik's day) easy chair, into which she sank more deeply than she intended, and he settled expansively in the ergonomically-friendly rolling armchair behind it, where, she realised, her posture in the easy chair afforded him a good view of her legs from ankle to thigh.

"Reverend," she said, "Can you answer a few questions about the Soul Patrol for me?"

"Certainly," he said.

Thelma brought out a notebook from her pink plastic tote bag. The notebook had yellow, pink, and blue daisies on the cover, and a matching pen with pink faux-cloisonné daisies welded to the clip.

"I have heard there is an Inner Circle which leads the Soul Patrol. Are you part of this circle?"

"Alas, I have not been honoured thus."

"Do you know who around here *has* been?"

"I believe that Reverend Goldring of the New Alliance of Jesus Closer to God is the leader of the Regional Circle. I'm not sure who else professes that way."

Thelma wrote, *Goldring. New Alliance of JC2G.* "Thank you. Do you have any reason to believe that you are being considered for a place in the Circle?"

"No, and in fact . . ."

Thelma waited.

"I believe I will not be. I've been told I am not 'executive material' until I have succeeded in bringing more people to investiture."

Thelma nodded. Then she got up with as much dignity as she could from the enveloping arms of the Naugas and pulled a straight chair over from the conference table to beside the desk. Settling herself there, she extracted a stack of pages from her tote-bag and slapped it onto the desk blotter.

"Well, in that case, Reverend Cutter," she said, "I have some things to say about the Soul Patrol."

"Call me Andy," he said, as he always did. "What about it? You had your investiture a year or so ago, didn't you?"

"Two years ago June, Reverend Andy," Thelma said. "Yes, I did."

"So what can I do for you?"

After diving back into the tote, Thel dumped her Soul Patrol T-shirt on top of the sheaf of pages.

"I quit," she said.

She sat back, satisfied.

The Reverend Andrew Cutter was not easily surprised. He often said so in his sermons. Today, however, he seemed overly vulnerable to the difficulties of the flesh. His jaw actually dropped for a second, and he sat up abruptly, before he wrestled himself back into control.

"Dear Thelma, I can't imagine why . . . what . . . you could be thinking!"

Thelma leaned forward. "Reverend, I've been doing some research. The Soul Patrol is not what I was led to believe. I want to show you this material, and I hope you will feel as I do, and I hope you will help withdraw our church from those supporting this . . . this *invidious* organisation."

"Invidious?"

She swept the T-shirt aside and began to spread out the bundles of neatly paper-clipped computer printouts in front of him. Bringing in the sheaves.

"Look. *Here* is the mission statement of the Inner Circle, which discusses in *very* un-Christian terms a number of unfortunate groups in our society: homosexuals, for instance, and homeless, and drug-dependent individuals, and sex workers. I know we hate the sin, but as you have so often preached, we should *love* the sinner. *This* is the Inner Circle's website. It's actually public. *Look* at its name. That's *outrageous*. God doesn't *hate* anyone: in fact, God doesn't *hate* at all. God is love. Hate's the realm of The Other One. How can they call it that, let alone write *these terrible things?*"

She flipped pages and tapped with her forefinger's lacquered, decorated fingernail on one paragraph where the text advocated violent "cleansing" of racial minorities by the minions of a "white God".

"God," Thelma said furiously, "*is not white*. If God made us in His image, all races are God's work. God is *not white!*"

"Sister Thelma, calm yourself," Reverend Andy said gently. He placed a hand on hers, stilling her, but she shook it off.

"This," she said, "is a list of Soul Patrol members convicted of violent assaults. They actually *brag* about it! Look at that chat forum, with all those posts about what they did! And they can't even *spell*."

Another clipped sheaf. The paper clips were in pastel colours and some of them were animal shapes. "Here are those convicted of hate crimes in jurisdictions where there is hate crime legislation, including here in Canada where they received more serious sentences because their crimes were hate-motivated. Reverend, these are not people who act as God wants his children to act. Jesus said, *Love one another*."

"Jesus also cast the moneylenders out of the temple," said Rev. Andy.

"Perhaps he did, but he didn't leave them bleeding from the ears and nose, or dead and crucified on a fence. He sat down with prostitutes, and he told a thief, *Tonight you shall be with me in paradise*."

"My dear, perhaps their methods can be a little extreme, but most of the Soul Patrollers do God's work. Look at your own wonderful work at the soup kitchen . . ."

"God said, *Thou shalt not kill*! He did not say, thou shalt not kill nice people. Jesus did not say we should only love those who are already on the road to salvation. Jesus called us to go among the outcasts and offer them help and salvation. *Salvation*, not swastikas carved on their faces, like this poor Jewish girl, or a bullet in the head, like this doctor from a street clinic, or brain damage from being kicked with steel-toed boots, like this poor, poor young lad." The grisly photos stared up from the desk far less accusingly than Thelma stared at Rev. Andy.

"I'm sure these are anomalies," he said. "Every movement has its . . . extremists. Misguided, perhaps, but their motivation . . ."

"Their *motivation*, Reverend, is *hate*. How can you condone —"

"I do not condone such acts, but I understand them," he said. "After all, do you not get frustrated when you cannot bring God to people who seem to willfully flout his commandments?"

"Frustrated, but not violent. Not murderous. Jesus told us to turn the other cheek, not strike in anger."

"Jesus also cursed the fig tree that bore no fruit."

"And you yourself told us that we were not to use that episode to infer that Jesus wanted us to kill Jews — or anyone else. In Luke, it is referred to as a parable. Now you are using it as an apology for these terrible people."

"I'm sorry you are so upset, Sister." The Reverend bent into his intense, attentive pose.

Thelma found herself surprised to be thinking the word *pose*. She had taken much comfort from Reverend Andy before, and he had been especially helpful when Thel and Ihor (Harold, but I often call him Ihor — she hates it) had received the results of the amniocentesis. Yet today he seemed to her to be too close, too damply warm, too blasé, too avuncular.

"I'm not sorry, Reverend. Jesus crusaded against the wrongs he saw around him. He said that whatsoever we do to the least among us, we do unto him, and he didn't just mean good deeds. If I were not upset[12] I would consider myself less than Christian. I want to know if you share my concerns."

The Reverend clasped his hands before him. To Thelma, waiting on the edge of her seat, he looked almost nervous. "Er, I can't rightly say, off the cuff, here. I would like to read your material, if you would leave it with me."

"I made these copies for you to keep. I am requesting you formally to take this material —" she tapped again, this time on

12. Note *her* correct use of the subjunctive. Thelma was well suited to do the homeschooling she had expected, until recently, to offer her child unassisted.

a page liberally ringed with daisies, with a carefully formatted letter printed in the centre in Freestyle Script, the same typeface she uses for her Christmas letters, but in 14 pt "—to the church council and to consider my *formal* request to withdraw our congregation's support from the Soul Patrol. I have a second request here to censure and shun them. That is somewhat strong, I realise, but I am horrified — *horrified!* — that they would commit atrocities *in Jesus's name.*"

"If you feel you need to make it a formal matter —"

"I do. And I certainly hope *you* will, as well. I'll be in touch with some of the councillors after I feel they've had time to look over their copies —" she slapped her manicured hand down on the stack of pre-clipped copies "— to see if they need any more information."

Thelma stood, collected her colourful belongings, and tapped to the door. Suddenly she stopped, swivelled, tapped back to the desk, and swept up the Soul Patrol T-shirt.

"I'll return this shortly," she said. "Perhaps if you would keep my resignation letter to the Patrol —" she reached over and tapped it: another floral Freestyle Script missive, enclosed in a matching envelope "— in your desk until Sunday? I would appreciate it."

"Certainly. Taking some time to reconsider?"

"Certainly *not*, Reverend. My mind is made up. But I have some matters to settle with them before I withdraw. A few details. Just to finish up."

"No problem. Until Sunday, then."

Thelma thanked her spiritual leader and shrugged into her wet coat. The sky was still low, but the rain had slowed to a steady, slow drizzle.

She only had to change buses twice to reach the New Alliance of Jesus Closer to God Church. On the way, shivering with the dampness, she took off her coat and put the Soul Patrol T-shirt over her blouse, carefully freeing the round-edged collar and smoothing it over the band at the T-shirt's neck.

When she arrived, she saw an SUV with the church logo on it in the parking space labelled *Rev Goldring*. She glanced briefly at the urban-brutalist facade of the massive building, then strode in her ruined sandals to the huge double door.

Squaring her shoulders, she heaved the door open and walked briskly into the darkness within.

98. WHEN WE RETURNED HOME . . .

When we returned home through the drying streets, we found two bedraggled, barefoot women sitting on the stairs just below my landing, comparing the damaged shoes they held soles-up in their hands.

They both had over-processed, determinedly-blonded hair which had been through a storm; both wore dangling earrings and blue eye-shadow; their hose was laddered, their narrow skirts had ridden up on their shapely legs, and they were laughing.

Thelma and Vikki had met.

ONCE IN A NIGHT AS BLACK AS PITCH ISABEL MET A WICKED OLD WITCH.

99. STRANGE BEDFELLOWS

Thel wouldn't tell.

"Get that big policeman here," she said. "I only want to talk about this once."

"She's pissed off," said Vikki.

"Please," said Thelma. "Anger is no reason to abandon basic civility."

"Sorry," said Vik. Hmm.

100. DICK-EQUIVALENT

Easier said than done. That big policeman had more than one case, and a life. Jian went back to Double Greetings to get takeout to feed our intrepid detectives, and I provided some clothes that, though they fit and look pretty good on me, did nothing for Vik or Thel except cover them with dry fabric and warm them up.

Finally Lance and Rog showed up.

Lance was annoyed. "What does Internal Affairs have to do with it anyway?" he was saying as they came up the stairs. "It's not like he's —"

"He's a witness in an investigation, you putz," Roger said. "You're lucky you didn't get suspended."

"Lookit, Staff, he's really —"

"He's The One? He's the Man of Your Dreams? Then he'll wait."

Were they talking about Denis? Apparently. That was encouraging. True love has been known to follow from a prohibition.

Apparently, however, Roger was taking moral high ground to which I had personal reason to know he might not be entitled. I opened my mouth, then closed it again as Lance said, "I told them I wouldn't stop seeing him, but I'd keep it cool while the investigation was active, and they said they'd make a note of it, and then dismissed the meeting. That's gotta mean —"

"That you were one hell of a lucky cop," said Roger. "Which puts you in good company, but let this be a lesson to you."

"What kind of lesson, Staff Sergeant?" I said, and he glared at me.

"A lesson that nobody ever learns," he said.

"Not to think with his dick," said Vik to us, grinning. "My business was based on nobody ever learning that lesson."

"Hmph," Thel said, but she was grinning too. Hmmm.

"Or dick-equivalent," said Roger. Why on Earth was he looking at *me* when he said it?

Thelma filled us in on her visit to Reverend Andy, and even put up with me giggling at the font and paper with which she had printed all her missiles . . . er, missives (she had copies for us all, too, which is how I know about the 14 pt Freestyle Script and the paper clips). When she got to Reverend Goldring of the New Alliance of Jesus Closer to God, leader of the Regional Circle of the Soul Patrol, however, I quit laughing.

"Thelma, for Christ's sake, you could have been killed!"

"It was for Christ's sake that I had to do this," she said with dignity, while Roger was rushing in at the same time with "No, no, highly unlikely . . ." so I had a chance to glare back at him — revenge for earlier.

"Besides," said Thelma, "He is definitely not involved. He is a dangerous idiot, and I'll be starting to do some work around opposing his Ungodly —" I heard the capital letter "— organisation, but I am quite satisfied that he is not one of the murderers we seek."

She really said "seek". Then she told us why she was so certain.

101. THE SOUL PATROL SO FAR

When she got to the New Alliance of Jesus Closer to God Church, the first person Thelma met was not Reverend Harper Goldring. It was his personal care attendant.

His personal care attendant was pushing the Reverend Harp Goldring's spare power wheelchair up the ramp of the purpose-fitted cavern that was the body of the church, a carpeted auditorium that was big enough to hold two thousand people but at the moment was empty and dim, the sound system off and the giant projection screens grey and empty.

("It's not because he's in a wheelchair that he's not a criminal," said Thelma. "That would be naïve of me.")

Rev. Harp's personal care attendant was a balding, sour-looking, lumpy man in his forties, wearing a Soul Patrol T-shirt that had seen better days, and a beige windbreaker.

("Yikes, you really *could* have been killed!" I said.

("Yikes?" said Rog and Jian at the same time, for different reasons.

("Nonsense," said Thel. "I was simply a damp suburban matron.")

("Damn suburban matron?" asked Jian seriously — maybe. I couldn't tell.

("Damp," said Thelma. "Damp. Wet. Are you people going to keep interrupting like this all the way through?"

("No, no," said Roger hurriedly. "Yes," Jian, Vik, Lance, and I said.)

Thelma remembered my description of my assailants instantly, and she admitted that a small frisson did occur, but my impression hearing her account was that it was more a frisson of the same towering annoyance that brought her there. She asked the Slob, as she immediately began to call him —

("Apologies, but *really*, his hair was *so* unwashed, what there was of it, and I don't think I owe him one hundred percent civility after what he did to you. Anyway, I am not calling him some of the things I *thought* when I realised who he must be . . ."

("Are you going to keep interrupting yourself like this all the way through?" I asked.

("Oh, hush up," she said, but I think I got a corner of a grin out of her despite herself.)

— where she could find the Reverend, and he said, "Gimme a minute here, this thing is friggin' heavy, pardon the expression, Sister."

"I am not a religious," she said. "May I help?"

"Nah, forget it. Yeah, second thought. Here, I'll open this here door and you push it in, okay?"

She thought the division of labour was perhaps a little off, but she complied. He locked the door to the closet in which they'd stowed the wheelchair and then led her up another ramp to a wide-doored, adapted office where she met Goldring.

Goldring was as charming as a man could be who had to gasp for breath every few words and who besides that was the regional director of a gay-bashing gang.

"Come in," he said. "I see you've met my able caregiver. Able, that's a pun. His name is actually Abel, Abel Jones. And you, Sister?"

Thelma introduced herself as a Soul Patrol member coming to the source. She glossed over the conversation a little bit. I had a feeling she might have been having some qualms of conscience about the way she played him like a fish on a line (and I know fish on lines: I used to go fly-fishing now and again with a dishy and famous-but-reclusive science fiction writer in Washington state, but that's another story), so she didn't go into as much detail as when relaying her encounter with Andy Cutter. Or maybe she was just getting tired.

Soon they were having a comfortable chit-chat, Thelma making use of her long legs again for emphasis, and the Reverend Goldring ignoring them.

("He really was," Thel said. "He was totally absorbed in his conversation. It was a little bit eerie. I really didn't realise until today how much one's . . . er, corporeal body . . . takes its place in interactions of the spirit, whether we know it or not."

(Vik snorted.)

Goldring took her through the complete history of the Soul Patrol in our region: how his brother-in-law had introduced him to the organisation, how Goldring had franchised it with promises of recruitment, administrative support, and space in the carpeted sports arena that passed for his church — Thelma had seen smaller warehouses in her job as a forklift saleswoman before her marriage — and how he'd sold the idea to local business people as a way to provide a kind of citizens' watch over their streets.

"Of course, Sister Thelma," he said, "the Soul Patrol is only part of the picture. We are an active church, a community church. We feed four hundred homeless people here every night —" Thelma wondered if they had to be white and non-homosexual to get their hot dogs, but she didn't ask "— and we work with the parole board to receive and place parolees who have paid their debt to society —" ("He actually *said* that?" Vik said, and Thelma laughed and said, "Would I lie to you? Those very words!") "— finding new work for them that helps them repay the community and change their lives. Why, Abel here is one of our graduates!"

Abel mugged a practised moue of repentance, and nodded his way out of the room backwards. Thelma got the impression he would have tugged his forelock had he had one. (She had read *Ivanhoe* — and seen the Monty Python movie about the Holy Grail, having mistaken it for a religious film and having been too shy to leave the crowded theatre once she realised her mistake.) However, she didn't believe for a minute that Abel was the changed man the Reverend obviously and proudly thought him to be. She knew what the Slob did on his evenings off.

Goldring then rang for a taller, more fastidiously-attired, more relaxed, but in her mind equally sinister sidekick with greasy hair in a pony-tail, so that this office helper, whom Goldring called Jordan (ha!), could go to the filing cabinet and withdraw for Thel a brochure extolling the programmes the church ran in conjunction with a number of other local churches. Thelma had to admit it looked pretty good — it was an ecumenical triumph, in fact, with far-right Protestant denominations cheek-and-jowl with Unitarians, Anglicans, Roman Catholics, and even a couple of mosques in a loose federation called Metropolitan Multi-Faith Foundation, which hired its own executive director and staff and had its own board.

It was when she ran her glance down the list of board members that it fell into place for her. She knew who was using the Soul Patrol, and inasmuch as she could, given that he had betrayed everything her religion stood for, and thus also betrayed God, by buying into the Soul Patrol in the first place, she felt sorry for the Reverend Harper Goldring.

The Honourary Patron and Founding Chairman was Laszlo Stinchko, and the Treasurer was Panda Stinchko.

She tried. She really did. "Are you aware," she said delicately, "that Mrs. Stinchko has had a slight . . . problem in the past with misdirected fiscal governance?"

"Oh, that can't be right," said Goldring. "Her record is quite clear. Best steward our organisation could have. Such a breadth of experience in the non-profit sector. So good with the numbers. A godsend."

So even with Harp's ability to forgive and employ, Panda had stopped short of revealing she was a jailbird. Thel, whom we are beginning to see was no slouch in the synthesis-of-information line, wondered ungenerously if maybe it had something to do with Panda not wanting to tip off the billionaire husband. Goldring went on.

"It's her first time with a church, and she has just been bowled over by our faith. She just sent us an e-mail that when she returns from her vacation, she plans to join our congregation. We do full immersion baptism, you know. I don't know what we would have done without her. We've had some financial setbacks, but she always seems to make sense of things."

Thelma was visited at that moment by a true revelation, akin to the holy visions of a number of other women over history: hers was a vision of the bank accounts of the ecumenical homelessness-alleviation council dripping — nay, flooding — funds into offshore accounts. (Amazingly, when she shared this moment, we all saw it too, and it later proved to be a true vision. This is the way prophets get their reputations.)

Thelma was almost moved to pity for Goldring and his church, but she didn't dare warn him further, so she led the conversation back to the Soul Patrol. She was at this point hoping that she could Make a Difference (I heard the capitals there too).

"Are you aware," she began again, "that the Soul Patrol uses some very muscular techniques for fighting sin?"

"God cleanses with fire and the sword," said Goldring with vicarious satisfaction, and misquoted Psalms, "The Lord smiteth mine enemy upon the cheek-bone; He hath broken the teeth of the ungodly."

Sitting perched on the seat-edge of my living room couch, wearing a blanket and my ill-fitting clothes, Thelma looked like a kind of female Galahad, with a little halo of goodness around her head. She sat silent for a moment after relating that Scriptural moment, then decisively broke the halo into little tiny pieces.

"It was at that moment," she said, "that I abandoned him to his fate. He deserves Panda Big-Fake-Breasts Stinchko and everything she's probably doing to his nasty little — cult. He can rot in Hell for all I care. May Jesus have mercy on me for thinking so."

And with a flounce of indignation, she settled back on the couch, and received our applause.

102. "OH BOY, OH JOY, WHERE DO WE GO FROM HERE . . ."

Most months, the Royal Canadian Mounted Police's "Phonebusters" team, which "liaises" (shudder) with local police forces and gets about 750 calls a day to their hotline, completes about 5,000 complaints of Internet and telephone fraud. The Nigerian letter, the rental scams, the home renovation hustles . . . the world is full of con artists. Credit card fraud, identity theft, fraudulent puppies (well, fraudulent people with non-existent puppies), offers to pave the driveway. New scams every day.

Phonebusters' bevy of civilian members gathers basic info and pass it on to a handful of investigating officers. Apparently fraud is like speeding only more so — lots of people do it, but very few actually get caught.

Our city police force, Rog said glumly, has two officers and one receptionist in the Fraud Department. They don't have time for little things like old ladies' life savings being syphoned off by systematic fraudster sweatshops in Nigeria, Benin, or the Netherlands.

No. The local force concentrates on *big* frauds. Frauds with numbers with six or more digits. Like for instance Panda Stinchko's previous conviction (under a far different name) for taking over $900,000 from a local non-profit organisation (bankrupting its humanitarian efforts in Africa and breaking the heart of its executive director, who not only had been convinced she was good for the board — do we see a pattern developing, anyone? — but also believed she was good for him, as they'd just begun dating[13]).

Those kinds of frauds have street cred.

Frauds with murders attached have *extra* street cred.

Roger had no trouble interesting the Fraud Squad. Only problem?

No complainant, no evidence. Just suspicions.

Keanu Reeves movies notwithstanding, two detectives and a civilian member stretched too thin cannot spare much time to investigate a crime that hasn't been committed yet — even a crime you can see barrelling down on its victims like domestic murder after a nasty marital breakup from a psychopath.

Back to Roger to investigate the murder.

Back to Maddy.

Back to us.

---

13. Obviously, Laszlo was cast as the husband in this iteration. BTW, Thel offered no data on whether Panda had also suggested bigamy or fornication to Goldring, though she opined in a shockingly non-charitable way that if Harp was so deeply Old-Testament, he probably thought *that* would have been fine too. But from what she'd seen, Panda's tits would do Panda no good if pointed in Harper's direction.

"Back to us," I said glumly.

"Oh, no no no . . ." said Roger. "No no. Back to Standard Operating Procedure. Please?"

It was two days after all the rainy revelations of the unlikely Bobbsey twins Vik and Thel. The full crew, as I was beginning to think of us, was sitting at one of the round tables of the Noodle Noodle Restaurant, another neighbourhood favourite, and Roger was giving us the news that the Fraud Squad, while interested, was overwhelmed.

Denis was watching Lance's every move with a concentration only equalled by Lance's focus on disregarding Denis's every move. The Rainy Night following the Rainy Day that his supervisors had cautioned Lance, he and Denis had had the "cool it" talk and then fallen into each other's arms and had to use a lot of manly self-control to keep their clothes on. Apparently it doesn't count if you don't undress, or so Denis had told me the day afterward in one of his excited "girlfriend" phone calls.

That intervening day had been otherwise grey and unrelieved, and I had spent some of it both depressed and grateful that I hadn't had to use my backup idea and Maddy's boots to go back out on the drag as a stalking horse.

But today some watery sunlight had forced its way through the cloud cover and accompanied me downtown, where I had been summoned on short notice to spend the morning in the lovely Mr. Spak's office, reading financial disclosures and signing papers. Apparently having money requires work, no matter my wish to be left alone.

Thelma had come along to the last half hour of the meeting, and as a result of discovering that they wouldn't have to remortgage their house to hire caregivers for the baby when the time came, was looking flushed and almost happy. One hand rested on her belly in that gesture that breeders use unconsciously and may even deny using, depending.

The surprise was Vikki, who had used the intervening day to go over to the college and switch from business to the early childhood and special needs education program, and to negotiate with Thel and Ihor — I may have to call him Harold from now on, if Thel keeps surprising me — the terms on which she was going to move into their spare room when Thel got to the inevitable beached-whale stage, so she could become their nanny when the baby came.

This was a pretty serious career change, and Jian was grilling her in an undertone on her commitment, her ability, and her suitability.

"Look," Roger said to the rest of us, "we've got —", only to be interrupted by Vik.

"Look, it's not as if I'll be wearing fuckin' fuck-me boots to the fuckin' park with the fuckin' stroller, all right? Why don't you just keep the fuckin' boots and give me a fuckin' break in exchange?"

We all looked at her, Thel as blearily as Bunnywit when he's interrupted licking his belly. "Language," she said absently, moving her hand to her shirt ruffles.

Vik looked back at our stares like a Gremlin after water had been applied. "What? Jian acts like nobody ever changed their fuckin' career choice before. I can do this, okay? For one thing, I usta take care of my mom's babies after she lost interest, until they got apprehended. And some of them were pretty fuck— . . . er, not so normal exactly, after all the drinking and dope she did. This kid is gonna be a piece of cake by comparison."

Thel looked a little bemused. I think she was parsing the differences between fetal alcohol syndrome and Down's syndrome. But she said nothing, only smiled.

Denis cleared his throat. "Works for me, girlfriend," he said, and Vik nodded at him almost as if she hadn't only two days ago called him a fucking limp-dick do-gooder who always thought the best of people. Lance had, we could infer, proved the former was untrue, but, apparently from Denis's reaction, she had been right about the second part. Still, now the sensible shoe was on the other foot, apparently.

"Can we have some focus here?" said Hep. "We are *talking*, I believe, about apprehending Maddy's killers."

"No," said Roger. "We are talking about *the police* doing our *job* and investigating Maddy's killing and everyone else staying the fu— . . . the he— . . . staying out of it. Right? Can I just get some kind of an agreement on that?"

"What kind of agreement?" Jian predictably asked.

"You got a secret past as a lawyer or something? I want some elbow room to work here without having to wade through a crowd of civilians."

"Is that all I am to you, Roger?" I asked archly, and — surprise — he glared at me again. "Hey, is that glare gonna be your default look from now on?"

The others laughed, and Rog quit glaring, but he didn't crack a smile. "Just promise me you'll leave it alone," he said. "Lance is already in trouble with the ethics cops, and the only reason I'm not is that Cummings isn't *my* boss, thank Chri— er, thank goodness."

"In other words, nobody noticed yet," said Hep.

"Sort of," said Roger.

"I told her to stop," said Hep righteously.

I thought that was pretty rich from a woman who cut off about thirty years of hair growth to go to a drag club in leather gear — and I said so.

"Stop all!" said Jian. "Fox eats its own vitals," with predictable reactions ranging from laughter to creased-forehead stares. "No use fighting," she continued unnecessarily.

"Yeah, we get it," I said. "And Hep? With due respect? I think we have accomplished our goal."

"What on Earth can you mean?" Hep demanded, flushing and slamming both hands down on the table.

"Well, your worry was that Maddy would be treated like just another dead prostitute. We've learned a few things since then."

"Which is for one," Roger interrupted heatedly, "that there is no such thing as just another dead prostitute in my goddamn unit, dammit!"

"Some of which are," I spoke over his outburst, firmly, "that there is no such thing etcetera etcetera for Roger, yes, but also that this crime is part of something bigger. Now we have all the attention to Maddy's death that you could possibly want. We have Roger's time and energy invested out of proportion to the number of killings in this town. We have Lance's undercover work tying in. We have the eye of Cummings, which while it is problematic for Lance's and Denis's social life is not necessarily a bad thing for the case. And now we have the attention of the Fraud Squad."

"What she said," said Lance.

"Hallelujah, she sees the light," crowed Rog with what I think was unnecessary enthusiasm.

"Which ordinarily would mean that I pretty much agree with Roger. We could try leaving it to the police now. And don't say anything, Roger, because I'm not finished."

I stopped to take a breath and savour the moment.

"Which *ordinarily*," I repeated for rhetorical effect, "would mean I agreed with Roger, except for two things. First, that the Bad Guys have my address. So far that hasn't meant anything except that I have to spend a *fuck* of a lot of money getting my Mendelson Joe repaired —" Lance shifted uneasily in his chair, and turned his eyes to his empty rice-bowl "— but it's an issue. Second, when those guys bashed me outside the club, they knew who I was. I can't imagine that they were spending their time following me around in their rôles as the angels of non-mercy for the farther-than-far-right-Reverend Harp-o'-Gold.

"So, there is some face-place recognition going on. So we may stop looking for them, but are they gonna stop looking for me? In which case, I'd just as soon be looking for them and find them first."

Another Pinter Pause, then an afterthought, "Oh, yeah, there is one more thing. The cops don't have time to look into Panda until she is a crime-in-progress. So we —"

"That is totally not what I said!" Roger used his Cop Voice on that. Impressive.

"— could look at what a civilian helper might achieve."

"Nothing," said Roger, still in Cop Voice, "and you could mess up a lot. We have ideas, and we even have plans, but they are none of you people's business. Look what happened when you stuck your noses in as far as you did!" He pointed to my head and then shook his finger as if that would work better.

"We, Victoria and I, could just go to that church for a while," said Thel, "and, like, get on some committees." Victoria?

"Yeah," said Vik. "Undercover, like."

"If anybody's going undercover anywhere," said Rog's Cop Voice, "it will be duly sworn members of the police service who are protected and empowered by law to investigate, and who operate within the rules of evidence. Or duly licensed private investigators who have equivalent protections, though I can't believe I'm even going there, given your tendency to hop onto bandwagons."

"You know you can't put a guard on me like they do in detective novels," I said, "and I have a legal right to protect myself."

"Not like a vigilante," said Roger.

"So the Internal Affairs guys *were* on your back then! You just didn't admit it."

Roger clammed up, blushed, then shook his head. "You're the fucking Energizer™ Bunny, aren't you? Can't you just stick with the 'I agree with Roger' part and cut out the bullshit? Give us all a break?"

"I'd be happy to do that," I said, "if not for points one and two."

"Which were the same point," said Lance.

"You think so?" (But only to cover the fact that he was probably right.)

"You have a bunch of cash now," said Roger. "Just go somewhere until this all blows over."

"Yes," said Jian brightly. "Like Panda Stinko did." I Cheshired.

"Oh, no no no," said Roger. "Amateur detectives in Thessaloniki? Even worse. You don't even speak the fucking language."

"I do," said Hep.

"She knows you," I said. "You can't go."

"I can do anything I please!"

"Except blow the police case by putting the Stink Bugs onto you," said Denis. "I vote we all cool it, and that girlfriend and her girlfriend go somewhere nice and neutral. Taipei or something. River cruise of the Amazon. Iceland. For a couple months."

"Sounds good to me," said Roger. "Meanwhile, we'll just wait until the Stinchkos get back, thank you all very much."

"Nonsense," said Jian. "For one thing, my *mother* lives Taipei. You *really* want somebody kill me?"

After a moment she said, "Or me kill somebody? Fifty-fifty chance, maybe."

That was pretty much it, though our conversation circled tediously for another half hour. Reluctantly, Hep and Jian and I agreed to give it a rest (and to call Roger *first* if anyone had, in Rog's words, "any more of your bright ideas"), Thel and Vik agreed that the needs of the baby came first and that they would be too much at risk at the Whatchamacallit Harp of Gold Gay-bashing Church, Roger agreed to keep us posted if doing so would not jeopardise an ongoing police investigation, and Lance and Denis just agreed, like a couple of big-eyed greeting card kids.

Thel wasn't happy though. She was still worried about the Soul Patrol.

"It's enough to give religion a bad name," Thelma grumped.

"Thel," I said, "sorry, but religion already has a bad name. Lots of bad names." She glared at me in the old way until she heard the next bit. "The way to help that is just to be yourself, and work in your own church. Get them to dump the Soul Patrol, as you promised Reverend Andy. Go through channels. Do your committee thing in your own back yard. Let your little light shine and all that."

"You don't believe that," she said.

"The little light part? Yes, I do. And the 'think globally, act locally' part, I totally do. The religion part? I don't get that and I won't pretend to, but I won't make any more fun of your 'getting it'. I think I've learned that much from this, if nothing else."

But I hadn't learned nothing else. I'd learned about Jian, and that was good, and I'd learned more about my family, and while that was not so good, I could stand it. I'd learned a lot more about cops and liked a lot more of them than I had when I was a lot younger — or even a little bit younger — and had had differently-shaded dealings with the police services of several cities.

And I soon learned, when I loftily offered to pick up the bill for dim-sum for eight and a steamed veggie plate, that Noodle Noodle had raised its prices by fifty percent since I was last there. And no more ten percent discounts for people who'd been coming there since God was a pup.

Sometimes it's the unexpected blows like that one that just make you lose your faith in people.

THE WITCH'S FACE WAS CROSS AND WRINKLED,

104. CHERCHEZ LA FLIM-FLAM FEMME

Which is not to say that I didn't *think* a lot about what someone, whoever, maybe me, could do — especially when I picked up the paper the next day and discovered a cute little photo in the fashion gossip of Laszlo and Panda Stinchko at a charity arts gala the night before, right downtown and not ten blocks from the Epitome Apartments.

To say I was cross at that wrinkle would be an understatement.

When Roger exacted that promise of inaction from all of us, he had to have known that the flim-flam femme fatale was back.

THE WITCH'S GUMS WITH TEETH WERE SPRINKLED.

105. BEWARE OF ALL ENTERPRISES THAT REQUIRE NEW CLOTHES

It was amazing how perfect Panda's teeth were.

They were even more perfect than her breasts.

They were more perfect than her couturier gown — or mine.

You heard me. I was in drag again, this time the real thing. Hep, Jian, and I had gone downtown and spent some of my money and some of Hep's on gowns for Jian and me. Jian looked just as dishy and just as trashy as she had on our club circuit, but in real brand names, not Denis's low-light-needing improvisations. And I looked — gracious, I looked like a socialite.

Which was important, because we had then spent pots more money on tix to a $1000-a-plate charity bash for the previously-mentioned multi-church coalition properly yclept the Metropolitan Multi-Faith Foundation, fondly known as M2F2 to its devotees, although to me that sounded like either an eighties disco band or a way to write a rude word without your mama finding out about it.

I had left a message on Roger's work voice mail just before we left, telling him where we were, honouring the letter of our agreement. I figured he had made it in enough bad faith that I wasn't bound to honour the spirit of it.

"Here's how I see it," I'd told his virtual ear. "First, I really did just inherit a chunk of money and in the normal way of things, if I hadn't been busy and also so pissy about the whole thing, I'd already have been looking for a charity to help me spend some of it so I can be poor and eat fish sticks again. And inner-city housing is a passion of mine. Look at where I live if you don't believe me. So it is perfectly natural for me to try this out. If I get recognised, I shelled out the bucks, I have the dress and the shoes, who's going to suspect a thing? It's a small town."

It seemed pretty small when we got there too. The first person I saw was Thel's Reverend Andy, the second was someone who'd been in juvenile detention with me once — I was there for swearing and having sex too young (and for free), he was there for boosting a car. Allegedly, as they say. Ha. He was now a magistrate, juvenile records not being permanent I guess. Or maybe he beat the rap. Is that still an expression people use? Beat the rap? Beats me: since being downsized, I get my argot out of cheap thrillers I read in the bathtub, with Bunnywit trying to knock them into the water every time I turn the page.

"How've you been?" he said. "What are you doing these days?" By this I realised that he barely recognised me and was doing the looking-for-clues tap-dance.

"Well, my parents died, so I inherited, of course," I said, "and it's a pretty steep learning curve."

He nodded sagely.

"You know," I laughed, "the folks kept me on a pretty tight leash, but I didn't care. I really thought I was above money somehow, until I had some. But you get used to it pretty fast."

"No kidding," he said. "But the flashy cars and the dames take it out of you just as fast. In my experience, anyway. You probably don't have the dame problem with guys. They probably line up even before the money, eh?"

Bob. Maybe he was just in juvie for bad manners. Or being a living cliché. Clearly, still loved flashy cars, though.

"Let me introduce you around," he said. "Still the same last name?"

"Yep," I said, and left it at that. To his credit, he didn't squirm. And he did in fact tow me over to the secret power centre of the room, where the mayor, a member of the legislature, and a member of parliament were in a cluster with four suits (well, tuxes), three women wearing a couple of tons of sequins between them, an earnest-looking bearded guy in a sports jacket and a pony-tail looking blithely unaware that he too should be tarted up, a slender young man in tails who was fending off three steel-haired magnolias who should have known better given the gaydar reading, and Laszlo and Panda Stinchko.

"Don't bother talking to little old me, dear. Here are the folks that matter. I'll leave you to introduce yourselves."

The mayor is a sharp, lean, smart guy — the first mayor in fifteen years for whom I actually had voted (I always vote, just usually not for the winner). He watched Bob's retreat, then smiled at me. "Hasn't a clue who you are, right?"

As we traded names and handshakes, the mayor looked at me, looked again, then, very quietly, murmured my name. "I didn't recognise you at first under all that makeup. I didn't think you were into this kind of —"

"Drag? I'm not. I have a reason to be here. Tell you sometime. Who's who in the zoo here, Your Honour?"

"Well, you must meet Pan," and he drew her by the elbow away from Bob, who had been sucked toward the twin poles of het-man magnet she had had installed on her chest.

When Panda bared her teeth at me, giving my dress the once-over simultaneously, I knew I wasn't in Kansas anymore.

"What a quaint gown?" she said. "So lovely? Retro?" To her, this stuff seemed to really matter. The question marks were ubiquitous, I think, not intentionally insulting.

"No, it's one of the new designers. I think he has promise. You know, just the right amount of disdain." (Instead of *What quaint tits, dear. Retro?*)

"How love— what?"

"Oh, you know, designers with disdain for the bodies they design for always produce such interesting results. The artistic tension is almost unbearable, isn't it? So how are you connected with this marvellous event?"

"I'm the treasurer," she said shortly, forgetting her girly question marks.

"Oh, then His Honour introduced me to the right person. I've just come into my inheritance, and I'm looking for a good recipient of a substantial donation in my parents' memory —"

That focussed her attention. "We must lunch?" she said. "I'd love to discuss it?"

"I may be off to Greece in a couple of days. Or Taiwan. Why don't you tell me a bit about the process now, and I'll ask my lawyer to call you and set up the details."

She flashed the teeth again, and again I noted their remarkable clarity, colour, and balance. Perhaps I should lunch with her, just to find out who the artist was.

"What kind of sum are we . . . ?"

"Substantial," I repeated, as if that should be enough, girl-to-girl.

Jian tapped up to me, her high heels clicking on the ballroom's dance floor.

"Oh, herro," she said to me, deliberately slurring into a stronger accent — a bad stereotypical one that never had I heard emerge from her lips in company before this moment — and almost unbalancing my bland façade. "We meet here too! How rovery. My husband wirr be so grad I have girrfriend to tark to. I am Ling Ling Chan," she said, extending her hand to Panda. I stifled my hilarity behind a convenient canapé. *Herro* indeed. Not only had she named herself after a prominent panda bear, pronouncing the Ls perfectly, but I knew she was doing the intro just to get Panda to commit to a version of "Stinchko".

"Panda," said Panda, "but everybody calls me Pan? Lotzi calls me Pan-Pan?" she continued unbearably, simpering at tall, handsome Laszlo who had appeared to claim her with an arm around her waist and a proprietary downward smile. His smile was three-cornered and feral. He was charming, reminded me of the head of the debating club in junior high school, and I hated him at once.

"Ling Ling the name of famous panda bear," said Jian. "Name after me. My husband make donation to zoo for keep pandas arive and thliving, breed panda babies. My husband very generous successfur businessman. I very lucky. Visit casinos in twenty-eight countlies so far. Always rucky. You have good casinos?" This was 'way too entertaining. I hoped they didn't catch on to her taking the piss.

Laszlo transferred the grin to her, beaming it very tightly. "How very naughty of you, Mrs. Chan. Yes, we have casinos. The high rollers go to the Palace, right downtown. But here, of course, the profits go to charity, not gangsters." Apparently Ling Ling seemed completely credible to him.

"Ah, rike this dinner. Chality. Tell me about this chality."

With an audience of two rich women to whom they could condescend, Lotsi and Pan Pan were in their element. While Studly Amor — of course that was who sylph-boy was — fended off his admirers and tried not to grab either of his patron's asses in public, Pan Pan and Stink Stink told us all about M2F2, from cradle to grave, and about every one of their new projects, from foundation to shingles — not the disease, but environmentally-inert, 100-year-guaranteed shingles made of recycled material and alternating with enough solar panels to light a small city. Of course, if you weren't hip to the new way of talking with eternally rising end-tones, you might have thought Pan-Pan wasn't sure about the age of the shingles.

"That would be on the new development, of course," said Lotzi, who had no trouble committing himself. Looking at Panda at his side, I wondered if he knew who he'd committed himself *to*, pardon the dangling preposition.

"Of course. What new development?"

"Well, we're holding several huge donations in trust?" said Panda, "including of course the city's grant? We're looking at a mix of low-income housing, neighbourhood businesses, social agencies, and schools? Lotsi is helping the city assemble the properties now? He's in real estate, you know?" She confided this to Jian, Jian's marital status granting girlfriend ranking. Besides, given the difference in his predator's grin when applied to Jian or me, Lotsi apparently didn't go for women of Jian's age, size, race, or type. Little did he know.

By the time they were done, it was pretty clear why there was plenty of motive to make sure one cheap hooker who had recognised Panda from before (and how the hell she did it I can't imagine, because this woman was a triumph of Barbie™-emulation surgery) never had a chance to tell anybody. I felt sick, which always mixes itself up with hunger in my gut.

"Look at that lovely buffet," I said to Jian. "I must get over there before His Honour eats it all!"

We disentangled ourselves, me with a promise to have the immaculate Mr. Spak get in touch with Panda.

His name relaxed the last of Panda's reserves, and she deigned to air-hug me on parting, as she said, "*So* glad we ran into each other? Do call and we'll have lunch?"

Lunch for people like Panda was a couple of surfers and a school of tuna with trawler included, but I smiled and said, "Sure. Have your people call my people."

And got the hell out of Dodge before I started laughing (or, worse, Jian did, and set me off).

106. SOMETHING IN THE WAY SHE MOVES . . .

The mayor was standing beside the buffet table, at a slight remove, looking intently at Panda and Laszlo. No-one will ever be able to say I missed an opportunity. (Otherwise known as "Fools rush in . . .")

"Well, Your Honour," I said to him, "it's quite the ambitious project."

"Yes," he said, but absently, preoccupied with Pan-Pan — and not her tits either. He was watching her talk to the next patsy — er, potential investor in the worthy project.

"Problem?"

"She seems . . . familiar to me, somehow. I can't figure it out."

"Maybe she is one of Charlie's Angels, retired," said Jian brightly, accent slipping. I shook my head slightly, and she said, "I find cocktair," and tapped off toward the bar.

I took the mayor's elbow and turned him to the table. "My cat would think he was in heaven," I commented, and drew him toward the astonishing buffet of luxury goods. We stopped by the lox and capers. "Quit staring and get some food," I said, sotto voce. "Can we talk in complete confidence, Gary?"

"Is this about why you're here in that . . . in 'drag'?"

"Yes. I came to see what Panda was up to. Gary, has the city already bought into this? And sent the money?"

"Signed, yes. Delivered, no."

"I didn't tell you what I'm about to tell you. Promise?"

"What? Certainly."

"You recognised her yourself. Right?"

"I what? Oh! Right. What?"

"Panda changed her name on marriage," I said, and told him her original name.

There's this expression, "blanched", often rendered "went white", signifying shock. Gary was genetically incapable of going white, but the blood did rush from his face, leaving him sallow and sick-looking under the fluorescents. He had been on the board of the non-profit that lost the almost-a-million. "Holy *fuck*," he whispered.

"Language!" I said. "And try to look happy. I just saved the city 28.8 million smackeroos. Don't know about the private donors, though. That's one for the Fraud Squad, who are apparently on the case."

Gary forced a campaign smile. "Does her husband know?"

"Don't know. Suspect so, but that's as much because he makes my skin crawl. He could be one of the patsies." I filled a plate, then my mouth, with smoked salmon, cream cheese, and capers on little crustless bagel-bread rounds.

"Pasties?" Mechanically, he followed my lead.

The salmon platter was centrally garnished with salmon roe. Mother and child reunion. Harsh. I scooped some roe onto one of the canapés. "Very funny. Just what those tits are made for. I said patsies, like victims. Listen, at least one person has been killed to keep this a secret, so watch your ass. Lovely ass, by the way. I love how you slimmed down for the campaign."

"I'll tell Leora. She made me. Why I'm not eating those." He waved his lox toward warming trays with the deep-fried wontons, stuffed mushrooms alongside escargot swimming in butter, spring rolls, and scallops on toothpicks next to vats of dip with avocado and crab — mmmm.

I laughed out of proportion to how either of us felt, and we moved toward the steam trays so I could make up for his neglect.

"Smile, or I'll step on your toe with one of these goddamn heels," I said. "If it gets out I told you, I might be murdered, and I'm not kidding, but I can't watch this train wreck happen without at least one word to the wise. And I know I can trust you."

He didn't have to ask why. He went for the salient point. "Murdered? Are the police on this?"

"Homicide *and* Fraud. One person has been killed already. But no fraud *case*, as such, to speak of — yet. The homicide will be traced to some dope dealer's hired goons, not Barbie™ and Ken™ over there, despite how their paths have crossed with the killers'. And the churches and donors and city will spend the next ten years picking up the pieces. Not to speak of your career going up in smoke."

"That's the least of my worries." He isn't, you might guess, your usual politician. After the original charity fraud, he'd remortgaged his house to take care of his share of the board's liability for unpaid salaries and several years' unpaid employer tax and benefits contributions. He was a rich guy, but not rich enough to have absorbed a hit that big. When he ran for mayor, it was on an anti-corruption platform that owed a lot of its street cred to his past experience, as his had been one of the shocked-face photos plastered all over the papers for weeks.

I knew this because the day before I'd looked up the whole back-story on Yahoo™, Google™, and in a real hard-copy news-paper archive, courtesy a reporter friend who'd been promised an exclusive interview when the story (I didn't tell her details, but she knows she can count on me) broke.

I looked over at Panda. "I'd swear she's had that leg-lengthening surgery too," I said, "like that performance artist who is getting surgically altered to look like Barbie™. Who could have guessed dumpy, quiet little Doris would turn into *that*."

"Well, if I can have a makeover," the mayor said bravely, "what's to stop her?"

I laughed again, with less effort, and he joined me. His professional face was intact again.

"Can you carry on without showing by a flicker that you know?" I asked. "Because if not, go home and get a Botox injection before you meet them again. I mean it. This has already been enough money to kill for. She won't hesitate a second time. I'm not even sure she hesitated the first time."

"I'll be fine." I believed him. Gary had been a lawyer before his election. These wouldn't be the first sharks he'd met — or to whom he'd had to show a pleasant face.

"Take good care of yourself," I said. "I'm in the book — call me. I'll get you in touch with the main cop guys who are looking into this."

"'Cop guys'. Well-spoken as always."

"Speaking of, no more swearing in public, right?"

"That's what Leora keeps telling me. You must dine with us sometime. Someplace where you can wear that thing again. Leora will laugh her head off when she sees you."

And she did, about thirty seconds later, when she came up, said to Gary, "Oh, there you are, sweetie! The Boys and Girls Club awaits . . ." and tucked her hand into his. After one sharp glance at his face, she looked protectively at the person who put him in that state, did a double take, and guffawed.

Recovering, she said, "Omigawd, you look *fabulous*!" and air-hugged me with far more warmth than Pan-Pan had. "What on Earth are you doing here, and dressed like that?" she murmured as we did the kiss-kiss.

"I'm in drag," I whispered in her ear. "Try to pretend I belong!"

She drew back. "Why, we see you at so many of these," she said out loud. "We *have* to get together!"

"That's what Gary was just saying."

"Sorry to run, dear, but I have to get Gary to his next appearance," said Leora.

"I'll call you tomorrow," said Gary quietly, and she looked at him again with a flicker of surprise. The Garys and Leoras seldom actually *do* call folks like me, unless they have to. We'd met when I was a social worker, working with troubled kids. You know how that goes. You're grateful at the time, but ever after? The sight of the one who kept your kid's butt out of detention and your faces out of the papers[14] is a reminder. Now I seemed to her to have upset Gary — angered him, from the way the pulse in his neck had come up — and I saw her wonder why, and why he was saying he'd call.

"I'll be there," I said. Which was sort of true. My cell phone number was on my voicemail message now: I was everywhere, or anywhere, anyone wanted me to be. Modern technology.

Gary patted Leora's hand. "Let's go, babe."

I turned back to the canapés and was making a serious dent in some water chestnuts wrapped in bacon when Jian happened by. That is to say, when Jian tried to pretend that she wasn't standing beside the sushi just to eat piece after piece.

"Mayor Gary get bad news?" she said. "Wife tell him maybe she fooling around with you and me?" After piece.

"That is so not funny," I said. "These shoes are killing me. Have you had enough to eat?"

"Not a thousand dollar worth, that's for sure." After piece . . .

So we stayed for the sit-down dinner, and even the entertainment. But somehow the knowledge that I was in the room with a stone killer and con artist who was setting up a fifty-million-dollar (minimum) fraud with one foot on Maddy's body put a slight damper on my appetite. Usually nothing gets to my appetite. I was kind of surprised. Maybe I was getting too emotionally involved. Ha.

---

14. I got their permission to say that much here, by the way — am not breaching confidentiality. Just in case you wondered.

107. *AN ESSAY ON MAN* ("WHICH INCLUDES WOMAN, OF COURSE")

Maybe you know me a little by now. You think, hey, she's a smartass fag-hag with low, anything-that-moves morals. You hear I have some kind of secret past where I wasn't as happy with cops as I am now. I have injection marks. Then you find out I know the mayor. That maybe makes you pause for a moment, but you think, Hey, she met him and his wife in the line of work. I inherit some money, but not enough to make me the new Paris Hilton — no more, in fact, than a university prof and his always-working wife would accumulate in a working life. I'm smart, maybe, and I'm even kind of interesting, but I'm not your kind of people.

That's because I haven't kept any secrets. Even with the body art, I completely could have charmed you if we'd met at the fundraiser, the gallery, or even in Roger's office. I would have fit there, and you would have liked me fine, with hardly any reservations.

But the *real* secret is, *everybody* has a past. Everybody has something that if they ran for office they wouldn't want to get out in the media. Everybody. People are funny that way.

Panda Stinchko had the best tits money could buy, and she had unbelievably-rich Laszlo, and they had a boytoy on lifetime retainer. She went to Thessaloniki in Lotsa Stinky's private yacht (or jet or whatever), for a couple of weeks of caving at Petralona, and I bet she got to go off the roped pathways there. She had designer gowns on a body that made them look good even if they had been designed by sadistic misogynist closet cases with a bad sense of humour. M2F2 was as close as she planned to get to the jail experience from now on.

As a result, she'd gone a long way to ensure that the real nature of her finishing school hadn't come out. A long, long, wicked way.

And here is my theory: if she had just told everybody from Laszlo on down that she'd once been in jail for fraud, full disclosure from the get-go, she would have ended up in the same place, but Madeline Pritchard the Youngest would not have been dead and my Mendelson Joe and my head would not both have big scars on them.

Because the fact is, if I met you today, and we spent some time together, knowing what you know now and what you might eventually find out about me, you'd probably still grow to like me. In his *Essay on Man*, Alexander Pope wrote: "Vice is a monster of so frightful mien, / As, to be hated, needs but to be seen; / Yet seen too oft, familiar with her face, / We first endure, then pity, then embrace." Setting aside the sexism of title and pronoun, and the old-fashioned rhyme scheme, he was right on the money.

We can get used to anything, and learn to like it, and the Internet is full of kinky porn websites to prove it.

People are funny that way.

HO HO, ISABEL! THE OLD WITCH CROWED, I'LL TURN YOU INTO AN UGLY TOAD!

108. AND ANOTHER THING . . .

Another thing people are funny about. People lie to the police.

Shocking, hmmm?

You, of course, my readers, paragons of virtue all, have never lied to the police. *Ha. Officer, I was only going fifty-two. Yeah. Officer, I swerved to avoid a cat.* Sure.

You think only criminals lie to the cops? Nope. Innocent people lie to the cops. We lie to the cops because we are all in some ways still five years old and afraid to Get Caught. Even if we haven't done anything. I myself have lied to the cops. Really.

Police are familiar with this phenomenon. They assume that everyone is withholding some Guilty Secret. It's a lot like the Dirty Little Secrets I was just talking about. Everyone has some legal transgression they don't want known. The college students have a home invasion, so they call the police (of course — they *are* middle class after all), but first they bury their tiny stash of marijuana and the rolling papers in the back yard. And wash their hands after.

What all these innocent, paranoid folks don't always get is that police officers Know What They're Up To.

And they don't care. Usually. I mean, if the cops investigate a domestic dispute and find a grow-op, there isn't going to be a hands-off policy. But if police are investigating a homicide or a fraud (or, in our case here, a homicide *and* a fraud) they aren't going to care much about a couple of outstanding parking tickets, a prior for soliciting, or even an outstanding warrant for something minor, like speeding or spitting. They want to get the Bad Guys who do the big stuff. (*Bad Guys* in this context includes Bad Women, too, of course.) They have situational ethics.

Of a sort.

Most cops.

After some time on the job.

On a good day.

Now because civilians don't know this, they (we) do a lot of unnecessary lying.

Like for instance, some women I know who run an art gallery, and their gallery got painted with hate messages against "dikes" and "fagots" one day when they left the back door unlocked and only a couple of people knew it was unlocked. But the owner was paranoid about her insurance, so she lied to the cops. This prolonged the investigation — until someone else came clean. Then the cops were able to prove it wasn't a generalised anti-queer hate crime, but a you're-a-bitch-and-you-dumped-me personal hate crime. In the end the perp had the full force of the law down on her. (Only a modest fine and a stern warning, but her name got in the papers, humiliating her further so the whole feud is now writ in stone, but that's the wages of crime.)

So this little parable is meant to illustrate that if you have something to tell the cops, tell the whole truth and nothing but the truth, and usually that is the best thing.

(Of course, the gallery owner has never taken tea with *me* again, either, because she is mad about me breaking ranks, but that is the wages of having a strong personal morality so I am willing to live with it. Besides, she *is* a bitch, even to those of us who wouldn't sleep with her on a dare.).

So.

109. LIES AND CONSEQUENCES

So. Remember Norman?

Norman went to Roger and gave a statement. He was pretty honest, though not as much as he had been with me. Roger had to assure him that no-one in homicide used the word *john* pejoratively. Which was a lie, but cops also believe in means to ends, if within the law, and this one was more of a fib. It's the social contract, right? So he established some info about Maddy's prior run-ins with the Dynamic Duo.

Vikki had also had some effect on the street folks who had known Maddy, and finally a few of those allowed to some beat officers as how they might have information about a girl who got killed, and so on. These folks lied too, but with a little joking and a little bullying, Rog was able to put together a picture of Maddy's last few days. Which had been pretty much as one might expect. Turn a trick. Wait. Turn a trick.

A few run-ins with what the other girls thought were two irate johns. Who weren't.

Then, the night of her death, Maddy getting into the car of the same two johns. She was laughing. They weren't.

On information received from an anonymous source, Pink was "surveilled" (a back-formed word I hate), and soon busted for trying to sell crack cocaine to an undercover narc. Not the brightest crook in the remand centre, that one. But in an uncharacteristic attack of wiliness, he offered to dish on some other

206

crimes he'd happened to notice while he was innocently visiting friends in the inner city bar Wing's.

He described a number of useful scenarios, including a hooker who was seen struggling in a cheap rental car with two "goons from S'toon".

Pink and the hookers had pretty good recall and descriptive skills.

Roger went and pulled in Abel Definitely-an-Alias Jones and Jordan Definitely-an-Alias Smith and put them in lineups.

"Those are definitely the men," said Hep. But she hadn't actually seen Maddy get in a car with them.

"That's them, I think," said the woman who had seen the "irate johns". "But I couldn't eggzackly swear to it. I was over on the other side the road, y'know."

The woman who had seen Maddy get in the car on the night of her death, and Pink, looked at the line-ups. When they saw Abel and Jordan Not-Their-Real-Names, she went pale under her too-thick makeup and he broke a sweat, and they both said the same thing.

"No, hey, man, sorry, I don't see nobody there I reckonize. Sorry, man. Can we get outta here?"

Grammatically speaking, they were right. They didn't see nobody recognisable. Our star witlesses saw two someones whom they recognised perfectly — and knew them or whoever ran them well enough to be afraid. To be very afraid.

Roger considered whether it was worth blowing Lance's street usefulness and Cummings's mystery investigation to put the creeps away for busting up my apartment, and decided it wasn't.

So.

A couple of hours later, Pink was back in Remand, the working girl (woman, that is, but it's the idiom — what can I do?) was back on the street, Roger and Lance were cursing (eventually, we all cursed — fluently!) and really depressed — and Abel and Jordan were back pushing the Reverend Goldring around, smirking to themselves as they did.

And people blame the cops for letting the Bad Guys back onto the streets. Ha.

The consequences of lying.

Sometimes minor. Sometimes, a shitload of bad.

ISABEL, ISABEL, DIDN'T WORRY,
ISABEL DIDN'T SCREAM OR SCURRY,

110. "WHO PUT THE RAM IN THE RAMALAMADINGDONG?"

Now here is what we have: We have two guys, Edouard and Darryl, known as Spot and Puff, also known as Abel and Jordan Not-Their-Real-Names. They have records, but mostly for such trifles as aggravated assault, robbery with violence, assault with a deadly weapon, and the like.

No-one has ever actually caught them outright killing someone.

However, witnesses can be intimidated, as we saw in the previous chapter, even by the reputation of such as Spot and Puff.

Edouard and Darryl were returned to the Supreme Church of the Misguided Goldguy by two police officers, one large and one average-sized, the large one being a tall muscular white female and the smaller one being a medium-height muscular Asian man. These police officers acquainted the Wrong Reverend Goldring with the fact that his protégés were operating under aliases. They urged him to be more systematic in his research about the felons he rehabilitated, for his own and the community's safety.

Goldring, we heard later, preferred to take the word of two felons that they were "trying to get a fresh start on account of how the cops will pick up anybody with a record and stick them in a line-up and try to frame them for any crap that's going down", rather than the word of a female and an Asian, police officers notwithstanding. His mistake.

Edouard and Darryl were not happy to have been discovered. Perhaps whoever they worked for was not happy either.

Later that week, they paid me another visit. This time, given the improved security on the fire escape, something which my fellow tenants resented as much as I resented the break-in that caused it, they came to the front door. It was later established that a neighbour let them in to the hallway, and as for my door? That's what crowbars and jackboots are for.

Jian was in the kitchen. So was my cell phone. Later I discovered she had 911 dialed before the crunching stopped and the kicking-the-door-open was done. She efficiently reeled off the address to the operator in a whisper. My screaming gave her a bit of cover.

Actually I was just screaming. I had no idea what she was doing, but I tried to make enough noise to warn her and alert a neighbour.

As I screamed, I dived for the handset of the land line, but the thugs went for me faster. Things got confused. I took some blows to the belly, and I got flung into the bookcase, and the coffee table hit my back and splintered — well, in fact *I* hit *it* as I got booted across the room. My nose was hurting now for some reason, and when they hauled me upright, I couldn't quite stand up for some reason. I ended up with one arm twisted up behind me by Puff, while Spot stuck his face in my field of vision, yelling. I missed poking out an eye with my other hand, but did manage to rake my fingernails down his cheek.

Puff put an arm around my throat. I bit it. He swore and

jerked his arm tighter under my chin, immobilising my other arm with a kind of half-Nelson effect. During the struggle my head had thumped something. Spot had four eyes, and a lot of pimples when you took what was there and multiplied by two.

"Where's the Chink?" he shouted. It took me a while to figure out what he meant, during which time he slapped me three times, back, forward, back. The backslaps hurt worse because of the knuckles. "Where's the fucking slope?"

"Out. Gym," I gasped. "The Y." I said it with conviction, which means I gasped more, drooled some blood.

He made a quick circuit of the apartment. I sweated. Jian was in the kitchen. But somehow in that minuscule place he didn't find anyone. (Later I discovered that Jian was lizard-climbing between fire escapes and breaking the window of my neighbour's apartment to get help.)

"Good," he said.

"What . . . do you . . . want?" At least, I tried to say that. Then I almost fainted when Puff yanked one wrist even higher. (Classic, but no less painful for that. Maybe Jian bent that way, but I doubt most humans do. Certainly I didn't.)

"You're getting on someone's nerves. Say goodbye."

"Goodbye . . ." I whispered hopefully, just before they threw me back into the bookcase and I passed out.

111. "WHEN I REGAINED CONSCIOUSNESS . . ."

Those of us who are old enough remember Dave Broadfoot on the radio, even sometimes while we are swimming up from a sea of pain and someone is calling our name and someone else is licking our cheek, we remember the stupid damned Air Farce and wake up laughing like a Robert Palmer song, wondering where our dog Cuddles is. And if you don't understand this, Internet search engines are your friend.

Except I was only laughing on the inside. Everywhere else was still screaming, but silently. I decided that this wasn't as funny as it sounded on the radio.

Several of my neighbours stood or crouched around me. Improvement over Spot and Puff. How many neighbours? Fuzzy, Jian crouched over me, slightly doubled, like a 3D film without the glasses to make sense of it.

"Ambulrance coming!" She must have been upset. She was messing up her her *L*s. That wasn't very funny either.

Bunnywit was licking my cheek. That hurt because he was licking where it felt like some knuckles had broken the skin. Little carnivore, was he licking my blood? Weakly, I tried to wave him away, but my hand only lifted a few inches, then dropped despite my best effort. (Later, I was told that no, my cheek was just bruised: the warm moisture I felt was Bun's saliva as he attempted to comfort me.)

"I'm . . . alive," I said to Jian. Saying *M* hurt, and didn't really sound right from my swollen-feeling and unresponsive lips. I heard Bun start to purr, then he gave a little mew and backed off, squeaking slightly in a most uncharacteristic way. "You're alove — alive . . . Bun's ali—" *B* hurt to say also. Lips again.

"I know," said Jian. "Shut up."

I had something important to remember. What was it? Oh . . .

"Call Thel . . . warn her . . . call Rog . . . tell him . . . not to tell anybody . . . see me . . ."

"You go to hospital."

"Call Thel . . . they know she . . . please . . ." I tried to get up, and she pushed me back gently.

"Okay, okay, I do now, just lie down, shhh!" Jian fumbled with the phone. Her hands were shaking.

"You sound . . . weird . . ."

"Fucking men, stupid men! Shut up! Hi, Thelma, pick up phone! Damn damn machine. Somebody come, attack us. They know you are her cousin. Call the police. You get this message when you are not home, don't go home. Go to Roger!" She pressed the off button, looked up behind me with relief.

"Here is paramedic."

This was so.

"Check . . . ID . . ."

"Yes, shhh, is okay." To them she began to explain, "Some men break in, beat her up. She had concussion before, not long ago . . ."

Some of her grammar was back, anyway. That was good. I would like to think I relaxed, but I believe I just passed out again. This was very boring, I decided later. At the time, it was very dark and deep.

112. WHEN I REGAINED CONSCIOUSNESS, REDUX

I don't want you to think I took being beaten up lightly. Before, when I was hurt far less, it was possible to think about it. Now I was badly hurt, and the mind has a way of skittering off terrifying topics. This is called dissociation. This is what was going on in my battered brain.

Really, I knew Spot and Puff came there to kill me. They then planned to go on to kill Jian and Thelma.

What I didn't know while I hung writhing in a clot of pain and morphia and fear and irrelevance and light and loud voices in the emergency room was that my neighbours had interrupted them, and by force of numbers in the narrow hall, with only slight injury to one neighbour, had prevented them from escaping downstairs. So they ran up. When the cops came, Spot and Puff were the only people trying to get down from the roof in a hurry. It made them somewhat conspicuous.

Some cop cars came down the alley in answer to the several 911 calls, from Jian and from some neighbours concerned about crashing sounds in my apartment.

Half the fire escapes descend to the alley, and Spot and Puff had picked one of them to descend before they saw the cops. When they tried to get back up to the roof and go down inside, the safety doors kept them trapped. The rest is obvious.

Jian and several neighbours were up for a line-up if needed, but turned out there was no need, with Spot's DNA under my fingernails and Puff's blood — from where I bit him — all over my shirt.

We all made cameos on the TV news. Except me. I was getting reassembled.

113. "THE ARM-BONE IS CONNECTED TO THE SHOULDER-BONE . . ."

Before I list the damages, I should say that when I mention pain, it's despite a number of injections and an IV. Pain is like the ocean. Sometimes there are tsunamis.

So. Total damage resolved by emergency room visit and subsequent three-day stay in hospital:

- One dislocated shoulder. It's amazing how quick the pain stops when the joint slips back in place. I didn't even have to have surgery. Just some sleight-of-hand with bent elbows and strange transverse pulling and suddenly, with a scraping sound I remember all too vividly amid the haze, about one-quarter of the pain went away. I think I sighed. Anyway, I heard a deep voice say, "Attagirl." Attagirl? What was I, a trained dog? I may just have said that aloud, as there was an inappropriate giggle from somewhere out there.
- Another cut on my head. Ow. Dammit. So much for my hair. A local anaesthetic made about one-third of the remaining pain go away. Attaboy. Maybe I said that out loud too. Inappropriate laughter again.

- One broken and two cracked ribs. Strapped up. I was very grateful at that as they — the ribs — stopped making a gritty scraping that I could feel as much as hear. "Attagirl," I said to the helping hands. What a card, eh?
- Scrapes and abrasions from head to knees. Most of them not needing stitches.
- A broken nose. That was wrenched back into place and the remaining pain diminished by half. I felt like Achilles chasing the tortoise. Asymptotic reduction of anguish.
- One dislocated little toe. They found that last, about a day after, when I woke up enough to say that my foot still hurt a lot. Crunch, another tsunami, and suddenly I was down to background pain level. Most of the time.

In the words of an old and silly song, "and after that, the weather started brightening-o."

SHE SHOWED NO RAGE AND SHE SHOWED NO RANCOR,

114. FULL DISCLOSURE 1: BORING

One thing I thought during the attack and recovery is worth repeating: the whole damned thing was boring. If you think I'm joking, think again.

Pain is boring, and chronic pain more so. It's there all the time, like a noisy neighbour playing goddamn show tunes. As a topic of conversation it's limited and repetitive, two qualities that in theatre, books, life experiences, and companions are not usually valued.

The drugs one takes to "manage" pain create an eternal twilight in which at best one wants to sleep and at worst one wants anything else but this. Combine this twilight of pain relief with hospital routine and hospital food and recovery-related activities: not interesting. Half the interactions with hospital people are about your toilet achievements, the other half the efficacy of the painkillers, which we have already established are . . . limited in scope.

Oh, sorry, carve about two percent off there for filling out the menus which give you a supposed choice of fare, and for discussing oral hygiene needs.

Equally boring in their way were the law enforcement housekeeping needs.

I was glad, in a twilit way, that Spot and Puff were in jail. I was glad they'd rolled over once caught and copped to the murder of Maddy.

I was a little more animated for the private discussion I had with Roger about the threat to Thelma.

"Who knew? Us and you and Lance. Is Lance dirty?"

"He told Cummings. Cummings told three guys on the drug squad. Mooney, Stanley, and Brady."

"And?"

"Brady."

"Just like in the song." But Roger was no ethnomusicologist and I was too twilit to explain about Duncan the bartender and Stag-o-lee and Brady the crooked cop and the women dancing in their loose Mother Hubbards and their stockinged feet. (If you think I was raving, remember, the Internet search engine *is* your friend.) I just lay there, tried not to nod, and later told Jian she was right, there *was* a crooked cop.

For Denis's sake, I was glad it wasn't Lance. Even though Denis got me into this, I didn't want his heart to look or feel like my head did.

Then Roger and Jian and Hep and I had a little housekeeping talk, and then after quite a lot more of the boring stuff, I was discharged from hospital. It was actually a little earlier than the doctor wanted, but my bruised face was looking the most Technicolor™ it was going to, which would play well to the cameras at the impromptu media conference Rog, the police media liaison officer, Hep, Lance, and I had spent a fair amount of time setting up to seem spontaneous.

BUT SHE TURNED THE WITCH INTO MILK AND DRANK HER.

115. FULL DISCLOSURE 2: NO COMMENT

The swarm of reporters, technicians, microphones, and cameras at the hospital door was worthy of a scene in a movie.[15] I was news. Yay.

Hep had come to wheel me out to her car. Roger was there to represent the police service's kindly, protective face. No other cops were on scene.

By this time Spot and Puff had been charged.

"How do you feel?" Stupid question, but I bravely smiled through swollen, split lips and allowed as how I'd felt better. In fact, I told them, I couldn't say I'd ever felt worse. They laughed politely.

"But in a way it's been worth it," I said provocatively.

---

15. I wonder who would play me? Probably some tapped-out child star trying to make a comeback. That one who saw dead people, maybe. What was his name? He'd look good as a female bisexual. Oscar rôle time? Just a thought . . .

They bit.

I continued, "The men who killed Maddy Pritchard and tried to kill me have confessed. We can rest easy knowing Maddy's grandmother —" I gestured weakly at Hep "— can find closure."

I'd promised her earlier that I wouldn't say *closure*, but if I had to do this, I was going to enjoy it a little. Her fingers dug into my sore shoulder. Accidentally? Ha. That's closure for ya.

"We understand the young woman was a drug addict. Is this gang-related?"

Roger stepped up.

"Maddy Pritchard was a recovering drug addict, it is true. But we think the killing was a random one, related to her high-risk lifestyle." Prostitution, everyone knew he meant.

"What about the attack on you?" one of them asked me. "Do you have a — high-risk lifestyle too?"

I tried a little chuckle. "I guess this makes it look high risk . . ." gesturing to my face and the bandages ". . . but no. I'm a retired —" sounds so much better than "wrongfully-downsized" "— social worker and a friend of the family. I was asking questions about Maddy's death, and we assume these guys heard about it and decided they were at risk. This was just . . . collateral damage, you might say. I'm just relieved that the case is cleared up and the killers are in custody."

"But you cracked the case."

"No, indeed. I can't thank the police more for their commitment to the case. But ironically, the police service didn't have enough evidence to hold the men until the attack on me. If they had just left well enough alone, they would have been able to — what's that expression in the movies? 'Beat the rap'?"

Hep intervened. "Yes, we must all thank the police service. They made it plain that they would put all necessary resources to work solving the case."

A sharp-faced size-two reportrix in a tiny perfect suit pushed her microphone at Hep. "How do you feel about getting your friend beat up?"

"Excuse me," I said sharply, "but the only ones responsible for the assault are the men who committed it. Suggesting anything else is blaming the victims." I've always hated those tiny perfect suits.

The seasoned crime reporter from the local daily, giving no indication that we had known each other for fifteen years, said seriously, "If you hadn't asked questions, you wouldn't have been beaten up — have you thought of that? Was it worth it to risk death?"

"If we could read the future, Dave, there are a lot of things we might do differently. For instance, these two men might have decided not to kill a young woman they thought of as just another hooker. I *can* say, though, that I would not have wanted my friend here to go through the uncertainty of never knowing why her granddaughter died or who killed her."

"So you're satisfied with the conclusion of the case."

"Yes, I sure am, Dave, and as soon as my bruises heal, I'll be even more satisfied." That got a little laugh too. Good.

David had one more question. "And you're both satisfied that the police have covered every angle of the case?" Dammit, the man had good instincts. Too good.

"I certainly am," said Hep. "More than satisfied."

"That's right," I added. "The police investigation was complete and thorough. One of the best I've seen, and I come from a profession which often sees crime and police investigations. They don't always turn out this well."

Roger stepped in smoothly. "Thanks aren't necessary, ladies." Ladies? Ha. I was *so* going to get him later. "The police service believes that every victim is equal and needs equality of policing. We work hard on behalf of every murder victim."

"Excuse me," I said, "but I really have to go home. This is about all I can take without an illegal level of painkillers." I left 'em laughing, and Roger answering questions about whether Maddy Jr.'s murder related to the murder of several other prostitutes over the years. When the doors swung shut behind us, he was saying something about the differences between that serial killer and this stand-alone crime. I know he was bullshitting, because the whole task force on those killings, which he also directs, had only solved a few, and has so little consistent evidence about the rest of the crimes that they could be stand-alone, copycat, or just accidentally-similar. But that's another story.

Hep took me home. There was one more scene that had to be played out to ensure our safety and Thel's, but it wasn't one we could play; Thel would be doing that herself.

Jian met me at the door, and hugged me, and started to cry. That started me off, and for the first time in the three-and-three-quarters days since I'd been attacked, I too wept.

It hurt to cry. Salt in my wounds.

But it felt good too. I was finally feeling something, emotionally, where it counts.

116. FULL DISCLOSURE 3: HAPPY HAPPY HAPPY ALL THE TIME

Of course you know what we were doing.

If the whole Panda Stinko thing was going to be successfully investigated, everybody, and I mean *everybody*, had to believe that we were all convinced it was All Over. No more inconvenient threats to either the Do Matrix or the Stinchko peace of mind could exist. They all had to believe that with the capture of Spot and Puff, everyone was happy.

No-one except Roger, Lance, the invisible Cummings, the two Fraud guys, and a select group of trustworthy if odd civilians (that'd be us) would know The Real Story. Any other police involved later would be thoroughly-trusted dead-square types whom Roger had known since he was knee-high to a grasshopper and would let shake his dick dry if he were paralyzed in a freak accident. You know the kind I mean. I wasn't even sure that Lance would be let in on it. He'd been the source of the intel (that's cop talk for information) that Brady leaked to the bad guys. He was in the cop version of the doghouse for that. But Brady had been left in place, just in case we needed a pipeline.

Between us, we figured we could make a fine set of false impressions.

117. FULL DISCLOSURE 4: TRUTH AND RECONCILIATION

On the record I will say that I was wrong about my cousin Thelma in so many ways. She is smarter than I thought, braver than I thought, and her religious beliefs are sounder and less wacky than I thought. I wanted to mention it for honesty's sake and so that it wouldn't sound self-serving when I told you about the following scene.

It was after I got home and I was recovering. This means lying on the couch moaning whenever Bunnywit jumped on my head, my abdomen, my ribs, my thighs, my foot — well, you get the idea.

Thelma had come over to tell a quiet little party of Hep, Roger, Vikki, Jian, and me about her part in the calming of the waters.

"First I want to say, cousin, that I have been thinking many unChristian thoughts about you, and most of them were wrong," she said to me, formally and awkwardly. I was feeling pretty awkward too.

"Well, back atcha, cuz," I muttered. Then, a little louder, "and don't worry about it. We're . . . past that now, right?"

"Not quite," she said. "I have to apologise, so here goes. I'm very sorry. And I have to say that I am sorry to Jian too, for some of my thoughts. I have learned a lot in the last few weeks. I feel like I was pretty stupid before."

"Um . . ." but in the interests of full disclosure, I had to come clean: "Actually, you were, kiddo. I'm sorry, but . . ."

"Well, I'm a little better now," she said briskly. Apology over; on to item two. "Now, about Harp Goldring."

"Is that his real name?" said Hep. "It sounds made up."

"Real," said Rog.

"You wouldn't believe that man," said Thelma. "Well, I guess you would . . ."

118. FULL DISCLOSURE 5: THELMA GOES BACK TO CHURCH

When she got to the New Alliance of Jesus Closer to God Church for the second time, the sun was shining and the concrete slabs and curtain walls of glass just looked like annoying architecture, not like the outside of an ominous cavern. It was cold and crisp, and Thelma was wearing one of those inside-out-sheep coats with boots to match, and sensible slacks. She carried the (laundered) Soul Patrol T-shirt in a little turquoise shopping bag that she had been given with a cosmetics purchase. She had wrapped the shirt in red tissue. Red, she explained to us, for sins-being-as-scarlet. A little private symbolism.

She had made an appointment. This time the Wrong Reverend Harp Goldring met her at the door with his new personal care attendant, a short, muscular Filipina Woman of a Certain Age, whose lovely face was enhanced with laugh wrinkles that clearly weren't getting a workout at the New Alliance of Jesus Closer to God Church.

The Reverend Harp wasn't smiling as widely. He already knew about Thelma's crusade to get her own church to leave the Soul Patrol. When they went into the office, the lovely and talented Lotsa Stinko lounged there in an Armani suit the cost of which would have bought the caregiver's family a house.

"I thought it was best to have my lawyer here," Goldring said.

("I almost had a heart attack when I saw him," Thelma said, "and it took all I had not to call him by name during the meeting. Because *of course* he didn't introduce him. But I managed to keep a straight face."

(I didn't even make the obvious joke — *how could she avoid having a straight face?* I'm a changed person. Ask anybody.)

"That's fine," Thelma said, "but this is not really an official visit."

"Hmmm?" The Rev's best smooth minimal encourager was a placeholder while Thelma moved the only available chair out of the one-down position in which it had been carefully placed. "So sorry," she said, "but when I face into the light behind someone's head I get a migraine. Except with Jesus of course."

"Of course," said Harp o' Gold without irony. I'd been suspecting it for some time, but this is when I became absolutely sure that Thelma had a sense of humour. Knowing that cast a different light on some of the things she'd said to me over the years.

"Now," she said, "I have two things to talk about. Let's get the nasty one out of the way first. This is my Soul Patrol T-shirt. I'm returning it to you. Since we met last time I have learned too many things about the wicked activities of the Soul Patrol to be able to remain a member. You should know that also, I will be pursuing all the proper procedures to call for eradication of the Soul Patrol from our church, and I will be bearing witness against the Soul Patrol wherever I can.

"But I came here to ask you to think carefully about your own soul, Reverend Goldring. You have been misled by two terrible men. They were the ones who attacked my cousin, not once but twice. They posed as innocent ex-inmates who were looking for a change in their lives, and they betrayed you. Can you not see that for men like that, whether they have been jailed yet or not, the Soul Patrol is like a permission slip from the teacher to do wicked deeds?"

"Well," said the Reverend, "I must admit I was pretty surprised when Abel and Jordan returned to a life of crime."

"I'm sorry, Reverend, but they never left the life of crime. They were using your church and the Soul Patrol as a cover for their criminal activities. You were, well, not to put too fine a point on it, Reverend, you were hoodwinked. Yes, hoodwinked."

Stinko the Suit chose this moment to intervene. "You are correct. The Reverend and the church had no idea these men were active criminals. They have done terrible damage to the reputation of our rehabilitation program[16]."

"Yes, I'm sure they have," said Thelma. "I'm sure you'll be repeating all your background checks and that kind of thing. But really, gentlemen, you have to think about the liability to which your relationship with the Soul Patrol exposes you. If they break the law as they carry out their misguided activities, and you are seen to be a part of it, it will do terrible harm to your wonderful outreach programs[17] and the big plans you have.

"And Reverend, you can't give freely with one hand and punish with the other. 'Vengeance is mine, says the Lord; I will revenge.' It is not for us to decide who enters the Kingdom of Heaven. That is God's work."

---

16. I know he would have spelled it "program", not "programme" as I still stubbornly do. Guys like that are big on short cuts, in my not-so-humble opinion.

17. I love Thelma's good grammar. "to which your relationship exposes you"! But alas, she would spell it "program" too. "You have to accept some changes in our national language as we join the global village," she said to me yesterday. Scary.

Stinchko interjected smoothly, "We don't support anything illegal. Trust me: we will look into this."

"That's all I can expect," said Thelma warmly. She was sure neither of them suspected a thing, but Thel thinks the caregiver's eyes crinkled at the corners with a hidden smile, and she got a laugh from all of us later too.

"Now, Reverend Goldring, on a personal level, if I may, I'd just like to express to you my deep, deep regret that you have had to undergo the betrayal by your personal, one might call them intimate, helpers that way. It was just terrible, and you must just feel so annoyed."

Annoyed didn't serve to describe the Wrong Rev's mood, given his expression, but she carried on blithely. "I just had to come and say that. I do feel for you, Reverend, even though we might disagree about some articles of faith. The fig tree, and so on. But I think all of us here agree that being betrayed by those closest to you must just be the worst thing ever. I just had to say how glad I am that those awful men are in jail and this is all over. And I do hope your big M2F2 project goes well. It will help so many people."

"Thank you, Sister Thelma," Goldring said. "We are hoping great things for it."

"Well, I'm going to do all I can to see that those people waiting for your help aren't disappointed," Thelma said brightly. "I've been elected to my church's board, you know, just night before last, and they've been asked to send a representative to the M2F2 Council or Board or Steering Committee or whatever you call it. I'm not really a business person, but running a home efficiently teaches you a lot about money, so I put my name in, and I'm hoping I'll be approved. Wouldn't that be lovely?"

"Lovely," said the Reverend, and he managed to almost sound sincere, Thelma said. Stinchko made a sound Thelma took as a stifled snort, which he then disguised as a cough. Thelma ignored him.

"I'm so looking forward to hearing whether I'm chosen," said Thelma, "and to seeing you there from time to time, Reverend."

Then she thanked them for their time, and Stinchko said that if she'd excuse them, the caregiver would show her out, as they had another meeting. Broad smiles all around, and Thelma even got a chance to have a private word with the caregiver on the way out and give her the phone number of the Mennonite Centre for Newcomers. "In case you need to leave this job someday," Thel said diplomatically. The woman nodded.

"Just don't marry him," Thelma said impulsively, thinking of mail order brides.

"No chance," said the woman. "Ha. I rather drink my own urine."

Whew. Ick. I guess Thelma was reassured by that. I sure was.

119. FULL DISCLOSURE FINAL: ARE YOU CRAZY?

Roger wasn't. Reassured, that is.

"Are you crazy? Getting on the board with those damned people? You were supposed to convince them this is over!"

"What better way?" Thelma said calmly. "I'm just a prissy do-gooder, you know. I actually am, that's not really an insult. Anyway I may not get my church's endorsement. But civilian oversight is a big deal with the police, why not with this too? And *she*" — indicating me — "can't do it, even though she wants to."

"She does?" said Rog. He looked at me blankly. I lay on the couch, wrapped in an afghan my mother had crocheted for my first grown-up sized bed and drinking, out of a Bunnykins mug, a medicinal Chinese herbal tea Jian had procured for me. Perhaps I didn't look enough like Jeanne d'Arc.

"Can't you tell? It's driving her nuts sitting here. She wants to right all wrongs right now. You *know* that."

Jian giggled. Hep snorted. I didn't do anything because moving hurt.

"Oh, yeah, I forgot," said Rog glumly.

"Look," said Thelma, "they're going to be more reassured that I'm out of their way if they see me occasionally in the church community. Doing good. Being a pain in the . . . the neck. Insisting on consulting the Bible. Letting them patronise me like they did today. Sister Thelma indeed. Tsk. I'm not *his* sist— . . . oh, darn it, I guess in God's eyes . . . well, you know what I mean."

And we all parted agreeing that we'd done all we could to let everyone know that we were Not a Threat.

A bunch of milquetoasts, in fact. Funny word, that, milquetoasts. Soaked with the *milque* of human kindness. Softies.

Isn't it funny how someone criminal is condemned as "a hard man" or "too sharp by half", while to be a softy is an insult?

I lay there, thinking about having been softened up by Spot and Puff, turned into a milquetoast. It's true. I was too soft for the hard life. I had breakable ribs and skull, thin snappable neck, bruisable skin and muscle. But still, Thel was right.

I could hardly bear even to pretend the crusade was over. Or to wait for the real ending.

120. "GOODBYE, HANK WILLIAMS, MY FRIEND / I DIDN'T KNOW YOU, BUT I'VE BEEN PLACES YOU'VE BEEN"

Vikki and Hep organised the memorial for Maddy Junior.

It was in the meeting room of the community centre where the working girls had their association and clinic, which was in the basement of a community church that broke (for the better) all the stereotypes of a church. Bunnywit had to do without his boots for the day as they became part of a little tableau of photos, chicken-shaped slippers, and other memorabilia.

Norman was there, and came over to me to say quietly, "I guess you got the envelopes." I looked at him, I'd say cluelessly, but the envelope had been full of clues. He went on, "Maddy left them with me last time I saw her. She wanted me to mail them if anything happened to her."

"Why didn't you tell me?"

"Maddy trusted me," he said simply, and I couldn't argue.

"Yeah, we got them, and they really helped. Thanks, Norman."

He blushed, but I wasn't going to believe he was Mr. Naïf ever again. "Fool me once, shame on you; fool me twice, shame on me," and all that jazz. We were interrupted just before it would be completely obvious that there was nothing more to say on the subject.

"Can everybody step into a healing circle and join hands?" Vikki called. She wore her street (as in on-the-street) clothes and her chicky slippers, and managed to look dignified. The room was small and crowded and compressed the circle.

I was sitting because I still couldn't stand for long. The circle formed raggedly, defined by two fixed points: me, and the other person who needed a chair, a one-legged older woman with a scarred, pockmarked face who parked her wheelchair not far from mine. Her tall, nervous companion held her hand in one of his weathered paws and Hep's hand in the other.

Hep held one of the working women's hands on the other side. I had been quickly introduced to Francine, Angel, Bobby, Serena, Jeffrey, Sammy, and Bonnie-Rae, and couldn't really remember which was which. There were at least twelve other people there who avoided being introduced to any of the straight(-looking) people. They were jittery and nervous with all the strangers and even a couple of cops around, but this was *their* place, and they were here for Maddy.

Hep was linked to either Frannie or Bonnie-Rae, a tiny thin woman who held Roger's hand. Roger's other hand was nervously pinched by Jeffrey (or was it Bobby?) wearing her best drag wig, who linked up to Norman in his dress-up brown polyester suit, who linked to me, who linked with Sammy (or Serena?), who could barely reach my hand because she stood so tall in her spike heels, and so on around the ragged circle until the tall, taciturn street artist — whose beautiful portrait of Maddy was propped up behind the boots — held the one-legged woman's other hand.

A First Nations Elder who had once been on the streets himself and now ran the clinic did a sweetgrass smudge ceremony, waving the smoke toward us with an eagle feather he had been given when he gave up the life and had been dry and clean for a year. At his instruction we scooped the smoke against us to wash our bodies, our hands, and our faces. The smoke swirled around our heads and rose up to hang below the fluorescent lights. I watched everyone's feet: from moccasins to high-heeled fuck-me boots, everyone mixed up and standing (or sitting, in my case) in a circle, and the smoke rising up like Maddy's spirit.

My eyes and nose stung with more tears. It was as if, having begun to cry a few days before, I couldn't stop. My tears fell without drama or noise. I wept for Maddy, for Hep, for my parents, for myself, for the world.

We all said what we wanted to say about Maddy. All I said was, "I never met her, but she changed my life." Love is powerful, the others said, and hate is wrong. For a moment we were all part of one life, one grief, and one family.

It never lasts, but it was a good moment.

ISABEL MET A TROUBLESOME DOCTOR,

121. IT AIN'T OVER 'TIL IT'S OVER

This is the moment where the director instructs the audience (with malice aforethought) to relax.

Maddy Junior's murder, the presenting problem, solved. The terrible twins, Spot and Puff, in jail. Vikki off the streets. My modest fortune claimed, and not yet spent back to zero.[18] Cousin Thelma a real, dimensional person to me, and to all of you. Mayor warned about Panda. The Fraud Squad on the case. Roger on the case (Roger that).

Shouldn't we just tie up all the ends now and close the book? Denis and his Adonis, Lance, live happily ever after. I heal up and enjoy my new income, not riches by any means but enough to keep me in real food and to keep Bunnywit from having to eat leftover fish sticks. Jian becomes independent.

---

18. That came later.

My Mendelson Joe gets fixed. Hep grieves and moves on (I do so hate that expression). It's all good.

But as some baseball guy famously remarked, "It ain't over 'til it's over."

I was listening to an old *old* John Hartford album, soothing my wounds with nostalgia for simpler times, when the phone call came. "Way up on the hill where they do do the boogie", with its social satire, was appropriate to the caller.

"Hi?" We had all hoped I'd be hearing that little-girl voice and its surrounding giggle again, that questioning lilt with the steel behind it. Still, I broke into a cold sweat even before she said — or asked — "This is Panda?"

"Panda Stinko! How are you?" I hope the recorder was getting this call. I hadn't even heard whether Roger had got the wiretap approved. She was efficient, this Panda machine.

"Just great! I was thinking we should have lunch this week? And discuss the project?" Lo and behold! She had let my evilly-intended pronunciation of her surname pass unchallenged! Goodness, what names people have.[19]

"Project?"

"You know, you were thinking of a charitable donation? To our M2F2 project? I thought we could meet and I could explain more about it?"

Really I should have said, "Sorry, you have the wrong number," and hung up right then. Things might have turned out better for a few people. But I didn't actually want things to turn out better for those particular people. I said sure, and set the date.

I hung up, waited out the cramp in my belly and the cold sweats — then I called Roger.

---

19. Mind you, I'm not in the position to be too snarky about names, given my own.

The wiretap hadn't been active yet. He was at my door almost before I finished getting presentable clothes on (ouch).

122. THE DEVIL'S BODY PARTS

It is always entertaining to watch Roger storm about. For one thing, he knows a lot of swear words in other languages. I'd be able to share them with you here if I knew how to spell them. They aren't the sort of thing you can look up in the Portuguese-English dictionary. Or the Chinese-English phrasebook. Or Dr. Anne Anderson's definitive dictionary of the Cree language, though I think I caught the word for "bitch".

The Finnish one, however, had been translated by the helpful newbie cop weeks ago, so I finally knew what it meant.

"Saatana perkele! I forbid it. I'll arrest you for obstruction of justice. I'll keep you in protective custody until hell freezes over. I'll —"

"Make me wear a wire?"

"What?" He stopped pacing around my living room.

"A wire. As they say on TV."

He glared at me. "Wire? It's all wireless these days. *Not* that I'm agreeing."

"But if you do — as you recall we have imagined this scenario already — if you do, you might hear her making promises of some kind, or asking me to make the cheque out to her, or something . . . and at the end of the lunch, I'll just say that I'll have my people call her people, and be done with it. I'm nothing to her but a source of money now."

"Oh, come on," Roger said. "They sent bad guys to kill you, for fuck's sake. This is some kind of trap."

"Maybe," I said. "No, don't give me that look, I mean it. Maybe it is. But what kind?"

His look indeed changed.

"What kind — and why — and wouldn't you like to know? A money grab from the greedy Pan-Pan, or a set-up for another actionable assault, or what?"

He sat down in the big armchair I'd bought to replace the one with all the blood on it.

"Look, I called you the minute she said 'Goodbye?' and hung up. Why do you think I did that?"

Roger grinned. "Because you are smart enough to be scared."

I nodded. "The cold sweat has mostly dried up but I shake when I think too much. And if you would only admit it, you are having the same reaction. It's why you're throwing this irrational hissy fit."

"Okay, I'm reacting badly. Thank you for calling me irrational. You are brave and brilliant. We are back on track with Plan B. All right?"

"Thank you. That is gracious of you." I even meant it.

I grinned back at him and we both snorted one of those half-laughs that meant we admitted and recognised our real and vulnerable selves, just for a moment. Or that we recognised we were both being fuckwits.

I got up and dot-and-carry limped to the kitchen to put the kettle on. I fumbled as I fussed with cups and tea. The box of Sleepytime™ teabags burst at all its seams when I tried to open it, and after I finished playing twenty-five pick-up I threw the lot in the sink and gimped back into the living room.

"So, I'm so smart and you're so smart," I said. "Now what the bloody hell will happen?"

"Beats the fuck out of me," said Roger, and went in to finish making the tea.

That's what I like about Rog. He's a font of comfort and good sense. Always has the answer.

Ah, well. The tea was good.

123. MY MENDELSON JOE

The phone rang into our companionable, tea-calmed silence.

"Hi, sweetie, it's Marta."

"Marta! How are you?"

"I am so good but not so your Mendelson Joe. I am sorry to say that the restoration has been only about seventy-five percent successful. This is because the rest of the painting had to be considered — the soaked-in damage of the many liquids on the canvas and so forth. I have sent it over to you by a messenger, but I vanted to let you know in person."

"Did Joe himself try the restoration?"

"No, but he gave permission for the person we chose; she is very good. Dear Joe does not feel there is much more to be done, unless he paints another on commission, and he is not eager to revisit such an old work. I told him it was unlikely, but that if you wanted, we would write to him."

"No, you're right," I said. "I don't want a copy. It's the original I loved. Love."

"I am sorry, my dear. I know how much you love it. I have reduced my invoice."

"Not your fault," I said. "I knew the salad oil was going to cause problems."

"Yes, that was terrible," she said. "She had great trouble with that, too, and also the sugar, strangely enough. Well, again, I am so sorry. I hope you come by the gallery soon."

"I will, Marta. Thanks."

I hung up quietly.

"Okay," I said. "That does it. They can get away with ordering me beaten and not taking the fall, but when they destroy my Mendelson Joe, they're in trouble."

124. BEWARE OF ALL ENTERPRISES THAT REQUIRE NEW CLOTHES, REDUX

Henry David Thoreau said that, in his 1854 classic *Walden*. Well, actually, he said, "I say beware of all enterprises that require new clothes, and not rather a new wearer of clothes." But the full quote's a little deeper than I needed to go to prepare for lunch with Pan-Pan-da-da.

I did need to buy some clothes that didn't look like they had been selected from a heap in the corner of a low-rent thrift shop. My usual style was a little too boho-pomo-oh-oh to impress a construct as dazzling as our Pan-doris.

Conventional fashion wisdom seems to be that if you don't lunch with the same people every time, all you need to look like a million dollars is one good suit and a cashmere overcoat. This is true for any gender: male, female, both, neither, or Denis.

After a morning spent at Holt's, I felt ready, though I now had a sleek black dress and contrasting jacket, not exactly a suit. I sent the haberdashery to the dry cleaner so it wouldn't look that new, and wore the boots to the Saturday market to give them patina.

I also had to do some non-fashion-related preparation. There are strict protocols for people who help the police. I wasn't a "confidential source", with protection from testifying. I would be something else called an "agent" — sounds very 007, but it just means that I could "wear a wire" (more later on how wireless wires are these days) and take direction from police (Roger and I both laughed at that, for different reasons) and testify if I wanted to. I was introduced to the Officer in Charge, Roger became a Cover Manager (jargon — doncha love it!) and also my Source Handler (I got some good jokes out of that), and there was a warrant prepared by an "Affiant Team" which allowed for the police to deal with any criminal activity that happened to be going on around our suspects, so they would be ready on the scene to swoop in if needed. It's complicated stuff, and I was glad the specialists could make sense of it.

By the time I alit from a taxi to keep my date with Pan-Pan, using a cane to help support myself on the high-heeled boots my fashion consultants had insisted I had to wear, and picked my way through the slush from the previous day's dusting of snow, I was about as prepared as I could have been. Given what we knew at the time. What happened later really was nobody's fault, as such. Certainly not mine, despite what Roger said later.

Panda had just arrived when I limped in, and she turned from the maître-d'hôtel's station to greet me as if I was her best friend who had just come back from a long trip. She swooped toward me, crying out my name, and grabbed me in a frightening hug. My head was buried in perfumed sable. Since the purpose was to suck me in, it was appropriate that I felt like pigment must feel when attacked by the Winsor & Newton Series 7 Round #10.

Heads turned. I recognised some faces from both the daily news and my chequered past, but none of them were looking at me. Panda, who under her furs was wearing cleavage, long black-stockinged legs, and not much else, drew all gazes. She also drew a bevy of assistants who relieved her of her furs gladly and deigned to handle my cashmere as a sorry second.

We were lunching at the Hardware Grill, a tasty upmarket restaurant in the historic building once occupied by a hardware store of the old school. But there was nary a sign of a bin of nails, and the only furnace ductwork was built in and had been exposed as a design statement. I didn't say to Panda, as we waved our lips beside each other's ears in the classic non-kiss of the moneyed class, that I remembered shopping here with my dad and mom and that the food better be damn good to make up for losing that experience.

I did say, "Panda, how lovely to see you again!" and look enquiringly at the short, bulky, expensively-suited middle-aged man behind her who had followed us to the table. Such was Panda's ability to bend light rays that he had been as invisible to me at first as I was to the restaurant patrons.

"Oh," she said, "I hope you don't mind, I brought a friend?"

"Not a bit!" I said, and turned to extend my hand. He pinched it between the fingertips of a huge be-ringed paw, in that mincing crab-claw grip that some men use on women, and squeezed. I was be-ringed too, and the half-handshake, as usual, meant the squeeze crunched knuckles and fingerbones and rings together into an unpleasant painfest.

I was almost prepared to give him the benefit of the doubt, and a short lesson on the correct handshake protocol for women (short form: be as committed to your handshake as you would be shaking hands with a man, and the rings will be okay). And as for the smile, maybe his face was just built that way.

But as he squeezed, he looked me over from the bottom up, with certain pauses and a smile I didn't like, and I thought, *This man never does anything accidentally.* I tried not to scream with pain, gave his hand as close to equivalent punishment as I could manage, and reclaimed my hand quickly. Then Panda settled my judgment by repeating my name to him, turning to me, and saying brightly,

"And this is my good friend Dom. Doctor Dominic Matrice? He has that marvellous clinic, you must know him, he does just *every*body? He did me!" and she gestured like Vanna White to her own boobs, belly, and hips.

Just then someone opened the outer door behind me, so my slight jump could have been the effect of the wintry draft blowing up under my coat. Silk underwear is bracing in winter.

It is also bracing to hug and shake hands with two people who so recently wanted you dead. And who still might, if you only knew it.

"Dominic, such a pleasure," I said. "I'd say you're an artist, but I'm sure Panda was just as beautiful before you . . . er . . . did her." Panda preened. (She really did!)

The maître-d' came back without my coat and Panda's — Do Matrix was a Real Man and hadn't worn an overcoat; his suit was his cashmere layer, making him all-in-one like a cheap shampoo — and showed us to our window table.

I sat down to lunch with two murderers.

HE PUNCHED AND HE POKED TILL HE REALLY SHOCKED HER.

125. "BAD HABITS ARE HARD TO BREAK . . ."

When Fake-doctor Matrice shook my hand, he didn't just crush my fingers. He also looked down at the inner hollow at the bend of my elbow. There are tiny scars there. Tracks. They're from repeated IVs during a childhood illness (the others I always keep hidden), but how was he to know that?

And he smirked.

For that smirk, I hoped to see him jailed for life. It was the gloating of a predator, meeting someone he thought he could conquer.

He didn't know who he was messing with.

Unfortunately, I did.

126. "CALLING ALL ANGELS: WALK ME THROUGH THIS ONE; DON'T LEAVE ME ALONE . . ."

After we ordered, I excused myself and dot-and-carried my cane and fancy new boots to the Ladies'. Luckily, it was a one-seater

— no potential to be overheard. I locked the inner door and leaned against it. I took a couple of deep breaths. I started the water running in the fancy high-concept sink.

I called Roger.

"Did you hear who she brought with her?" I demanded when I heard his voice. I tried to neither squeak nor shriek.

"Who is this?" he said.

"Very funny, asshole. I am having lunch with the two most dangerous people on the planet!"

"Don't worry, there are people on the planet more dangerous than Do Matrix."

"For fuck's sake!"

"Relax! You know there's someone watching you."

"A drag queen again? Very comforting. Matrix will recognise him right away."

"No, some very unobtrusive young officers. Call me if they don't do their jobs."

"What?"

"You know, if they drop any of those busboy bins they carry around, or don't let you taste the wine first before they slosh you a glassful."

"Suffering Chr— . . . Roger, this is serious."

"Look, they're trying to find out how much you know. They can't kill you there, in front of all the movers and shakers, disrupt their power lunches. We're listening. You have back-up. Just play along like we planned, and everything will be fine."

"Right. Fine."

"By the way, the marked money? To my astonishment, Fraud has actually approved in time for the operation. Someone will get the bills to the credit union before you get there. So *that's* great, anyway."

My Spidey-sense was adding another tingle to the frissons of pure terror that had already played Rachmaninoff on my vertebrae.

"What's that? There's something else, isn't there?"

"Um, not as such. I'm handling it."

"Don't come the raw prawn with me, Roger!"

"Um, well, it's just . . . um, it seems that Cummings had an operation going on Matrice. We suddenly had crosstalk on the radio — our undercover guys and their undercover guys are tripping over themselves all over the kitchen there. And the street. We're in the OIC's office trying to sort it out now."

"You mean there's a total clusterfuck going on."

"We're working on —"

"And someone is listening to your end of this, so you're trying to cover your ass."

"We're both live on the wire, you idiot. But I warned them about your language. And really, it's not going to be a problem . . . our guys are there for you, no matter what Cummings is doin—"

"Oh, for fuck's sake." I shook the phone until the display came on and found the little red dot that shut him off. I almost flung the phone into the toilet, but since it was also one of the devices that was transmitting everything to the rest of the cover team in the van around the corner, I restrained myself.

Annoyance had re-stiffened my backbone, but I still felt like a Star Trek red-shirt on an away-mission. I turned off the water in the ridiculous design-conscious sink, covered the pinpoint camera I was wearing with my scarf while I used and flushed the not-as-design-conscious toilet, washed my hands in the stylish-but-barely-useful sink, and ran them through my hair to dry them and refresh my gelled JBF look.

I got back to the table, offering breathy, Panda-influenced apologies, to find the appetizer already there: two rounds of chevre, maple syrup, and some other cunning little additions staring up at me from a triangular plate in the centre of the bamboo and linen woven placemat.

"How lovely!" I said. "Good recommendation, Panda! I love pretty food." I tried to turn the dish's blank, accusing cartoon stare into a protective overseeing, but since that didn't work, I picked up the little fork and cut a wedge out of one eye so the face was winking, turned to Dominic, and said brightly, "So! Are you also involved with this wonderful housing project of Panda's?"

"As a consultant only. Panda asked me to give some advice on the addictions side. I was a medical doctor working with addictions before I founded my chain of wellness clinics. Now administration keeps me too busy to actively practise."

Nicely put, I thought: always good to avoid admitting you were defrocked, or whatever they call it for doctors. You are *so* going down, you smarmy creep . . .

Wedge out of the other cheesy eye: now they looked furtive. "I know what you mean. Since I came into my inheritance, it seems like I almost have a full-time job just deciding how to deal with all that money. You know, people think all there is to being rich is just play. But it's a serious responsibility."

Panda looked at me expectantly, hanging on my every word. She was smiling warmly as if she were finding a new friend. She *was* beautiful, in a terribly *organised* way, and I remembered Tammy's Boys and Bi's. I remembered that they knew about Jian and me. She was using wiles on me. She thought. Little did she know.

"You know, I was a social worker until a year ago. I was very involved in advocacy for the poor and differently-abled, and housing was always *such* a problem. If anything good has come out of the sad events of the last few weeks, it's my awareness of M2F2. And then meeting you at the fundraiser — it was like a message to me. Here's someone who really cares, who is really *doing* something with her money. I can learn from you."

"Well, a lot of it is Laszlo's money," she said modestly. "I just provide, like, guidance? But really, even someone as wealthy as Laszlo, just one person, unless you're Bill Gates you can't give enough to solve the problem. It has to be a community effort. Private and public money. A synergy." Demonstrating, she interlocked her talons.

In the sense that you like a snake better when you can see it than when it's hiding in the underbrush, I liked her better when she abandoned her fake valley-girl intonations. Now she sounded smart enough to be a con artist.

"I know I can't give as much as I'd like, but with that synergy thing happening, what I do give will do a lot more good. The main part of the estate is tied up in probate for so long! It's just driving me crazy. I'm living out of a safety deposit box!"

"What on Earth do you mean?"

"Well, it turns out my folks kept a safety deposit box in my name. Before they ... died ... they mailed me the key and location. The box had about a million and a half dollars in cash in it. The probate judge ruled that it was a premortem gift and I could use it while I waited for the bulk of the estate to go through probate. Which is good, because I have been limping along in this bizarre little apartment, you can't *imagine* the squalor in the hallways, I mean, picturesque is one thing and uptown funky is one thing, but really . . . never mind that. I do have money available to donate at the moment, but the problem is, it's cash."

"Cash?" Panda sounded as if cash had never touched her fingertips.

"Yes, I'm afraid so. I was going to ask if you would come by the bank with me, well, it's the provincial credit union actually, user owned, you know, that's my preference. Anyway, come by and I'll turn over my first donation. But I do need an official receipt from M2F2 of course. For tax purposes."

"Well, I did bring the receipt book. I am the treasurer, of course. As it happens, we have an account at the credit union too. So much more community-oriented. So we can just deposit it there right away, and I can give you the receipt. We haven't had a cash donation before, but as long as there's a paper trail, I'm sure it will be all right."

And that was just over the chevre appetizer. We spent the rest of the meal hearing Dear Doctor Matrice's ideas for the rehab facility, and his theories about addiction, lifted pretty much verbatim from Dr. Gabor Maté's book *In the Realm of Hungry Ghosts*. Including the examples, slightly misquoted.

"Why, a client of mine told me he had to steal $500 per day of goods to fence for $100 to pay his habit. So one client in a harm reduction facility, not stealing to get his drugs, saves $182,500 of theft in the community over one year. $183,000 in a leap year!"

I laughed dutifully. It sounds better when Dr. Maté, who is a brilliant man and a remarkable crusader, says it, than when it is parroted by a slick, snide criminal with a drug-dealing empire dependent upon these very addicts and their thieving habits. Hypocrites-Я-Us.

I immersed myself in the tomato, avocado, and caper palate-cleansing salad that separated the spicy soup from the crème brûlée. My palate definitely needed cleansing. I was going to have to take a shower when I got home, just to wash off the bullshit.

Doctor Faketrice shut up while the waiter came and fired the tops of the crème brûlée with that little hobby torch they use. Did you know that flame-related injuries are the most common hazards facing a wait-person? Flambé, brûlée — dangerous stuff.

The little torch seemed harmless compared with my companions.

THE DOCTOR'S TALK WAS OF COUGHS AND CHILLS, AND THE DOCTOR'S SATCHEL BULGED WITH PILLS.

127. . . . HE PUNCHED AND HE POKED . . .

Do Matrix was a skilled interrogator, and Panda darned near as good. They took me through my parents' tragic deaths (a matter of public record), my reluctance to claim my inheritance (considerably revised for their consumption), who that lovely Asian woman was they saw me with at the gala ("a good friend" *nudge nudge wink wink* whose husband's a rich broker in Singapore, and who stays over sometimes . . .), my family ties (fishing for Thelma, but instead I gave them the dead brother and some distant cousins in Hawai'i), my plans for the future (I ran a nice trip to Thessaloniki up the flagpole and got: "Oh, I *must* give you some tips, I've just come back; we stayed in the dearest little hotel?" This woman was a menace), and even my old job and my connexions with the police (a careful two-step there, because Roger had been coming to my house often, but insinuations of sex are such a *good* explanation for almost all anomalies of that sort — I took particular pleasure in those inventions and hoped his dozens of colleagues listening in ragged him about it for the rest of his life).

When the doc got up to go to the men's room, he managed to stumble and fall heavily across me, and the ensuing oh-so-accidental grope would have found a wire if I'd been wearing one; all TV-and-movie cop bidness appeared to have fooled the Bad Guys as well. (Have you noticed? Real cops usually laugh when they watch *CSI*. Especially in Canada.) Nobody wears body packs any more when even the Hammacher-Schlemmer catalogue sells pens and cell phones and lipsticks that can transmit to satellites, for fuck's sake. Guess Doh didn't have much free time to shop online.

Somehow, in all the talk, I managed to learn almost nothing about either Panda or Dom. Funny, that. If I hadn't been wise to it, I as a new and minor heiress might even have felt flattered that these two smooth, cashmere-clad, wealthy, powerful people were focussed on little old me. As it was, I understood that they expected their hourly rate for this lunch to be in the six figures each.

We even discussed my recent brush with death. I downplayed my rôle, and told them the media-conference version, slanting it heavily in the direction of pulling old-boy strings by using my "relationship" with Roger to press for a solution to Maddy's death. They understood old-boy networks and fucking for profit. I played innocent on the reason the men targeted me.

"I just didn't have that much to do with it," I complained. "I'm so glad it's over now, and those men are in jail. Even so, I have such a hard time sleeping. I hope that by the time they earn their parole, they have given up any resentments they might still have. I simply don't understand why they would go after me instead of just letting sleeping dogs lie. The police really didn't have *any* evidence until I was attacked and then those men confessed."

While rubbing that in, I tried to sound prissy, upright, justice-favouring, and sensible-shoe-wearing (oops, flunked that one! Well, the heels were comfortable, as long as I stayed sitting down). I was just a harmless little social activist (forget the cynical, tired, and frightened amateur crimefighter with no credentials, a lot of healing bones and tissues, and an unwillingness of almost dissociative magnitude to wonder about the clusterfuck Roger was sorting out back at Cop Central). Harmless.

I have to give Panda credit for her astonishing acting ability. She put a hand over mine, she comforted me, and if I hadn't known, I'd have believed her.

"You poor, poor thing! That's just so terrible? Those *awful* men? Are you in much pain?"

Dominic was almost as good, but as he sat back and listened to my recital of my physical woes, there was a slight quirk of one corner of his mouth that I knew was a supressed smile.

"The aftereffects will be difficult to recover from," he said. I resisted correcting him on his dangling preposition. (Harmless me. Not even associated with the Grammar Police, let alone the real ones.) "You should come by my clinic. No charge. I'm sure we could do something for you. We have physicians and holistic healers working together on all sorts of problems. Are you on any painkillers or herbal remedies?"

"Like comfrey for healing bones?" I know nothing about herbals except Denis's herbal facials, but I've read my Dick Francis. "Yes, I'm taking a range of things. The painkillers are a problem. The ones they allow me don't work very well at low doses, but I don't want to become dependent. It's so easy to take more than I should . . ." And just the slightest arrested glance at my inner elbow for him to notice: feed him a little weakness there.

His smile was bloodcurdlingly condescending. "You could

consult with some of our professionals . . . Well, no pressure, but the offer's there . . ." He wrote on the back of a card and handed it to me.

I turned the card over to see what he'd written: "The full treatment for pain. No charge. DoM."

I smiled. *The full treatment.* I can just imagine. I'd have more tracks, an expensive habit, and I'd end up as thin as Panda. Sure.

"We have some excellent cosmetic surgeons, too, if you should ever decide to get rid of your tattoos," he went on. "Say, why don't you come over for a tour after you and Panda are finished at the bank? Panda's got some special product there waiting for pickup anyway, so you could hitch a ride with her and we can have the limo take you home."

"That's a fabulous idea! They did wonders for me," said Panda. "You know, I had the usual butterfly and heart things from when I was a teenager? They just didn't suit me any more."

And they made you too identifiable as Doris, I thought. I smiled some more. "Thank you so much, Dom — I can call you Dom? I think I'll take you up on that," I said warmly.

Soon it was time for "Oh, my goodness, the time! We must get over to the bank!"

"Just let me powder my nose," I said, grinning because I love using that line when I don't wear any make-up.

In the washroom, I sat down on the toilet and called Roger again.

"We're leaving now," I whispered. "You heard that? I have an invitation to partake of the full range of services at the good doctor's holistic spa and drug palace! Isn't that swell?"

"Don't go! Cummings is —"

"Oh, they won't dare off me in front of all the rich and famous, disrupt their power facelifts."

"Very funny. We don't want to get in the way of —"

I wasn't about to listen to his troubles. *La la la la.* "La la la la. So, have your people come in after me if I'm there more than an hour, 'kay?"

"Go right home after. Take a cab, not their limo."

"Roger. I'm not *that* nervous. Or stupid."

"We'll be following the money."

I had a sudden adrenaline surge that almost flattened me. "You haven't put anything they can find in it, have you? I'd be dead!"

"No, we're doing it the old-fashioned way. Recording the serial numbers."

"She says they have an account for M2F2 at the credit union. They may not even leave the building with it."

"We have it covered. Try not to rubberneck looking for the cops when you get in there."

"Neither that nervous nor that stupid," I said. "Gotta go."

I flushed and washed and erased the two calls from the call log of the phone. Just in case. See how far I had come technologically? (I could even play that little bubble-shooting game that came with the phone. Cute, primitive, and addictive, just like Dr. Dough's herbal remedies. I'd wasted hours on it while lying on my couch waiting for my bones to knit — comfrey-less — and my bruises to turn new colours.)

Panda was waiting outside the door. Had she been there long? I stood outside after she went in, listening as I put on the coat the waiter brought me, but I couldn't hear a thing. Either she was just standing in there, or the double door was enough sound insulation. When she came out shaking her hands dry and I only heard the end of the flush while both doors were briefly open, I relaxed. The waiter handed her the cascade of red sable and she shimmied into it.

"Such fun," she said. "We must do this again?"

"I'd love that," I said. When hell freezes over, I thought.

But I wasn't done with Panda, Lotsa, Studly, and Doctor Doom.

128. GIVE ME ALL YOUR MONEY IN A BROWN PAPER BAG

The safety-deposit box that Roger and I had set up did indeed bulge with cash, all of it carefully catalogued. So marking hot money is out of fashion, eh? Who knew?

All that happened, however, was that I gave the money to Panda and Dr. Dom in the presence of a silent, suited gentleman who came out from one of the offices in the bank to escort us into the vault and hold the safety deposit box. He looked a lot like Roger. He looked so much like Roger, in fact, that later Roger would be able to testify in court that he had witnessed the transfer of a huge (to my mind) chunk of change that I was giving M2F2 in the person of Panda and Doh Matrix. Then this bank functionary walked across the floor of the bank, carrying the money because Our Panda wasn't getting her paws dirty. He handed it to Panda herself at the teller window, despite her fastidious shying-back, and stood by deferentially, listening to Panda tell the teller her account number and watching her hand over the money all by her widdle self and sign the deposit slip.

Oddly enough, the account she put it in later turned out to be a personal account in the name of Panda Stinchko, jointly held with a woman who no longer existed but who had once been convicted of fraud.

It had been a huge stroke of luck that Panda's account was at the same financial institution (not the same branch, of course: that would be unrealistic) where I held my money. But even if it hadn't been, Roger had planned to go with her, to carry the valise full of cash, as a safeguard and a courtesy from one banking institution to another. It would have turned out the same: him with his little lapel camera and mike to back up the bank's security cameras, watching her put what I was there to swear was a charity donation into a private account controlled by Panda Stinchko and Doris-That-Was.

Bingo. Doncha just love it when a plan comes together?

You would think that criminals would be smarter. But apparently there is always that ego flaw. Panda was now used to someone carrying her luggage.

THE DOCTOR SAID UNTO ISABEL, SWALLOW THIS, IT WILL MAKE YOU WELL.

129. SIGHTSEEING IN THE CLINIC OF DR. DOOM

We were now done, you might think. Now Roger can arrest Panda and everyone can relax.[20]

But we weren't really done, on the spot, that day, for the following reasons:

1. I was still standing there in the credit union with Panda and Dominic.
2. I'd promised to go to Dr. Doom's clinic for a tour.
3. As far as the law went, Dr. Doom was still an innocent bystander.
4. Panda could still lie her way out by saying that she held

---

20. Of course, there was something weird going on with Cummings and his squad that was intersecting, so even if we were done, they weren't, but I had no data on that and no idea what Roger was finding out from his OIC (which means Officer in Charge, if you hadn't yet put that together).

the money in trust, and Dom would back her up. We had to wait until something happened to the money.

5. Ergo, we needed more evidence.

So I went to the clinic.

I have to say, if I hadn't known what Dr. Dominic's sideline was, I'd have been impressed. After someone reputable takes it over, it'll be awesome.

It wasn't overly fancy, but it was homey in a way that said not only money but thought and good taste had gone into designing it. There were day surgery sections with comfortable recliners and personal attendants; overnight stay suites with every luxury you can imagine, including massage and foot waxing, and there were areas where appointments were kept on time by friendly, pleasant medicos, nurses, and other professionals. Personal attendants guided each "client" through their stay.

There were also public clinics: one consulting on skin diseases and facial or other surface malformations; a mastectomy-recovery clinic; an addictions-recovery wing for the rich and another for everyone else, but with little difference between their fitments (for a change). There were several semi-private wards for public health care patients. And downstairs, there was a spa.

Later, I said to Roger, "When Doctor Doom goes down, what happens to all that?" His cynical reply, "Baby plastic surgeons with new diplomas and visions of sugarplums dancing in their heads will be taking numbers to bid at the assets sale." And that's more or less what . . . ah, but let me stay in the moment. Because the best moments were just about to happen.

130. I LOVE IT WHEN A PLAN COMES TOGETHER

At the end of the tour, we ended up in Doctor Domino's private office. He had a desk the size of a pizza oven. He gave Panda a little wrapped package of "product" that looked a lot like a bunch of tiny Ziploc™ baggies with white powder in them to me.

Then he turned to me. I was still wearing my coat, and in preparation for departure I had drawn on my silk-lined kid gloves (Kelly green, in case you are trying to assemble a picture.)

"I've been noticing that you still seem to be in pain," he said.

I bit my tongue so as not to quip, "New shoes." Instead I looked away stoically into the middle distance (represented by a large painting, I think a Guillet, on the wall beside the Sally Ohe kinetic sculpture. Oh, this place was an art-lovers' dream too. Later I bid on the Ohe at the asset sale myself[21].)

"Never mind," I said bravely. "My goodness, Ohe's 'Puddle' — I thought that was privately-purchased decades ago. I meant to tell you how fabulous the decor is — the whole clinic is beautifully designed."

"Oh, yes, Panda did it," he said offhandedly. Reflect on that. A person smart enough to design a medical facility properly and make it look inviting to all comers, be they rich or charity cases, and smart enough to manage huge sums of money well, and she turns to crime. Why?

"But don't put me off, dear. I know you're suffering." (For that "dear", I hope he has several years added to his sentence. Postmortem.) "Let me see if I have anything that will help you."

He opened a locked cabinet on the wall behind his desk, and with his own, ungloved, distinctively-fingerprinted hands, drew out a few more packages.

"Here are some of our herbal preparations. For pain," he said, handing me a packet of several dozen tablets wrapped in a smooth paper that took his slightly-greasy-post-lunch fingerprints beautifully. "Take two or three of these every four hours.

21. Successfully. It's in the roof garden of the Epi-tome now, in the little glasshouse.

And here's something for a soothing soak in a warm bath, to help the bruising —" a fat packet of white powder, which later proved to be Epsom salts (you can't win 'em all) "— and if you're having breakthrough pain try two of these —" more tablets marked with the clinic logo, which would prove very useful later in court "— every night for about three weeks. For any trouble sleeping, use this tincture of herbs in a glass of water —" it's amazing how well a glass bottle takes prints "— and by then the pain should have let up.²²"

And into my gloved, non-fingerprint-making hands, one piece after another, he placed the key evidence that was going to put him away.

Practising medicine without a licence, or even just dispensing controlled drugs without a pharmacist's certification, was just the first charge. The herbal pain reliever was oxycodone, the dosage suggested would have tranquilised a horse, and the chemical signature matched a batch that was circulating on the street. (Isn't it nice to know that different batches of drugs have different chemical profiles and can be matched like DNA?) Though the powder was just a soothing bath additive, the "breakthrough pain" preparation was a kind of Ecstasy, prepared and pressed into tablets in Matrice's drug lab, which the stupid otherfucker had located in the clinic annex's basement for the convenience of executing our warrant. The sleeping pills, a few of which were out there on the drag too, in the very same kind of teeny-tiny baggies they put your craft supplies in (so cute when full of beads, so nasty when full of greed), were the kind of narcotic that needs a triplicate prescription signed by everyone from the doctor and patient to God.

So, speaking of God, Hallelujah.

---

22. By then I would have been stoned out of my gourd, had I been a civilian, not an "agent", and also stupid enough to follow his directions.

ISABEL, ISABEL, DIDN'T WORRY, ISABEL DIDN'T SCREAM OR SCURRY. SHE TOOK THOSE PILLS FROM THE PILL CONCOCTER, AND ISABEL CALMLY CURED THE DOCTOR.

131. "CHAIN CHAIN CHAIN, CHAIN OF FOOLS . . ." OR, AT LEAST, EVIDENCE

We discovered all that pharmaceutical information later — but I knew, from the expression on Dr. Matrix-Fell's[23] face, that we would. The expression, I would say, was of an extremely unpleasant Persian cat who thinks the mouse in front of him is his. Had he actually been that cat, he'd have been licking his lips.

Later, I would be the cat, smiling as I watched him go down the gullet of the legal system. But that was later.

For now, I put the packets reverently into my cashmere pockets.

I thanked the not-so-good not-doctor.

---

23. I do not like thee, Doctor Fell,
The reason why I cannot tell,
But this I know, and know full well,
I do not like thee, Doctor Fell.
— written 1680 by English satirical poet Tom Brown, after Martial

I thanked Panda for taking all that marked bait-money off my hands and putting it into a traceable private account that had the advantage of linking her two identities.

I air-kissed Panda, and endured another grinding of rings into flesh from Dr. Matrix.

I promised to return for a second visit to follow up on whether the medication worked. I went out of his office arm-in-arm with the solicitous Dr. Doom and made an appointment with a receptionist who remembered my name later.

I declined the loan of Panda's limo, having had enough of the expensive stink of hypocrisy-on-wheels.

I left the clinic, smiling to several more of the new-best-friends to whom I'd been introduced on the tour, and who were making a point of remembering my name because I looked like a million dollars (or several million: ain't inflation the pits!), and I hailed a suspiciously-available taxi.

To the taxi-driver suspiciously resembling Roger, I said, "Whoopee-ki-yi-yay! Driver, take me to an evidence locker and an interview room!"

After a brief glance in the rearview mirror at what I was waving about, he whipped around the corner to the van which awaited us there, where I finally met Cummings,[24] in the company of some very competent police scientists.

Later, in court, that direct chain of evidence would be important. The prosecutor even subpoenaed the clinic staff who saw me leave Do Matrix's office, walk out, flag a taxi, and get into it.

It was just great.

Dough wore the cashmere suit in court, but it didn't help.

---

24. Cummings has enough broomstick-up-the-ass in his cop-affect to render his homophobia highly suspect as denial, but he's a good cop.

132. YOU DON'T SHEAR THE SABLES TO GET THE HAIR FOR THE BRUSHES, YOU KILL THEM.

Panda wore the red sable coat to court every day. It didn't help her either.

Her husband should have come with her, in a show of support. He'd stood by her on the day of her arrest. I was still at the cop shop when he swept in on the point of a phalanx of lawyers and demanded to see his dear wife. But alas, when Panda was in court, Laszlo was busy elsewhere.

When he first arrived, while lawyers and their client were discussing statements, Cummings was executing the warrant on Dr. Matrice's clinic.

What Roger and his team hadn't known until their undercover operations and surveillance frequencies clashed was that Cummings had been about ready to take Dom down for drug manufacture and dealing.

Drug manufacture these days includes theft of raw materials from pharmaceutical manufacturers' warehouses. A few of Dom's thieves had been picked up and had already rolled on their boss in exchange for lesser sentences, just like in the movies.

Cummings also had some evidence of the ownership of the clinic with its foolishly-convenient basement lab. Co-incidentally, it involved Laszlo Stinchko's numbered company — the clinic was one of the "other properties" we'd all barely noticed.

But Cummings had been waiting on his warrant because he wasn't satisfied. Laszlo as owner and even Dom both had plausible deniability. *Why, officer, we had no idea those bad men were doing that nasty thing in the basement of our wonderful, humanitarian clinic!*

What had changed the order of magnitude of the bust, however, was the evidence I'd shovelled from my cashmere coat's pocket into the hands of the lab people. Dom's fingerprints iced the cake.

It took an astonishingly short time for Dominic Matrice to decide that he too would give evidence against his boss, on whom he hoped to blame everything.

"He's the owner! I took all my orders from him!" he said on videotape.

"Please name the individual for the recording," Cummings droned, his voice giving away nothing.

"I'm talking about Laszlo Stinchko," said Matrice. "I hope the fucking queer rots in hell." Ungenerous soul of savage mould and destitute of grace.

(Never say I don't have a classical education.)

133. "HAPPY FAMILIES ARE ALL ALIKE; EVERY UNHAPPY FAMILY IS UNHAPPY IN ITS OWN WAY."

I happened to be observing when Cummings came into the interview room where Lotsa Stink was supporting his poor wrongly-accused wife. I was watching on the closed-circuit video that has replaced one-way mirrors in interview rooms. I'd convinced Roger that I should be there because I was still an agent, because I could flag points where Panda might be lying about our encounter — and besides, I was curious. What can I say — you should know me by now. Rog does — and he let me stay.

I can't say Laszlo was providing support in quite the way Panda hoped. His jaw was tight, and he was clearly not happy to discover that his trophy wife was tarnished with a criminal record and an active career as a con artist. He had a tense exchange with her upon their meeting until their lawyers reminded him he was under surveillance. The cameras had then been turned off for a private spouse-to-spouse-to-lawyers confab which left all of them looking the worse for wear.

Panda was still playing him, though, and he was bearing up.

He allowed the cameras back on and sat with her, corroborating her evidence whenever he could, using his legal training to cue the tame lawyers, and generally spreading the very best butter around the interview room.

Roger had turned the interview over to a woman interrogator and had come to join me at the other end of the video when a knock disturbed us.

"Come," he said shortly, still watching the screen.

Lance came into the room, Cummings behind him. They were both grinning, which suited Lance's noble features but on Cummings looked like one of those guys on Mount Rushmore had just cracked a smile. Looking at that smile, one felt that later Cummings might need reconstructive surgery, but that he would be damned sure it had been worth it.

"A word with you?" he said to Rog. "Alone?"

They all went out.

Okay, weird timing, but for all I knew, it was a surprise birthday party for Cummings. I did wonder, but with nothing else to do, I went back to watching the monitor. So I had a front row seat when Cummings and Lance entered the room.

"Laszlo Stinchko, you are under arrest for possession and trafficking of narcotics, manufacture of controlled drugs, accessory to murder, accessory to theft over $5,000 . . ." It was a lovely list.

Panda didn't think so. Her high-frequency shriek challenged the microphone and speakers.

Cummings turned that smile on her. "You mean you didn't know that while you were busy ripping off a few million from the homeless, your loving hubby here owned Doctor Death's drug lab clinic and the money you were syphoning off from him is as dirty as hell? And I bet Mr. Millions here had no idea you were ready to take all the money and run. The two of you are a match made in Hell and you didn't even know it."

"Owned? Drug lab?" Ouch. Glasses would have broken if any were nearby.

"Siphoning? Run away?" That was Laszlo, almost as loud and almost as high-pitched.

Roger filled him in on that one. "We've got proof that Doris here, you know her as Panda, has already taken you for a ride for a few million, *and* has her escape route ready."

That was all it took.

It's strange but true. Neither of them had a clue that the other was a criminal. They'd both used Dr. Doh without ever getting in each other's air space. And we were all in front row seats as they spelled it out for each other in clear, loud, forceful tones. The incriminating statements flew hot and heavy despite the lawyers' warnings — and the recording continued to run while the lawyers continued to sputter background to the main act.

It was really splendid, just about Hollywood quality. It's to the credit of our honest, principled, professional police force that the video isn't on YouTube going viral.

The cops stood back and let the cameras catch the escalating hostilities.

Finally Laszlo yelled, "I'll fucking kill you, you fucking two-timing bitch," and reached for Panda's throat, at the same moment she leapt toward him, talons extended, crying, "You're dead, you fucking piece of shit!" and the fight went physical.

Even then, Roger and Lance, Cummings, and the woman who'd been doing the interview were a tad slow to intervene and pull the erstwhile Dream Couple apart.

Out of concern for officer safety, of course.

It couldn't have been because of how hard they were laughing.

No. These are law enforcement professionals we're talking about.

134. THE FUTURE, NOT LONG AFTER

Everyone was delighted that Lotsa Stinky hadn't known much about his lovely trophy wife with the interrogative lilt to her conversation, and that she hadn't known about him, because it made for two cases of vengeful annoyance that were very useful to the Crown Prosecutor.

Probably the only beneficiary in that family was Kurt Amor, their little playmate, who proved to be unimplicated and unaddicted but not unclever, and has already signed a book and movie contract.

So someone landed butter side up.

But not Doris, and not Laszlo.

Doris had to give up the sable coat (except during court) for jail-appropriate attire. It's possible the Crown eventually possessed it, after her conviction, as occurred with the jewellery, cars, cashmere, Laszlo's money, and all the other ill-gotten fruits of the parallel crime sprees.

Laszlo faced a list of charges as long as my arm, including conspiracy to murder, since Panda blames it on him and vice versa. He won't be spending time in any more Mediterranean resorts with his trophy non-bear and their toy-boy for a while — like for decades. His lawyers tried to make him clam up, but every time he appeared in court, he got mad at Panda's duplicity again and shot his mouth off. Oh, he is *so* going down.

As for my new BFF Panda, the cops got their bait money back, and the city's, and almost all of M2F2's money didn't go into the vortex, but I'm afraid they still haven't found the rest of Doris's little stash of bamboo leaves, a.k.a. skimmed-off currency. You can't win 'em all.

Still, when a person gets convicted for conspiracy to murder as well as for fraud, she goes to jail for quite a while. When she eventually gets out, she'll be quite a bit older, she won't have a wealthy husband — and she'll probably need another makeover. It's true, she'll still have those tits, and if she can get to her secret stash, she will be able to afford a modest sable stole if she's careful. So she got away with part of it.

But she didn't get away with the city's money, nor with the charity's money, nor with the cops' money, nor with my money.

Win. Win win win.

135. MEANWHILE, BACK IN THE PRESENT

Remember I told you that more happens in a story than can be captured in the ongoing narrative? Well, one of the things I'd done between bouts of BlockBreaker™ and crimefighting, back before the action hotted up again, was to write a letter and make some phone calls.

Just after Roger dropped me off at home the day of that lunch, many long hours after I'd gotten into the borrowed taxi with him, my cell phone rang.

"Jian Li-Po?"

Only one group of people thought my cell telephone number had anything to do with Jian. My heart thumped — whether with dread or joy I couldn't tell. I'm still trying to figure that out.

"I'm her agent. May I help you?"

The call went every bit as well as a call of its sort could, even though it was taken entirely in the scruffy halls of the Epi-tome Apartments.

By the time I was saying goodbye, I was ready to unlock my front door.

Jian was waiting.

"How it go? What happen? You are late! Got your message, thank you, but what? What? What?"

So I told her everything, from the Kolinsky hug at the Hardware Grill to the evidence from the police lab, which, for a change, had been able to give our afternoon's work its priority. Then I told her about the secrets that Panda had kept from Lotsa and Lotsa had kept from Panda, and the moment of revelation, and like the cops and me, she laughed until tears came to her eyes.

We hadn't had the arrests, the trials, or the verdicts that were to come, but we had the certainty that these would all take place. We could rest on our laurels.

We chose something much softer than laurels, however.

When we were done celebrating, which took an hour or two and involved some acrobatics, I lay in Jian's arms floating with pleasure and well-being. Sucks to you, Dr. Doom. Your medications are as nothing compared with the love of a good woman. In this case.

"I'm going to miss this," I murmured. "When you go."

Jian sat up abruptly. "What you mean, go? I not going anywhere."

"Well, you might," I said. "I got you an audition with Cirque du Soleil. If you ace it, which I don't see why you won't, you'll probably be on tour. Macau? South America? Europe? I hope you don't get Vegas, that's too tacky."

That was about all the talking I got to do before the attack of the gymnasts began.

136. AS EXPECTED . . .

She aced the audition. The world was her oyster again.

Damn. I was in a conflict of interest position again. I was really, really going to miss her.

"I come back often," she said. "Okay?"

"Often," I said. "Okay." But I knew she wouldn't. Not often enough to feed a real, day-to-day relationship, anyway.

So — "I can visit you too," I said. And later, often, I did.

137. A TOAST TO MADDY

We had our celebration party at my place. It was soon enough after Christmas that I decided to detox us all by ordering in a lot of sushi and green tea ice cream. (I hate Christmas carols too. Feliz fucking Navidad and that nasty little drummer boy.)

Hep was first to arrive, carrying a big wrapped box she insisted I had to open later, and a little box she handed to me as soon as I had hung up her coat.

"Before everybody gets here," she said, "I want to . . . well, Maddy wants to thank you. This was hers. I gave it to her when she turned eighteen." Inside the box was a silver ring engraved *MP*. It was a tiny ring, just big enough for my little finger. Hep said it had fit Maddy's third finger, but she had been skinny and small.

"Don't you want to keep it yourse— . . ." I began, then stopped. Then I put the ring on. "Thank you, Maddy," I said, "and thank you, Hep."

"All you have to thank us for is a few scars," she said.

"Don't be bitter," I said. "If I hadn't done this, I wouldn't have met Jian, and maybe she'd still be on the streets instead of on her way to fame and glory. Denis wouldn't have met Lance, and oh, by the way, do try to notice the commitment rings tonight. And . . . Panda would be in some tax haven with no extradition, spending her millions. I'm not sorry."

"I regret to say," Hep said, "that I'm not really sorry either. I'm old enough to understand that it wasn't me who bashed you, so it's not *my* fault. But I have to say I wish we'd —" but whatever it was she wished we'd, it never got said, because the doorbell announced the next guest.

I'd invited anyone who had anything to do with the case — except the Wrong Reverend of course. The peripheral people, a few cute investigating officers and the like, declined with thanks.

Alas, mayor Gary and his wife were on a business development mission to somewhere warm, though they sent regrets and a really nice, really expensive bottle of sake. I'd even invited Cummings and any date he cared to bring, and it was him at the door, but he showed up alone.

"Couldn't decide which ex-wife to bring, so it's just me," he said heartily (read: nervously), but he perked up when he saw Hep, who has kept the brush cut, and was looking smashing in teal velour. It took him half the evening to realise she was a bleeding heart liberal tree-hugger, he was so taken with her cleavage.

Roger was next, also with no date, but with no excuses about that either. He hugged me.

"Well done, girlfriend. But you never heard me say it. Officially you are a pain in the ass," he said. He had a gift too, or really, three: teddy bears wearing cop uniforms for Jian, me, and Bunnywit. Bun loved his and had its uniform off before we'd finished eating, Jian took hers on tour, and I used mine later for a "YMCA"-themed teddy-bear diorama I made for a silent auction at the Pride Centre.

Denis and Lance came in next, together and waiting for us to notice their new rings.

"Commitment rings?" Hep asked, sounding spontaneous. "*Very* nice." Cummings pretended not to notice.

"Engagement rings," said Denis.

"Well, wedding rings, as of next Saturday," said Lance. "You're all invited. Even you, Staff!" That was to Cummings, who cleared his throat and blushed, probably with horror at the implications of his department having the first out married gay cop in the police service. But I tried not to underestimate Cummings. After all, he was there, and in the ten minutes since he arrived, he hadn't said one homophobic thing. And he manfully (and I use the word in the best possible sense, not that any of them is great) shook Lance's hand, and Denis's too.

Before he had time to put his foot in his mouth, Thelma and Harold and Vikki were coming in, shedding scarves and boots and good cheer. Thelma had brought two platters of hors d'oeuvres made with cream cheese and walnuts and bacon and so on, all wound up in knots and held together with toothpicks. They were delicious, but I felt guilty every time I ate one, thinking of the amount of time it had taken to assemble just for me to demolish it in one bite. Not guilty enough not to eat them, though.

Harold — "call me Hal!" he said to Roger — soon was swapping sports stories with Cummings, and they drifted off to the kitchen to watch Cummings's pocket TV (say what?) when some game came on, leaving the rest of us dipping our maki in tamari and discussing the case.

"What ever happened with the rest of the clues?" I said. I pulled out the old list.

2 (two) thousand-dollar bills (magenta purple, with the pine grosbeak on them) with a hot pink heart-shaped sticky-note reading *Vikki?*

"You thought those thousand dollar bills had Studly Amor's prints," I said. "You were waiting for better comparisons. Come up with anyone else we know?"

"Do Matrix," said Roger. "We figure they were a preliminary payoff for Maddy when she threatened to expose Pan-Doris."

"'That's all I have on me today but I'll send my guys to pick you up for the real payoff later?'"

"That's what we figure. But with confessions, no need to accumulate evidence."

"But what about Studly?"

"The other prints overlay the ones which resemble his. No other connexion. And he claims he knew nothing — volunteered for a polygraph and passed." Given how a psychopath or a sociopath can game a polygraph, not the best exoneration, but.

1 (one) thousand-dollar Hong Kong bill (orange) with lime-green sticky-note, *Jan?* [unidentified-as-yet prints. counterfeit?]

"I wish Maddy had used more sticky-notes," said Roger dourly. "Counterfeit Hong Kong bills equal counterfeiting somewhere, but all I can imagine is that it comes from the source of the controlled substances."

"You do mean *drugs*, don't you?"

"Don't be a smart ass. Anyway, there's no use giving it to you, Jian, except as a souvenir. If you want it as a memento we might be able to release it after court, on the basis that Maddy wanted you to have it."

"That's nice," said Jian. "I want that."

1 (one) clipping from the classifieds of an unknown paper, for escort service

"*Intro Deluxe?*" I said.

"No big deal," said Lance. "We don't have the slightest inkling that Studly, I mean Kurt, knew what was going on. He thought he'd died and gone to escort heaven. What every sex worker dreams of: being adopted by rich clients."

1 (one) clipping from the *Sun* gossip page, with photos of several people at an event in an upmarket art gallery

"Remember that clipping?" Roger said. "Well, of the five people in that photo, three of them are in jail and the other two were very, very embarrassed when we told them where their money went."

"Has any of it showed up?" Hep asked.

"A lot of it had to stay in a trust account until the city matched it with their funds, so the donors were lucky," said Roger.

"Poor Studly," I said. "Do you think he will go back to TV?"

We laughed, all but Roger, who said grumpily, "Don't laugh. He has an agent and a book deal. The guy's fucking illiterate, and he thinks of nothing but his own dick, and he's going to be a celebrity."

"Do you think he needs a wardrobe consultant?" Denis chirped, and Roger and Lance glared at him, but Denis, being Denis, is constitutionally unable to have or keep a straight face, and he collapsed in giggles. "Gotcha!"

Thelma, however, was thoughtful. "Wardrobe and make-up consulting for celebrities," she said. "Now wouldn't *that* be a good home business for Victoria and me."

"Home business?" said Vikki and I, in ragged unison.

"A person has to keep busy," Thelma said. Vikki looked at her with a mixture of incredulity and hero-worship. I hope I never have to regret introducing them. I hope they remember the little people.

1 (one) photocopy of a business licence for a numbered company, with signature of owner/proprietor
1 (one) brochure for a chi-chi club downtown.

"The numbered company that Lazslo Stinchko used to run the club? Also part owner of Dr. Doom's clinic." Roger licked his finger and made a hatch-mark in the air. "One for the Fraud guys. And one for Maddy, in a way, because numbered companies are normally hard to track or something. But with this one clear, it was easier to make a paper trail to the other one. Don't ask me how."

"How?" we all chorused immediately. Roger shook his head, but he couldn't help letting a little bit of smile twitch the corner of his mouth.

1 (one) Ziploc™ bag (sandwich size) with samples of a white powder [not present]

"The white powder?" I asked. "We assume it matched Dr. Doom's stash?"

"Yeah," said Cummings from behind me, making me jump. "But useless by itself, because no provenance."

"Unlike my immaculate continuity of evidence," I bragged.

"Yeah, yeah, you're the fuckin' cat's ass of evidence," Cummings growled, and Bunnywit miaowed.

Even Cummings laughed at that.

Bunnywit turned his back to the room, his posture saying, *I practically solved the whole thing for you, and you laugh. Later I'm going to pee on something you hold dear.* I coaxed him into better humour with a piece of tekka-maki, though, so I think my new clothes are safe for now.

1 (one) Ziploc™ bag (sandwich size) with a used condom [not present]

"Hmmm?" I asked after I read out that list item.

"DNA matching is expensive and we have a confession," said Roger. "So we didn't go there. But I wonder from something one of the Heavenly Twins said if Maddy didn't trick one of them and save the evidence."

"Eww," said Jian.

"Ditto," said Hep.

"Not about condom, but about having to touch one of them," Jian clarified.

"I know what you meant," said Hep. "Ditto."

"No shit," said Vikki.

"Language!" said Thelma.

1 (one) Ziploc™ bag (sandwich size) with a cut-up plastic cup (not present)

3 (three) round paper clips, which had slipped off whatever they were clipping
together and were loose in the bottom of the envelope (not present)

"Same with that cup and the paper clips," said Roger. "If we had a guy, and knew where she got the cup or the clips, maybe they would mean something."

"Still pieces of sky," Jian said.

"Yep."

"But she tried," said Vikki.

"She more than tried." Surprisingly, it was Cummings, not one of us, who made the best speech of the night. "She was a smart girl, and if it hadn't been for her, we all woulda been up shit creek. So I say, let's raise a beer to Maddy."

And, except that for some of us it was sake not beer, we toasted Maddy.

138. GOING IN OPPOSITE DIRECTIONS, REDUX

One other thing that happened —

One day while Jian was getting ready to go (which had included lots of practising, lots of fussing about costumes, and a new haircut courtesy the Cirque costumer — this day she was practising), the doorbell rang.

I was still living in the Epitome Apartments.

I could have afforded to move, but I didn't want to.

I did, however, have the intercom and door buzzer fixed and a security camera system installed, all anonymously, so that tenants no longer have to go downstairs to let their guests in but can still see if the guests are who they say they are. And I have the lovely multicultural tabby lawyer on a quest for the owners, to make them an offer. This will use up my inheritance, but it is a housing project.

Anyway, the doorbell rang.

After I checked the security cam monitor, buzzed the visitor in, and checked her ID through the new peephole in the door, I opened to a courier from a national chain with a large, flat, thin, rectangular package in her hands.

I signed for the parcel, which I was not expecting, and which was from Emsdale, Ontario. (Where?)

Jian came to the door behind me, wiping sweat off her forehead and chest with a white towel and grinning in a way I found provocative in both senses of the word.

"Oh, it comes! Hen hao! Open it!" she ordered, and I did.

It was a painting.

It was a painting by Mendelson Joe.

It was called, "Coming Back from a Long Trip".

In it, two brightly-dressed people, one with a distinctly Chinese cast of features, flew toward each other down a long, winding road.

It was the opposite of my mended-but-never-the-same "Going in Opposite Directions". Where that one, even before its accident, was sad, this one beamed joy out into the room.

With it was a scrawled note.

From Mendelson Joe.

Himself.

SORRY TO HEAR THE TERRIBLE FATE OF 'GOING IN OPP. DIR.' – SORRY TO HEAR THE RESTORATION ONLY PARTIAL – NEVER MIND! LEAVE THE DISTANT PAST DISTANT AND GET ON WITH LIFE! TIME TO REVISIT THAT IMAGE/IDEA ANYWAY! LOTS OF YEARS GONE BY, AND NOW WE'RE ALL IN THE HOME STRETCH. HOPE YOU ENJOY THE PAINTING, AND THAT ~~GIRL~~ WOMAN OF YOURS – SHE'S QUITE SOMETHING. THANKS FOR LIKING MY PICTURE ALL THESE YEARS –

M. JOE

"After Cirque du Soleil audition, I go find him. I go commission this. For you. So you know I come home again. Sometime. Even if after long times pass."

It was that, after everything, that made me cry.

She had to dry my tears. The white towel and the creative use of a number of body parts did the job.

But every time I look at that painting, still, I choke up.

139. THE LAST WORD IN MYSTERIES

Jian was reading this manuscript today, just before I drove her to the airport.

"Is your name Isabel?" she said.

"No," I said, surprised. "Why do you ask?"

140. COURAGE, DEAR READER, WE NEAR . . .

. . . the end.

— 30 —
[a.k.a.]
finis

THE ADVENTURES OF ISABEL
— OGDEN NASH

Isabel met an enormous bear,
Isabel, Isabel, didn't care;
The bear was hungry, the bear was ravenous,
The bear's big mouth was cruel and cavernous.
The bear said, Isabel, glad to meet you,
How do, Isabel, now I'll eat you!
Isabel, Isabel, didn't worry,
Isabel didn't scream or scurry.
She washed her hands and she straightened her hair up,
Then Isabel quietly ate the bear up.

Once in a night as black as pitch
Isabel met a wicked old witch.
The witch's face was cross and wrinkled,
The witch's gums with teeth were sprinkled.
Ho, ho, Isabel! the old witch crowed,
I'll turn you into an ugly toad!
Isabel, Isabel, didn't worry,
Isabel didn't scream or scurry,
She showed no rage and she showed no rancor,
But she turned the witch into milk and drank her.

Isabel met a hideous giant,
Isabel continued self-reliant.
The giant was hairy, the giant was horrid,
He had one eye in the middle of his forehead.
Good morning, Isabel, the giant said,
I'll grind your bones to make my bread.
Isabel, Isabel, didn't worry,
Isabel didn't scream or scurry.
She nibbled the zwieback that she always fed off,
And when it was gone, she cut the giant's head off.

Isabel met a troublesome doctor,
He punched and he poked till he really shocked her.
The doctor's talk was of coughs and chills
And the doctor's satchel bulged with pills.
The doctor said unto Isabel,
Swallow this, it will make you well.
Isabel, Isabel, didn't worry,
Isabel didn't scream or scurry.
She took those pills from the pill concocter,
And Isabel calmly cured the doctor.

ACKNOWLEDGEMENTS

More than forty-five but less than fifty years ago, my first "real job" as a child care worker with teenaged girls fanned my nascent sense of social justice into a lifelong flame of justifiable anger — at systems, at colonialism, at sexism, at racism, and at myth-making about families and cultures and what we owe and give our children. All my writing, even this, is fuelled by that fire.

For the last almost-two-decades, I've lived in the wonderful inner-city neighbourhood of Boyle Street, and this book is dedicated to my diverse and wonderful neighbours (and a few who weren't so wonderful, but are at least educational), and to my partner Timothy J. Anderson, with whom I've shared almost two decades of life here in our big green working-class heritage house. We have also had help contributing to the house's entropic process from some dogs and a cat.

I want to thank all the people I've name-checked, quoted, profiled, parodied, and used as inspiration. I hope you have fun tracking down as many of the references as are not so completely personal as to be opaque: I have had a great deal of fun writing these books. Some of them were written in hard times, and the alleviation of humour was water in the desert.

I want to thank all the readers over the years who read them for fun and to check for mistakes in structure, typos, and assumptions. Particular thanks to S. C. Chan for an exceedingly helpful and rapid sensitivity read. Also thanks to the police, with whom I interacted for seventeen years on a civilian liaison committee, and particularly Kevin G. but also other sworn and civilian members of EPS and other police services, who took time to advise me on proper procedure, how a civilian helps with undercover, and what not to do. Any deviations from their advice are for the sake of story and Aren't Their Fault. Thanks to all the social workers from 1973 on, especially Derwyn Whitbread, Joanne Oldring Sydiaha, Gail Gilchrist James, and Marvin Karrel. Particular thanks to Barb Beaulieu for re-connecting after many decades and sharing a recent friendship. Thanks to Kitty Vendetta, Sparrow, and other punk cats I've known, and to Kayt, who should by rights star in the movie but who is busy saving the world, one kid and one dog at a time. Thanks to all the mystery writers I've loved to read — from when I was seven and first cracked the cover of a Nancy Drew to just last night — including those whom I now call friends, and those who kindly read the manuscript and provided quotes. Thank you to the Alberta Foundation for the Arts and the Edmonton Arts Council, who at various times provided funding for this series. Thank you to my agent, Wayne Arthurson. Thanks to everyone at ECW Press for choosing and doing such a great job with the book. Thanks to my family, without whom I wouldn't have the love of books, the brains, the heart, or the soul to do my work, and to beloved friends both departed and still with us, who love me as I am. More or less.

Our nameless friend will be back in *What's the Matter with Mary Jane?* and *He Wasn't There Again Today*.

CANDAS JANE DORSEY is the award-winning author of *Black Wine*, *A Paradigm of Earth*, *Machine Sex and Other Stories*, *Vanilla and Other Stories*, and *Ice and Other Stories*. She is a writer, editor, former publisher, community advocate, and activist living in Edmonton, Alberta.